The sun is 190 times larger than the earth . . . and we are totally dependent on its light and heat for survival.

ECLIPSE!

Minneapolis, Denver, Phoenix, and Salt Lake City were mysteriously without sunlight, as were Los Angeles, San Francisco, and Seattle.

The blackout wasn't limited to the western United States. The Sunstrike, as this unprecedented event was soon to be labeled, hit Alaska and Mexico as well.

And there was no immediate word from any scientific source on what had caused the Cimmerian nightfall.

To those astronomers across the United States who found themselves watching an inexplicable hemisphere-wide nighttime during a period when their portion of the globe was facing the sun, there was to be a still more disturbing development when contact was made with observatories in Europe, Asia, Africa, and Australia, where normal nightfall was occurring.

Inconceivable as it seemed now, not only had the sun disappeared, but the moon as well!

The earth was in a total eclipse—but no one knew why—and even more horrifying was the thought, *Would we ever see the sun again?*

SUNSTRIKE

GEORGE CARPOZI, JR.

PINNACLE BOOKS • LOS ANGELES

This is a work of fiction. All the characters and events portrayed in this book are fictional, and any resemblance to real people or incidents is purely coincidental.

SUNSTRIKE

Copyright © 1978 by George Carpozi, Jr.

An original Pinnacle Books edition, published for the first time anywhere.
First printing, September 1978

ISBN: 0-523-40365-8

Printed in the United States of America

PINNACLE BOOKS, INC.
2029 Century Park East
Los Angeles, California 90067

SUNSTRIKE

CHAPTER I

Experiment in Survival

For a dozen successive and saturnine years since they were grafted prematurely on the National Football League schedule, the Tampa Bay Buccaneers and the Seattle Seahawks had been the doormats of pro sportsdom and the butts of every pun and derogation contrived by fans and scriveners.

Even more outlandish was the intractability that Jimmy the Greek had adopted toward the two teams from the opposite shores of the land. Never once in their combined 336 regular season games since the bicentennial year of 1976 had the country's omnipotent oddsmaker ever favored either club to win by even a point.

But now in their thirteenth year, Tampa and Seattle had not only forged spectacular winning seasons but had gone on to capture their respective conference championships. They had trampled over point spreads against them stacked higher than the peaks of the Sierra Madre range towering so imposingly upon Pasadena's breathtakingly beautiful backdrop.

1

This was Super Bowl XXII and the teams that had wandered so long in the desert of losers were now, thrillingly, at last battling for the exalted crown of professional football.

Incredibly, after four periods of regulation play the Sea Hawks and Buccaneers had trench-slugged each other into a 21-21 standoff that contributed an added element of improbability to the already dizzying experience of the record-breaking Super Bowl crowd of 104, 392.

Now a sudden-death fifth period—only the second in the twenty-two years of this gridiron classic—catapulted the 1987 season to an even more exciting and wondrous windup on that warm, sunshiny Sunday afternoon of January 17, 1988.

And when the head linesman blew his whistle to launch that historic fifth quarter only two persons were gripped by an unconventional but intractible urge to leave the Rose Bowl . . .

Sandra Sheiler and Mervin Kotler shared more than ordinary eagerness to get away from the game, however reluctantly, and reach their car somewhere out in the sea of vehicles inundating the parking lots. They were already more than a half hour late in leaving the stadium.

"Oh, why didn't we take off after the third quarter?" groaned Sandra in her melodious, deep voice that somehow always caught first-time listeners by surprise. For a young woman of nineteen who barely reached 5-feet-1 in stockinged feet and weighed almost a hundred, Sandra's contralto tones were incongruous for someone of her size.

"We beat the traffic but we're still gonna be late," Kotler sighed heavily. "The good doctor is bound to have an apoplectic fit."

He turned to his companion and glanced down at her from his six-footer's vantage point. A measured frown creased his lean craggy face.

"Maybe he'll count us out . . ." Marvin started to say phlegmatically.

"Oh, no!" interrupted Sandra with palpable alarm. "Don't say that, Merv . . . why, why don't we just stop and phone that we'll be late? . . ."

"That'll only make us later and make him angrier. No way. Just let's hack it as best we can . . ."

Kotler looked at his wristwatch as they finally reached the car.

"Four forty-five," he grumbled as he unlocked the door. "If we're lucky we'll only be twenty-five minutes late . . ."

It was only a twenty-five-minute ride from Pasadena on the Hollywood Freeway to Los Angeles and the campus of the University of California at Los Angeles. But it was an impossibility for Sandra and Mervin to rendezvous with Dr. Gordon Lyle Simms on time, since the appointment was for 5 P.M.

Even if they arrived ten minutes late, Sandra and Mervin feared, that would end their participation in a historic project for which they had been preparing nearly a year. . . .

The project was the brainchild of Dr. Simms, professor of space science at UCLA and the outstanding pioneer in the development of life-support systems for America's far-reaching space program, which was now on the threshold of a bold new venture—a landing by a ten-member team of American astronauts and scientists on Mars.

While he had cut dramatic new ground on many occasions in his long and distinguished undertakings in the development of survival techniques for humans removed from their natural habitats, the program Simms was about to conduct now was vastly different than anything he'd attempted in the past.

For more than a year, he'd been preparing a group of students at UCLA for a subterranean mission designed to test the ability of humans to tolerate a year's existence in an evironment of total isolation from civilization.

Simms had singled out a dozen young men and an equal number of coeds from the sophomore and junior classes for this unique, indeed unprecedented experiment. He was to set them up in residence in an abandoned coal mine in Kentucky, which snaked some three miles into the bowels of the earth.

Their isolation was to be total. Contact with the surface would not exist in any manner whatsoever. There'd be no telephone communication from either end, nor would there be television or radio to keep them apprised of events in the outside world.

The group, labeled WAMIS (Women and Men in Survival), would exist, literally, in a world of their own.

It was, of course, an experiment sanctioned by the National Air and Space Administration and funded by the agency to study the effects of long periods of isolation on the human body. A hefty $10-million budget had been appropriated for the experiment, and Dr. Simms had not overlooked a single need for the two dozen men and women he had picked for the project.

His selection of the group had been a lengthy, painstaking process. It was begun a year earlier in January, 1987, with the start of the Spring semester at UCLA. As chairman of the Space Sciences Department, Simms virtually had a free hand in picking candidates who were to be his guinea pigs.

He had no problem convincing university president, Oakdale Hurst, and the board of trustees that it would be to UCLA's perspicuous advantage—and prestige—to sanction its students' participation in the survival experiment. Especially not after he apprised the school's hierarchy that NASA was prepared to provide an additional $5 million for a space survival science center that would be built on the campus to serve as the chief experimental site for all future survival tests.

In the initial planning, Simms was to have conducted his isolation experiment with the

UCLA students at the projected new center, whose completion was expected in 1989.

But then, for reasons of haste to get the project going "in the interest of accelerating the advances in the space program," as he put it, the professor prevailed upon both NASA and the UCLA administration to accede to his suggestion to conduct the year-long isolation experiment in the Kentucky coal mine.

Two other persons besides the twenty-four students were picked as participants in the experiment—a doctor with considerable experience in space medicine and a registered nurse, who also had worked for a number of years in the NASA-UCLA joint study of space survival techniques.

The doctor and nurse were to care for the students' health and welfare during the year-long isolation, and also monitor their day-to-day reactions in that protracted period of confinement.

The twenty-four students finally chosen for the 365-day "live-in," as some of them called it, were the survivors of a nine-month selection process that, at the outset, involved 336 candidates who had volunteered for the study.

In that period of weeding out the most qualified for the subterranean experiment, Simms and his team of doctors, psychiatrists, psychologists, and scientists put the volunteers through rigorous, indeed excruciating tests, to establish their ability to withstand the long period of isolation called for in Operation WAMIS.

Simms's motivations were never questioned because of his many distinguished years of achievement not only as a professor and chairman of UCLA's Space Sciences Department and his work for NASA, but because of his overall reputation as a scientist.

Yet, there were a few raised eyebrows at the way Simms had precisely selected his twenty-four "guinea pig" finalists—exactly twelve women, exactly twelve men.

NASA Administrator Maitland Thurber was one of the first to pass a remark about that makeup. It came in a phone call to Oakdale Hurst, prompted by a teletype message to the space center in Houston identifying the twenty-four finalists for Operation WAMIS.

"What the hell is Gordon pulling here?" Thurber asked, more in amusement than displeasure. "This makes it look more like an experiment in conjugal survival. I hope he's given those boys and girls instructions in birth control . . ."

Hurst chuckled. "It's my understanding that sex is not to be engaged in," he quipped. "But just to inject an ounce of prevention, I've advised Gordon to provide a handy supply of Ovral and Ortho."

Because all but one of the twenty-four candidates for the experiment were over twenty-one and emancipated from their parents' apronstrings, they signed their own consent forms for the experiment. Only Sandra Sheiler, who was twenty, was required to get parental consent. But that posed no problem, since her father was a propulsion engineer at North American Rockwell, where the third-generation space shuttles were being turned out.

"My wife and I would have even welcomed the opportunity to approve a flight to Mars if that was what Sandra had wanted," Manny Sheiler told a reporter from the Los Angeles *Herald Examiner*, in one of several feature stories the newspaper had published about the preparations for the WAMIS experiment.

"But we're delighted to give our daughter our blessings for the underground survival experiment. We're confident that the risks are minimal because of the extreme precautions that Professor Simms has taken for the safety of the group in this study."

Indeed, Simms had not overlooked any safeguard in preparing the site for his unexampled experiment.

Simms selected an abandoned coal shaft in Ravenna, an old mining town in central Kentucky, because it was of the drift variety—dug at an approximately 45-degree angle into the earth by the "room-and-pillar" method, creating rooms dug out adjacent to the main shaft, or gallery, at periodic intervals.

It was in those rooms that coal was mined. And when, finally, all the available coal was taken, the rooms were left with wooden props or pillars supporting the mined-out roof as the digging proceeded to new depths into the earth—and new rooms were created.

The rooms were dug systematically like the

blocks and alleys of a city, and the tunnels extending to the rooms led along the seams of coal. The coal in the pillars was extracted by subsequent working, which could be likened to top slicing, in which the roof was caved in by successive blocks.

After a room was excavated and evacuated of its coal veins, the pillars were removed and the roof allowed to fall in. The removal of the pillars was critical, for some of them supported firm 45 to 85-foot-thick seams of coal. If they hadn't been removed, then about a third of the coal in the room would not have been mined.

Throughout his exhaustive search into the innards of many abandoned mines in several states around the country, Professor Simms found none as suitable for his unprecedented experiment as the coal shaft in Ravenna. One of this Kentucky mine's most appealing features was the enormous size of the room at the last working face, a shade more than three miles underground from the portal entrance.

Simms was rather amazed to find the room in what he judged to be a perfect condition of safety. The wooden props or pillars installed to hold up the roof during mining operations were still in place, and there was a ready explanation as to why they had not been removed like the supports in most of the other rooms along the length of this tunnel that had been worked bare of coal during the mining process.

Like many other government officials around the country, Gerhard Trowbridge, the administrator of the Kentucky office of the U.S. Bureau of Mines, had cooperated with Simms in his search for a suitable mine. The graying, fiftyish mining expert had communicated with Professor Simms upon locating what Trowbridge judged was a mine that met the parameters set down by the UCLA space scientist.

Trowbridge was one of about a score of Bureau of Mines administrators with whom Simms had gotten in touch and asked what facilities mines in their state provided for his experiment. Only eight states came up with what the professor deemed were suitable accomodations worth looking at. They were, almost all of them, in the southeastern region of the country.

It was in early January of 1987 that Simms came east to search for a suitable site, even as the selection process for his two dozen guinea pigs was being conducted on the UCLA campus by his assistants. . . .

CHAPTER II

Locating the Site

"This mine was one of the country's most productive bituminous veins," Trowbridge informed Simms on his arrival at the Bureau of Mines state headquarers in Louisville.

"It was worked to death during the fuel crunch of the Seventies, but then when President Carter's energy reforms finally put the country on a self-sufficient footing with nuclear power and compacted waste recovery systems, well, as you know, coal became even more obsolete than oil and gas for energy."

Trowbridge explained that the Hillman Corporation, which had operated the mine until 1983, very quickly abandoned it after losing its profitability in the face of dramatic solutions of the country's energy crunch.

"They went out of business so fast that they didn't even backfill the shaft as the law required them to do. I went after them with all kinds of writs, but that Chapter Nine proceeding ended all their obligations."

Leaning over his desk and peering intently

at his visitor, Trowbridge sucked in a deep breath.

"But that's your big break, Professor," the government official smiled. "It's one of the few mine shafts I know of in the state that provides the specifications you set forth in your letter of inquiry. I'll be delighted to get that mine off my back, and that's why I phoned you so quickly . . ."

One of the key conditions Trowbridge laid down to Simms in offering him the use of the mine was that he had to assume the obligation of backfilling the tunnel after the experiment was concluded.

Of course, that was a minor matter to Simms, since the cost could easily be covered by NASA's $10,000,000 appropriation for Operation WAMIS.

Trowbridge volunteered to escort Simms to Ravenna for an inspection of the mine. They flew the ninety miles in a Bureau of Mines jetcopter. The 360-mile-an-hour Sikorsky twelve-passenger whirlybird made the hop in a breezy fifteen minutes.

The main building and other structures on the ground that once teemed with activity when more than six hundred miners toiled in the tumbrils of the earth, chopping and blasting for the "black gold," now looked like the remains of a ghost town.

The rusting chain link fence was decorated with a large, plasticized sign bearing black block letters on a white background proclaiming that the mine had been seized by the Internal Revenue Service and warning that trespassers would be prosecuted.

Trowbridge, who brought a portable miner's lamp from the copter, reached into his pocket, selected a key from a batch on a chain, and proceeded to open the large lock on the fence gate. He then led Simms to a building that had a fading, peeling sign over the door, which read, MINE ENTRY.

At the portal, Trowbridge flicked on the portable battery-charged light and aimed the beam at a panel of circuit breakers. "The electricity's still on," he said in an even voice. "We're required to keep power on in case of emergency."

He threw several circuit breakers and the mine shaft tipple was at once illuminated. Then he led the way to an all-steel electric car, the conveyance that transported the miners to their working places on a bed of rails. The car was on a track siding.

"Have to check its batteries," Trowbridge said. "The car's been laid up so long that it may have run out of juice."

"What happens then?" Simms asked.

"We give it a very fast charge," the government mine official smiled. He pointed to an outlet near the circuit breaker panel.

"That'll energize the batteries in the car in a matter of a few minutes."

As it turned out, the batteries were low; the car motor wouldn't turn over.

Trowbridge took a cord that looked like a

heavy-duty electric wire and connected it from an outlet on the car to the one on the wall aside the circuit breaker. After a brief few minutes, he turned the key in the electric car and the motor began running.

As he disconnected the cord from its terminals, Trowbridge stood back openly admiring the humming engine of the coal miners' passenger car.

The pride in his voice was almost edged with smugness as he gripped Professor Simms' arm.

"This goes to show what wonders an old expert like myself can do when it comes to restarting a mining operation."

That drew an easy laugh from Professor Simms, now in a high state of excitement generated by the imminent prospect of inspecting a mine he hoped would be suitable for Operation WAMIS.

"Get aboard, Professor," invited the Bureau of Mines official with a ready grin. "I'm ready to drive this car right to the center of the earth."

Simms hopped onto the car and sprawled on the floor under the horizontal steel protective roof, which had been installed to protect miners from falling nuggets and chunks of coal from the shaft's overhang.

"I'm ready when you are," Simms said excitedly. "When do we go below?"

"Right now," Trowbridge responded eagerly. "We're on our way."

He shifted the motorman's control to the

right and the car moved slowly from its siding onto the main track leading into the mine.

As the car proceeded a few more feet, the tracks suddenly took a downward pitch.

"What's the angle of descent?" Simms asked with more than ordinary interest.

"Same as on the incline," joshed Trowbridge good-naturedly. "It's forty-five degrees either way . . . but a lot faster going down, let me assure you."

As the car continued on its descent into the bowels of the earth, its path was illuminated by the brilliant headlight over the front bumper coupling. The beam cast an eerie glow in the tunnel despite the lack of luminosity or reflection from the black coal on the surrounding walls, ceiling, and floor.

Glancing behind the car into the inky darkness, Simms almost shuddered.

"It sure as hell is scary looking back where we've been," he said with a touch of tremulousness.

"Never look back, Professor Simms," counseled Trowbridge. "There's enough to concern yourself with what lies ahead."

"Why . . . why . . . what do you mean?" Simms exclaimed.

"If we don't keep our eyes on the tracks ahead, we could run into a wall of coal. You know there are collapses now and then . . . even in the abandoned shafts. That's why the Bureau of Mines insists on backfilling all tunnels after they've been worked clean."

The fifteen-mile-an-hour downhill ride came

to an abrupt halt when the beam of the headlight on the front of the car all at once exploded into a huge circumference of brilliance. Trowbridge and Dr. Simms had reached the end of the line. They were at the entrance of the last room at the bottom of the shaft.

"Oh, heavens!" exclaimed Simms as Trowbridge aimed his own portable light into the room for additional illuminination. The thick, rough-hewn timber posts were all in place and the prevalence of thick, rich-looking veins, or seams, of coal were still intact on the ceiling, walls, and floor.

"They had barely worked this room," Trowbridge said matter-of-factly. "It's a pretty darned ideal spot for your experiment, if I have understood what you're planning to do."

Simms shook his head agreeingly. He hopped off the car and took slow, cautious steps along the craggy floor into the room. He was trying to judge the dimensions of this underground vault.

"Here," the government mining engineer offered, "take my light and look around."

"Thanks," Simms said, gripping the handle and playing the beam upon the different areas of the room. He drew some swift conclusions about the size of the place: at least fifty feet deep, some thirty-five feet wide, and a ceiling of perhaps eleven or twelve feet.

Then he examined the timber posts up close. He pushed an outstretched palm against a few of them to test their firmness.

"If you want to move those supports,

Professor," Trowbridge suggested just a bit chidingly, "you'd better get a sledgehammer. They're not going anywhere, I can promise you that much."

Simms wheeled around and walked back to the car with quick eager steps.

"Tell me, Mr. Trowbridge, will it be possible to install partitions in here, say by utilizing the pillars for support? The reason I ask is that we're going to have twenty-four college students, plus a doctor and a nurse who'll be living in complete isolation for a year. So what I'm inclined to want are small cubicles for bunk beds and for other facilities for the individuals' comfort."

"Certainly you can compartmentalize this room," Trowbridge assured Simms. "But what accommodations will you provide for sleeping?

"I plan a dormitory-type arrangement . . . that is, two-in-a-room separate setups for men and women. It should be as nearly comparable to what those kids are accustomed to back at college."

"Sounds okay," Trowbridge nodded. "But what are you thinking of in terms of life support? I'm not just talking about food, water, sanitation facilities, and medical attention. You know the oxygen in here will never hold out for that many people. And you can't possibly depend on drawing the outside air through that three-mile shaft. Can never happen . . ."

Simms returned the light to Trowbridge with a broad grin.

"That's the least of our concerns," he said with an air of eminence. "We have something that'll produce oxygen for as long as there is a demand down here for a life-sustaining atmosphere. I helped develop a nuclear-powered, multi-purpose engine for NASA no larger than this . . ."

Simms held his hands apart in front of him, palms facing each other on a horizontal plane at a distance roughly that between the ends of his shoulders; then in a vertical position extending from the top of his head to his waistline.

"It's only this big," Simms went on, "but it can put out more energy than the Tennessee Valley Authority. So it has the capability of furnishing power for all life-support systems. I'm speaking not only about providing the requisite energy to run the oxygen-producing equipment for however long the experiment is conducted, but also to generate electricity for illumination, for cooking, and for whatever other uses it will be called on to serve . . ."

Trowbridge was genuinely impressed. Yet he still couldn't believe an engine so small had the capacity to perform for the year that Operation WAMIS would be conducted.

"How long can the engine run without refueling?" Trowbridge wanted to know. His tone was skeptical, almost as if he didn't expect the professor to offer a valid response.

"That will depend on the demands that are put on it," Simms said with a broad smile and a casual tone. "It has a minimum life of heavy usage without requiring a new core of uranium of slightly more than one-million years. On the other hand, if it isn't run at full capacity, it conceivably could keep on producing energy for about two-and-a-half million years . . ."

"Wheeew!" wheezed the Bureau of Mines official. "I had no idea nuclear engines had reached such an advanced state of compactness and great capabilitiy."

"Well, I hope to tell you they have. Moreover, we wouldn't be preparing for that mammoth voyage to Mars without such a power plant at our disposal. We certainly couldn't keep a dozen astronauts and scientists alive for the eighteen months they'll spend going there, living on the planet, and returning home safely."

Trowbridge shook his head in amazement.

"I believe you, Dr. Simms, but still it seems so far-fetched . . ."

The professor shinnied onto the car. "I'm ready to run for daylight, Mr. Trowbridge . . . that is, if you are."

"If you will shut off this front headlight after I've turned on the the one on the other end, we'll be ready to roll, Professor," Trowbridge said. He maneuvered himself under the low protective roof in a half crouch and went to the back of the car.

"There, Dr. Simms, we're set."

With the beam illuminating the tunnel for the return to the top turned on, Simms shut off the other light and joined Trowbridge at the controls on the other end.

"All set, Professor?"

"All set. Let 'er roll."

The car started to move. But its speed was greatly reduced now. Simms estimated the car was traveling on its 45-degree uphill climb at no more than five or six miles an hour.

Trowbridge sensed Simms's awareness of their lagging speed.

"It'll take a while longer to get out of this hole than it took us to get into it," Trowbridge said consolingly. "You can figure about forty minutes—unless gravity gives us an unconditional surrender."

"I doubt that," laughed Simms. "But I'm in no hurry any longer. My months of searching for a suitable site are over."

Trowbridge turned with surprise. "You mean you're going to do your thing in Ravenna?" he asked with a lilt in his voice. The government official seemed overwhelmed that, after all the searching around the country for an appropriate locale to conduct Operation WAMIS, he should have been the man to finally locate a site for Professor Simms.

"Yes, Mr. Trowbridge," Simms said with a deep sigh, "I'm going to do my thing, as you put it, right here in Ravenna, "Yes, indeed, right here . . ."

He turned to Trowbridge, wrinkling his forehead in contemplation of what he was about to ask. "How deep did you say the room is?" he inquired. His tone was hesitant. It was as if he were searching for reassurance that he had heard correctly earlier.

"Three miles and a little more. I'm not exactly sure. But we can check that easily. I have a map of the shaft and rooms excavated during the mining operations."

"Oh, that will be be most helpful," Simms said politely. "I certainly will appreciate having the precise distance."

"But . . . but . . . why must this experiment in isolation be conducted at such great depths in the earth?" Trowbridge stammered, his curiosity suddenly stimulated by Simms' obvious compulsion to want his human guinea pigs installed in such an extreme subterranean vault.

For a brief moment Simms was taken aback by the question. Incredible as it would seem, no one at NASA, at UCLA, nor indeed among any of the students participating in the experiment, had asked that question: "Why must Operation WAMIS be carried out so far underground?"

Of course, Professor Gordon Lyle Simms knew very well why he wanted his group isolated so deeply into the ground. But he hadn't counted on being questioned about it by anyone.

Now he had been. Gerhard Trowbridge had asked. And Simms couldn't respond as readily as he had when asked to offer some logic for picking an even number of men and women for the experiment. Oakdale Hurst had put the question to Simms, half-kiddingly, after that discussion with NASA's Maitland Thurber.

"I believe in women's liberation and women's rights, as well as equality of the sexes. That's why I've selected an even number of men and women," Simms explained in a tone that betrayed no other motivation.

But what could he say about selecting a three-mile-deep coal mine for the project? In actuality, any closed, soundproofed aboveground facility would have served the same purpose—and would not have subjected the persons taking part in the experiment to the greater risks attendant upon living in isolation so deeply in the ground.

After all, even a nuclear engine can fail. Suppose it did? What chance would the twenty-six men and women three miles underground have of coming out alive—especially since they will have had no contact with the surface for a full year?

Some observers—including the science writer of *The New York Times*, Walter Madigan, who observed that it was "madness to allow Dr. Simms to risk these young people's lives in such a dangerous undertaking"— frowned severely on the mission.

But Simms defended his motives.

"If we are to put people on far off planets and ask them to remain there for months and even years at a time, we must first be aware of their capacity, their resourcefulness, their ability to survive in adverse and restrictive facilities. So we must try out that life in isolation right here on earth."

His argument made sense to many in the

scientific community and he was supported by both NASA and UCLA officials because his motivation was laudatory. Such a test of human endurance in isolation had never been attempted. Certainly the time now was right—what with the mission to Mars so close at hand.

Of course, the results of Operation WAMIS would not begin to be known until the end of the year, but they would provide vital data in determining to what extreme period the twelve settlers on Mars might be expected to remain there. For, by then, the astronauts and scientists will have only been living on the Red Planet a mere three months; their first three months after their July 4 launch will have been spent in space traveling the approximately 35,-000,000 miles to their destination.

Thus, by the beginning of 1989, NASA and all other scientific and astronomical bodies studying the progress of the group on Mars will have available the beginnings of the study from Simms's group, which will have by then emerged from its year-long isolation. The daily logs recording their physical and mental reactions to their long period of solitariness would be available and provide a guide to what the Mars settlers could expect to experience in their pioneering sojourn on that inhospitable body.

Although virtually all the details pertaining to the isolation program were apparently known to the officials who had sanctioned the project, there was one factor that had not been discussed: the actual depth of the underground site that Simms wanted. It had been assumed the professor's search for an abandoned mine was for something like fifty to a hundred feet under the surface.

But no one even remotely gave thought to the likelihood that the students and their two medical caretakers would be entombed in a habitat three miles in the ground.

Even when Simms was on his search for a suitable mine, he did not trumpet his requirement for a deep site. He merely examined the locations that the U. S. Bureau of Mines engineers had to offer in the many states he had toured before arriving in Kentucky. The professor looked at mines in Alabama, Arkansas, Georgia, Pennsylvania, Tennessee, Virginia, and West Virginia, but none suited him—chiefly because they were too shallow.

It was only when Gerhard Trowbridge took him into the three-mile shaft at Ravenna that Simms's heart skipped a beat—for he had at last found exactly what he was looking for.

But now, he had been asked why—why did the underground site have to be so deep?

The silence following Trowbridge's question was almost deafening. Only the hum of the motor pulling the car on its uphill climb to the tipple of the mine broke the stillness.

"I say, Professor Simms," the mining engineer broke the hush. "Don't you want to tell me why you must put your people so deep in the ground?"

Simms looked at Trowbridge with a narrowed gaze.

"To be perfectly frank, Mr. Trowbridge, I didn't ask you to find me a shaft this deep, did I?"

The professor's voice was almost defensive.

"But you took me down here and it just so happens that the vault at the bottom is better than any site I've seen anywhere. So that's why I've decided to settle for it . . . that is, if you will let me have it for this noble experiment."

There was something evasive in the way Simms responded, Trowbridge told himself. The day before, Garth McGuire, his counterpart in Wheeling, West Virginia, phoned as a courtesy to Simms to arrange his visit to Louisville. In discussing what the professor was looking for, McGuire commented rather cryptically, "I don't frankly know what he really wants. I showed him that old Mulholland-Burns shaft in the Mannington area. And you know what huge rooms were left in that mine. But none of them seemed to suit him. Well, he's coming to see you tomorrow. But I don't know if you'll be able to satisfy him . . ."

Trowbridge knew the Mulholland-Burns mine well. He'd been with the Bureau of Mines office in Wheeling until early 1987, when he was given a promotion and shifted to Louisville. Garth McGuire then came in from the Tulsa, Oklahoma, office to take over.

Although he pretended to accept Simms's explanation, Trowbridge felt an uneasiness about

25

the professor now. Certainly in light of his conversation with McGuire, it seemed to Trowbridge that Simms had passed up a far more suitable site in Mannington for this deep-draft shaft in Ravenna.

Trowbridge didn't believe Simms's explanation was given in total honesty, especially not the way Simms looked away when he spoke. Yet it was an explanation that Trowbridge had to accept. For what motivation could he attribute to Simms's rejection of the mine in neighboring West Virginia for the one they were touring?

"Hurray!" cried Simms all at once. He spotted daylight looming ahead. The car had reached the top of the shaft and the end of the tunnel was in sight.

As they neared the track siding, Trowbridge made one final observation about Simms's decision to use the Ravenna mine.

"Professor, I'll say this much about your choice of this location. You certainly won't need to worry about keeping your people warm. I'm certain you must have noticed how hot it gets down there."

"I did notice that," Simms smiled with an edge of arrogance. "It must have been my subconscious telling me that this was the best place for my group. You know that these winters we've been having for the last dozen years certainly auger the coming of an ice age . . . and I surely wouldn't want those kids of mine freezing."

Besides that edge of arrogance, Gordon Lyle Simms's voice also exuded an unmistakable smugness. He seemed pleased—too pleased—with his find. . . .

CHAPTER III

Eastward to Ravenna

"This is the height of irresponsibility. You had no business going to the Super Bowl on this critical day of our departure."

Professor Simms was furious with Sandra and Mervin for arriving eighteen minutes late at the rally point in the School of General Studies on the UCLA campus.

They stood listlessly in the center of the room where they had approached Simms as he was outlining last-minute directions and details about Operation WAMIS.

Before the two latecomers had arrived at 5:18 P.M. on that Sunday, January 17, 1988, Simms had decided in his own mind that if some insoluble hitch had deterred Sandra and Mervin from joining the group, he'd carry on his experiment with the remaining twenty-two students and Dr. Floyd Wayne Savage and Registered Nurse Veronica Trees.

The errant couple's arrival, however late they were, heartened Simms. Yet he didn't betray his feelings. He wanted to exhibit anger

29

to impress not only Sandra and Mervin, but the others in the experiment, about the seriousness of the work that lay ahead.

"We're very sorry, Professor," Kotler stammered, trying to explain what had happened. His voice was doleful, almost pitifully so.

"We had planned to leave the game early . . . but the score was tied . . . before you knew it, the fourth period had ended."

"And the score was still tied, right?" Simms interrupted.

"Yes, sir."

"Well, I can't understand why you didn't stay for the rest of the action," Simms continued beratingly. "How can you walk away from the Super Bowl when you don't know the final outcome?"

Mervin and Sandra glanced shamefacedly at Simms.

Simms sat back on his haunches now in the hardback chair behind the desk and glowered at the students for several uncomfortable seconds. The others in the group glared sombre-faced at the proceedings. No one even dared whisper to anyone during this confrontation.

Then all at once Professor Simms exploded with laughter.

"I think you've been through quite enough," he said airily. "I don't think I should torment you any longer. Your repentance is quite obvious. All is forgiven."

Applause and shouts of "Hurrah!" broke out among the other students. Even Dr. Savage and Veronica Trees, the nurse, cheered approvingly.

Simms broadened his smile. His face was uncharacteristically enigmatic. He stuck a large cigar into his mouth that he'd pulled out of his plaid sports jacket. Then he struck a match, puffed feverishly on the Havana, and finally blew a large blue cloud out over the gathering.

"This, ladies and gentlemen, is the moment of truth," he said in a cornball opening that was not altogether out of character for him. Much of his dialogue had the polished but pedantic coloquialisms that might have titillated undergraduates on the campuses in the 1940's, but certainly he was not "with it" in this era that was rapidly heading toward the twenty-first century. But Simms had a captive audience in this instance and his listeners listened sharply to his every word.

"You are about to depart on an unprecedented journey. You are going to serve in roles that no one has every played before. It's extremely difficult for me to say at this point in time precisely what your pioneering achievements will contribute to mankind. Yet, I'm confident that by the time you've completed your historic journey into the great unknown, our exploration will have helped all of you to emerge with glorious achievements which will be recorded and remembered by civilization for all time."

Professor Simms was now ready to spring a surprise on his group. He had saved the announcement as the piece de resistance before the boarding of the jetliner at Los Angeles International Airport for the flight to Kentucky and the group's year of entombment in the earth.

"If you'll all step outside," Simms said equably, "we will take you to a big surprise before embarking for the airport."

The twenty-six people who were to take part in Operation WAMIS quickly emptied out of the School of General Studies. They walked onto the stone veranda outside the building.

As they waited for further instructions, their attention was drawn by a Greyhound bus that was stopped in the street, its motor running and its side covered with a large banner proclaiming, GOOD LUCK, OPERATION WAMIS.

As the members of the team glanced at the bus with combined surprise and amusement, Simms emerged from the building. He gazed at the group, smiling and winking.

His expression was at once both cheerful and doting. For the first time he actually betrayed emotions and feelings for the people who had volunteered to go through this long period of sacrifice for his project.

"This is a treat I want you to enjoy totally," Simms said in a tremulous voice. "We're going to have dinner at Perino's . . ."

There were sudden gasps among the group. The prospect of dining in one of Los Angeles's most exclusive restaurants was a totally unexpected surprise, a dividend no one anticipated.

Perhaps the view of what the company expected at most in the way of food was expressed best by Rita Logeman, one of the most voluble women in WAMIS.

"I could have bet my twenty-thousand-dollar dungeon dowry that old Professor Simms was going to depend on United Airlines's radar range quick-defrost fare for our nourishment. But he certainly fooled me."

Rita's reference to a $20,000 dungeon dowry was the contractual agreement that each of the twenty-four students had signed with Dr. Simms for their participation in Operation WAMIS: They were each to receive $20,000 for their year's involvement in the project.

Another twenty-one-year-old brunette, Rita's equal in pert good looks and shape, yet hardly as cerebral or as talkative, touched off muffled laughter with her out-of-character comment. "The professor's gesture reminds me of Leonardo da Vinci's mural in that monastery dining room someplace over there in Italy."

Elaine Pernick's statement puzzled everyone until Jack Kelly, always quick to bite at riddles, asked what she meant.

"I'm talking about *The Last Supper*, dumbo," guffawed Elaine to everyone's amusement.

The frivolity came to an abrupt stop after the passengers had seated themselves in the bus and they sighted Dr. Simms coming aboard.

No one would dare mouth even the mildest derogation, even if only in jest, in the professor's presence. He was intense, severe, and virtually humorless. At fifty-one, he had settled deeply into his ways. He had a firmness and intractability that tended to discourage virtually all disagreement and argument not only by his students, but by colleagues on the UCLA faculty and NASA as well. Contributing considerably to that forbidding portrait of severity was his appearance, shaped by a full head of white hair above a slender, tall forehead, narrow hooked nose, and thin, parched-looking lips.

Unquestionably, he was quite professorial looking, but the image of austerity was by far the most dominant characteric of his physiognomy.

As he took his seat behind the bus driver, Simms turned and shouted toward the back of the bus.

"Everybody with us?"

A chorus of voices responded in near unison, "All here!"

The bus cleared the huge, sprawling UCLA campus and headed eastward into the heart of the city for Perino's restaurant on Wilshire Boulevard. The trip was pleasantly swift because traffic into downtown L. A. was extremely light that late afternoon, a typical Sunday pattern.

Conversation was quiet and, for the most part, the passengers confined their remarks to the people sitting beside them.

Maitland Thurber, the NASA administrator who had raised a curious eyebrow about the even numbers of men and women Simms had chosen for Operation WAMIS, might have found it a strange turn the way the passengers actually paired themselves in the bus.

If a roll were taken of the impromptu seating arrangements, one would have found the row of seats on the left of the aisle with four sets of coeds sitting alongside each other and two others beside male companions.

On the right side, Dr. Savage and Nurse Trees were in adjoining seats directly behind Professor Simms, a bachelor who had no one beside him. The other seats were occupied by two coeds squatted beside each other and the remaining eight male members of the team keeping each other company.

It would seem from this spontaneous occupancy of the bus seats that the evenly numbered men and women going into their year-long isolation hadn't yet found a permanent involvement with members of the opposite sex to any extent that would produce credence to Thurber's suspicions about widespread sexual entanglements.

Of course, the experiment hadn't yet begun. At this point in time, the bus with the greyhounds painted on its sides and the banners drawing attention to Operation WAMIS had only reached Perino's now.

Dinner was a ball under the crystal chandeliers and amidst the elegant decor. Professor Simms had made all the arrangements for a banquetlike feast that consisted of pre-dinner cocktails, appetizers, soups, and full-course meals that gave his guests a complete range of choices on the menu's extensive list of entrees.

The meal was followed by desserts, beverages, and even after-dinner drinks. The only discordant note in the fête came at 9 P.M.

"I'm terribly distressed to interrupt this lovely affair," Simms said with regret in his voice. "The time is approaching and we must be off to the airport."

Had he been at the restaurant that evening, Maitland Thurber might have had more grounds to cackle, "Ha, ha, I told you so," than had he taken tabs aboard the bus. The seating arrangements at the tables had been set up for men and coeds in alternate chairs in each of the twelve-person groupings.

Shortly after 10 P.M., a United Airlines twin-engined Corsican Jetfire airliner lifted off the west runway at Los Angeles International Airport and climbed into a sky lit by a full moon and a canopy of twinkling starlight.

Four minutes after takeoff, the captain's voice came over the loudspeaker. "We are at eighty thousand feet and our air speed is Mach three, or approximately twenty-one hundred knots. Our estimated time of arrival in Louisville is eleven-fifteen. We're glad to have you aboard, folks, and we hope you'll enjoy your trip."

This was Flight 834 and it was a nonstop hop between Los Angeles and Louisville. The 215 passengers aboard had filled virtually every seat on this three-tiered, wide-bodied jet that had gone into service as a domestic carrier for all of the nation's airlines in early 1987.

The impact on the environment had been negligible and, consequently, the public accepted this plane, which flew three times the speed of sound and without a whimper.

That contrasted markedly with the fuss and furor raised a decade earlier when the Mach II Concorde introduced the supersonic transport age to America.

Residents of communities surrounding Kennedy International Airport in New York rose up in arms over apprehensions about the noise of the Concorde engines—yet their fears were never justified. The plane flew into Kennedy and departed at decibel levels lower than most of the accepted Boeing 707s and 747s.

One key force that brought the Corsican Jetfire into immediate favor was the silencer shield, a conelike device fitted over the back or exhaust end of the plane's twin-jet engines, each mounted on the outermost extremities of the tail assembly.

That device reduced perceptibly an engine's deafening roar—by 50 percent, in fact. It had been developed jointly by the General Electric Company in Schenectady and the Grumman Aerospace Corporation on Long Island. But G. E. took over mass production because Grumman had to concentrate on another project.

The aerospace firm was the successful bidder on the $5-billion contract for the Satellite Space Station Complex, a gigantic gravity-force laboratory that was to be placed in earth orbit in 1991 with a capability of supporting 250 space explorers.

It was to launch America's colonization of space, a program encompassing far larger and more sophisticated space stations that would be orbited around the moon and planets in the solar system.

But in this year of 1988, NASA's timetable in space was limited to just that one venture—the mission to Mars. The launch was scheduled for July 4, 1988, at Cape Canaveral. It was to be a banner event with the President of the United States attending the liftoff for the ten pioneering astronauts and scientists taking part in that sensational venture to Mars.

"Ladies and gentlemen, we are beginning our approach to Louisville," the captain's voice interrupted the silence that had prevailed abroad Flight 893 for more than an hour since he had last spoken to the passengers after takeoff from Los Angeles.

"Please fasten your seatbelts and shoulder harnesses and extinguish your cigarets."

Flight 893 came in for the landing in Louisville. Dr. Gordon Lyle Simms had brought his human guinea pigs virtually to the threshold of where their pioneering experiment was to begin.

All that lay between the debarkation from the plane and the boarding of the electric car that was to take the twenty-six members of the experimental team into the the tumbrils of the earth for a year's experimentation in survival was an overnight stay at the Holiday Inn Motel at the airport.

CHAPTER IV

Life Support Systems

Ravenna's residents were both bemused and amused when the news reached them that the old Hillman Corporation mine had been selected for an experiment to test the durability of humans in isolation.

The Louisville *Courier-Journal* dispatched a reporter-photographer team to the old abandoned mining town to do in-depth stories about the newly chosen site for Operation WAMIS, as well as gather local color and reaction among the 600 or so townspeople.

Since the closing of the coal mine in 1983, Ravenna's population had declined dramatically. More than half the people left after the area lost its chief industry and deprived them of opportunities to earn a livelihood.

However, those who remained ultimately found employment in a sprawling twenty-first-century-type chemical plant, which the Union Carbide Corporation built in Ravenna for the manufacture of low-density polyethylene used for a whole range of products, from trash bags to communication cables.

The new industry injected life into a community whose economy was threatened with catastrophic consequences. As a result of this infusion of some 2,000 new jobs, a resurgence into prosperity was experienced not only by Ravenna but a number of depressed communities along the banks of the Kentucky River.

But the prospect of twenty-four college students coming from Southern California to spend a year in the old coal shaft caused the natives to suffer considerable confusion. They certainly didn't view the experiment with much favor.

"We couldn't work longer than seven hours down in that tunnel without having to come up for fresh air," an ex-miner from the Hillman bituminous operations was quoted in a *Courier-Journal* interview. "I can't see them college kids living down there for even a week. That professor is sure taking a big and stupid chance with a lot of lives, let me tell you. They're all gonna die down there and they don't need an experiment like that to find out."

Another citizen employed in the local bakery, called the Pastry Chef's Delight, found the whole idea about the experiment a puzzling happening. "Why do they have to bring them all the way from Los Angeles to Ravenna to pull off this nonsense?" he wanted to know. "Don't they have any abandoned gold mines from the Rush of Forty-nine left out in California?"

One of the more jocose cracks was uttered by Ravenna's only barber, a perennial wit named Angelo Palladino. "They should give those kids picks and shovels while they're in the mine and let them dig for some coal," he suggested straightfaced. "Then they will be doing something useful while they are killing a year down there . . ."

The disparagements from the gallery had no effect on Gordon Lyle Simms's timetable for getting the mine in shape for its lodgers. The professor figuratively thumbed his nose at the local gentry's remarks, which he labeled "intemperate and stupid."

He also cast a critical finger at the *Courier-Journal*'s editorial stress on belittling stories about the project.

"The editors richly deserve the Pulitzer Prize because they have certainly laid an egg on this story," he cackled at the newspaper.

At the same time he steadfastly refused reporters and photographers from all media access to the mine.

"This is a serious business and it is a project that bears on the security of our nation," Simms pontificated. "The press can get its stories and pictures after we've completed our mission, but not before. Right now the mine shaft is off-limits to everyone—and it will be until the experiment is over."

Meanwhile, Simms proceeded, undauntedly preparing the room at the bottom of the shaft for its twenty-six occupants. His policy from the very outset was sparing no expense to make the underground site everything he planned it to be.

One of his first goals was selecting a contractor whom he could rely on to do the job properly. That objective was seemingly realized when Simms entered negotiations with the Plandome Construction Company in nearby Lexington.

The professor was delighted to discover that Redmond Friedrich, Plandome's president, was prepared to offer total cooperation. Friedrich agreed to direct special attention to the Ravenna project and assign his best workers to perform the structural fabrication that would get the mine in shape to accommodate Operation WAMIS.

The plans that Simms had shaped initially in his mind for the layout in the underground vault were formulated by him in rough drawings, then laid on the desk of an architect's office in Covina, California. The architect, Paul Samuels, needed a mere three weeks to prepare finished blueprints.

The layout lent itself to extensive usage of prefabricated materials. Lightweight aluminum wall partitions were selected as dividers for numerous units Simms had incorporated in his design.

Dr. Simms was concerned not only with his human guinea pigs' survival but their comfort as well. Thus, he spared no effort to assess his mastery over the many potential perils and distresses that can lurk in the dungeon he chose for the experiment. He took every precaution in the name of safety.

Working around the heart of the life-support system—the nuclear power plant-generator—the professor designed an atmosphere for the underground environment that not only drew oxygen from the surface three miles away through a five-inch plastic pipe laid along the mine shaft rails, but also independently manufactured an auxiliary supply of oxygen by the potassium chlorate-manganese dioxide method.

As an additional safeguard, the air was also to be cleaned and scrubbed of carbon dioxide by a highly refined system of lithium hydroxide and activated charcoal purifiers.

One of the earliest problems that confronted Simms neither surprised nor caused him great concern.

After the room at the bottom of the shaft was finally measured, its precise dimensions were found to be sixty by forty feet. That wasn't far off from what he guessed it was when he gauged its size visually on his first visit to the mine. Of course, it wasn't nearly large enough to accommodate all the life-support equipment required to sustain his group for a year. But that condition was readily corrected when Simms made use of the next-to-last room along the shaft. Although it had been caved in after it was worked clean of all its coal, the room was reexcavated for Simms into a hollow.

After the ceiling was shored up, large and

cumbersome equipment such as a walk-in refrigerator, plentiful canned and packaged nonperishable foods, and other apparatus and supplies were installed in the newly dug room.

Since the storage area was less than fifty feet from the vault at the bottom of the shaft, no extraordinary arrangements were required to transport the stores to the experimental station. Yet Simms wanted his students and medical team to enjoy the fullest conveniences. So he provided a battery-powered handcart for hauling materials on the mine's train rails from the storage room to the residential quarters in the vault.

For the day-to-day, indeed hour-by-hour, scientific studies of the twenty-six men and women in isolation, extensive and sophisticated monitoring equipment was procured to examine and measure the effects of that protracted human disconnection from the world.

Simms designed the coal mine chamber as a modular installation for total research flexibility. The plan encompassed three kinds of modules—for utility, living, and experiments.

Of course before any partitioning was done, a concrete floor was poured to level the jagged surface that was left by the mining of the coal. Over that completed smooth cement surface an indoor-outdoor-type green carpet was laid.

The lightweight aluminum wall partitions served to compartmentalize the room into the three designated modules. Once those separations were achieved, further partitions were shaped in each of the modules.

The most extensive number of units was dictated for the living quarters. A total of fourteen five-by-eight-foot cubicles was built as sleeping quarters. Twelve cubicles consisted of bunk beds designed to accommodate six paired men and six paired women.

In that layout, separate accommodations were provided for Dr. Savage and Nurse Trees. They were set up in two single-bed cubicles of the same dimension as all the others.

The abandoned coal mine vault was further reconstituted with walls, which sectioned off a spacious laboratory where the significant tests upon the participants in the program were to be conducted.

In that laboratory, extensive provisions were made for continuous testing of the twenty-four students' blood count, as well as their respiration, blood pressure, and other physical characteristics and vital signs that would register on scales, which would tell precisely where their levels stood.

The rest of the layout included a modern kitchen equipped with two heavy-duty electric ranges and a pair of microwave ovens to facilitate quick and efficient preparation of meals, a dishwasher, a twin restaurant-size sink with cold and hot running water, and other paraphernalia covering the gamut from pots and pans to crockery and silverware. A washer and electric dryer for laundering clothes were also located in a small walled-off section of the kitchen.

The life-support room, which housed the nuclear-powered engine-generator, oxygen producing equipment, and the cooling and heating units, was built next to the laboratory but outside the sixty-by-forty-foot vault. It was put at the end of the rail bed in the shaft itself, thus affording direct hookups to both the plastic conduit carrying air from the atmosphere to the oxygen pumping equipment and the power cables to the storage room on the next level.

Most importantly, however, by not putting this machinery in the vault itself, valuable space was released for other essential functions that were programmed for Operation WAMIS.

One of the significant benefits accruing to the occupants' further comfort by that design was the doubling of the area initially allocated for bathroom facilities. In his original layout, Simms had provided toilet, sink, and showers in two tight compartments—one for the men, the other for the women—that had a capacity for three users at any one time.

With the revised design, the professor created two relatively spacious bathrooms, each measuring nine-by-twenty feet. The fixtures in each were identical—three toilets, three sinks under six-foot wall mirrors, and two shower stalls. Thus, each bathroom now could accommodate as many as eight persons who might find a need to use it simultaneously.

Simms also provided ample room for dining in the large concourse surrounded by the sleeping cubicles. Four picnic redwood tables and individual matching chairs for the twenty-six occupants were installed there.

A further tribute to Dr. Simms's assiduous attention to detail in creating the safest possible environment for the year-long survival challenge was the extent to which he provided safe drinking water and a proper waste disposal system.

The latter installation was achieved with a grouping of eight septic tanks placed in the portion of the mine shaft running downhill beyond the vault. This section of shaft was unfinished; it was not timbered nor was rail laid on its floor. The coal miners had begun digging that shaft just before the Hillman Corporation ceased mining operations.

Had the company continued in business, the shaft eventually would have been extended further than the thirty lineal feet it now ran, and would have ultimately terminated in the area where still another room or vault would have been excavated to extract more tons of coal.

As it was, the unfinished shaft was an ideal spot to store the septic tanks. And since it was downhill from the occupied vault, gravity served to carry all waste water easily into the series of septic tanks.

Perhaps the most remarkable—and yet most questionable—provision Simms arranged for his people in isolation was fresh water. The professor's demand met stiff resistance from Redmond Friedrich.

"Dr. Simms, it is an absolute waste of money to dig a ninety-foot well from the bottom of the mine shaft," the Plandome executive protested. "We have some of the best drinking water in the state of Kentucky here in Ravenna. All we have to do is lay a pipe down the shaft and you will have an endless supply of clean, healthy H_2O."

But Simms wouldn't agree. "I don't want the people in the experiment dependent upon any life support from the outside world, "Simms insisted.

"But you are taking air from the atmosphere, aren't you?" Friedrich argued.

"Not so," Simms corrected. "The airline to the surface is only a backup system. We are actually going to produce our own atmosphere down there. We will not pump outside air into the environment unless the potassium chlorate-manganese dioxide method should suffer a breakdown."

Simms's will prevailed and Plandome Construction sub-contracted the Dow Well Digging Company from nearby Beattyville to sink the pipes for the underground water supply. Simms had determined from U.S. Geological Survey maps that an underground table of fresh water lay at a depth of 11,650 feet beneath Ravenna.

This water table was one of several hundred deep bodies of water in the shape of lakes and streams that were formed 20,000 years ago during the Pleistocene epoch, or the Great Ice Age, under the continental United States.

Although the shaft to the underground chamber was three miles long, the distance in a vertical direction from the surface to the room was two miles, or 11,560 feet. Therefore, boring the hole to reach the water was a relatively simple matter. It entailed the sinking of a ninety-foot shaft. Yet it was made a great deal more expensive because the well-diggers had to work in confined quarters. Nevertheless, the well was dug and Professor Simms didn't have to depend on Ravenna's water supply.

As the end of 1988 approached and Operation WAMIS was nearing its date with destiny, only a handful of finishing touches remained before the survivial test center would be ready to receive its tenants.

For Redmond Friedrich, that time couldn't come soon enough. He had had his fill of dealing with Dr. Simms. True, NASA had given his firm $1,985,000 in business for work performed in the Ravenna project. Yet Friedrich had never experienced anything quite like his encounters with Simms in all the years in the construction business.

"We could have saved the government nearly fifty percent," Friedrich complained to the sub-contractor, Walter Dow, the head of the well-digging firm. "But Simms was unconscionable and, I truly believe, stupid. He insisted on installations and equipment that were totally unnecessary and wasteful."

Dow nodded in agreement.

"I'll be damned if I can figure why I had to dig this ninety-foot well to provide water. Simms certainly frittered thirty thousand dollars down the drain when all he needed was a two thousand-dollar copper line to feed water from Ravenna's water supply."

What Walter Dow and Redmond Friedrich were discussing was a mere extension of the antagonism—and suspicion—that Simms had aroused in Gerhard Trowbridge at an earlier time.

The U. S. Bureau of Mines official didn't believe Simms was acting in good faith or in total honesty—not after turning down the mine in Wheeling, which Trowbridge considered far more suitable and more readily adaptable for Simms's purpose.

And now, as the Ravenna mine was being prepared for its twenty-six occupants whose arrival was just days away, Dr. Gordon Lyle Simms had caused still more suspicions to be cast on his motives in a project, which, on the face of it, seemed to be completely aboveboard and ostensibly motivated by the most laudatory of intentions: the furtherance of America's space program.

Yet, on the very eve of the year-long entombment of the two dozen UCLA students and their doctor and nurse overseers, there was that gnawing girdle of mistrust that some highly placed observers had wrapped around Operation WAMIS.

But what did it mean? . . .

CHAPTER V

Operation WAMIS Begins

Monday, January 4th, 1988.

A chill winter's day. During the night, the skies over Kentucky had blotted out the stars and the crescent moon. Now at dawn the clouds were gray and heavy with moisture. In some areas of the state a powdery snow was already falling.

At the Holiday Inn, the switchboard operator checked the time. It was 7:55 A.M. Her orders were to put in 8 o'clock wakeup calls to each of the fourteen rooms that Dr. Simms and his group were occupying. She proceeded to ring the rooms five minutes ahead of schedule because it would take at least that long to meet the deadline with the last of the calls.

Following Dr. Simms's instructions issued the night before, the overnight bags everyone had brought on the flight from Los Angeles were toted to the main lobby and deposited on a luggage cart provided by the motel.

This arrangement wasn't for convenience but security. The bags were picked up at the motel by a United Parcel Service truck and delivered to the old Hillman Corporation office complex at the mine entrance in Ravenna. When Simms arrived with the group, he would examine each bag before it was taken below. He would seek out contraband, such as portable radios or other devices, which could be used to establish a communications link with the outside.

Simms was consummately set on thwarting any slip in his plan to keep the group in complete isolation. So extensive were his precautions that the students' luggage, containing only clothes and toiletry articles, had been examined personally by the professor on the UCLA campus, then sealed and turned over to NASA, which in turn transported the suitcases to the mine in Ravenna. There, after a second inspection the luggage was placed in the appropriate bedroom cubicles assigned to the individuals.

This same precautionary procedure applied to Dr. Savage and Nurse Trees, who were no exception to the rule. They would have no contact either with the world above for one whole year.

After depositing their overnight bags on the luggage cart, the twenty-six people in his group joined Dr. Simms, who led them into the motel dining room for breakfast.

"Order anything your hearts desire," Simms said, gesturing grandiosely with his hands. "After this, you kids are going to be subsisting on a regimented menu. I can't truthfully say I envy that, but I'm certain I don't have to tell you again what your sacrifices are going to mean."

Arrangements for transportation from Louisville to Ravenna had been made long beforehand by Dr. Simms. Thus when breakfast was over and the group left the motel, they found a chartered bus waiting to take them to a landing pad at the western terminus of the Louisville airport.

There, a giant Air Force fifty-passenger Bell Aeronca jetcopter, dispatched from nearby Fort Knox, was standing by to airlift Dr. Simms's group directly to the mine in Ravenna.

"Oh, wow!" shrieked Sandra Sheiler as she gazed down on the landscape when the helicopter began its descent. "This sure ain't God's country."

She was catching her first glimpse of the rugged, snow-covered countryside of Ravenna's mining region, and it was a sight she'd sooner forget. The jagged rock of the landscape jutted out in a frightful tapestry of severe and angry prominences. The light dusting of the new-falling snow hadn't yet covered the ugliness of the mountain fissures that lay in dark shadow. Even when the carpeting of white was thick, it still never completely obscured all of the portions of the land tableau, which was most unsightly.

Sandra's initial impression of the ground below was shared by most of the others who had glanced at the scenery from the copter windows.

"I hope it's a bit more cheerful underground," Frank Waller muttered unhappily. "This sure doesn't look like the Garden of Eden."

His companion on the flight, Linda Ronson, a twenty-one-year-old sophomore from Los Angeles, turned to the chubby young man beside her—he was twenty-two years old and from San Diego. She spoke to him with an acknowledging half scowl.

"Don't be dismayed so soon, Frankie. Haven't you been told never to judge a book by its cover?"

"Yes," Waller, a junior majoring in economics, said snidely. "But if the inside is anything like the outside, I fear some heavy and dull chapters lie ahead for us."

The comments were voiced in uniformly muffled tones. Everyone was careful not to let Dr. Simms overhear their derisions. All were aware how long and hard he had searched for the site and the many months of preparation put in to ready things for the experiment. No one wanted to hurt the professor's feelings.

Within seconds after the chopper hovered over Ravenna it went into into a precipitate descent. All sense of elevation evaporated at once. It seemed the ground was about to swallow up both aircraft and passengers.

The chopper banked sharply when it dropped to its settling altitude of approximately one hundred feet and then swung along the shore of the Kentucky River. It was flying like a conventional airplane coming in for a landing. Actually, the mammoth jetcopter was too heavy to make vertical landings from great heights. It was designed to make its approaches like a winged aircraft, and only then could the pilot put down in a perpendicular descent for the remaining short altitude.

The copter landed on the flat soot-covered front yard of the decaying Hillman headquarters building. Even before the pilot had cut the main rotor, Dr. Simms lurched out of his seat at the front of the cabin, walked with tight, eager steps to the front hatch, lifted the lock-handle, and threw the door open.

A cyclonic gust of air and snow-covered coal dust churned up by the massive overhead blade slammed against the professor and even sprayed some of the passengers in the forward part of the cabin.

The whine of the rotor was almost deafening, yet Simms seemed to ignore the annoyance of both the blast and the noise.

"Last stop!" he shouted in a loud, excited voice. "We've arrived! Last one off is a bum!"

Laughter and cheers exploded as everyone reacted at once to Simms's uncharacteristic proclamation. They scrambled out of their seats and surged toward the exit as the pilot finally switched off the engine.

One by one they scampered down the four-step ramp, which had slid out of the belly of the cabin automatically after the hatch was opened.

As they stepped on the ground and gathered

in small and large separate groups, the students circled and turned restively, craning for a glimpse of the mine shaft they would be entering.

Floyd Savage and Veronica Trees exhibited no less excitement and curiosity than the twenty-four subjects of Operation WAMIS. The plain truth of it was that the doctor and nurse were just as surely going to be tested in this environment of absolute isolation from the world as the others in the unique experiment.

To be sure, they were considerably more mature than the body of students who were their charges. Both Savage and Trees had been in the NASA-UCLA jointly sponsored space survival program for the better part of seven years.

Savage had joined the space program as a medical researcher immediately after graduation in 1979 from Johns Hopkins Medical School.

The lanky, handsome, blond-haired graduate doctor was only twenty-six years old at the time—and he had the distinction of being the youngest medical researcher ever to enter America's space program.

In his years of service since, Savage had worked most closely with Dr. Simms and played a vital role in helping bring into fruition many of the advances in life-support systems for the space program that were credited exclusively to the professor.

Simms had chosen Savage to take charge of the twenty-four students in Operation WAMIS not only because of his infinite expertise in space medicine and survival techniques, but also because of his dedication and loyalty both to the space program as well as to the professor.

For several years now since he came to UCLA, Savage had heard Simms saying to him: "I will reward your work and dedication some day with recognition, glory, and wealth far beyond your wildest dreams . . ."

In the beginning, and for a period of time afterward, the young doctor experienced repeated exhilaration and enchantment whenever he heard those promises from a superior he respected highly.

Savage's loyalty to Simms remained unswerving, yet he gradually began to wonder in precisely what mannner Simms might make good on all his vows.

The professor, Savage told himself, certainly had it within his power to turn the spotlight of recognition on him, and perhaps to some limited extent help the young doctor achieve some measure of glory. But how could he ever hope to endow Savage, as Simms had put it repeatedly, with "wealth far beyond your wildest dreams?"

Eventually, Savage came to regard that part of the pledge as just so much talk, a mere figure of speech that had no real meaning. Moreover, Savage had never desired to achieve great wealth; if he had coveted riches, he certainly wouldn't have hooked up with the NASA-UCLA space program. The $31,500 annual salary he was currently receiving certainly didn't auger any immediate or even long-range prospect for gaining membership in any millionaire's club.

Veronica Trees had joined the space survival program the same time as Floyd Savage. The pixie-faced, slim-figured brunette, with the small shy voice and studied, enunciating-every-word quality, had graduated from Georgetown University's School of Nursing the very year that Savage wound up his medical studies at Johns Hopkins.

They had never bumped into each other in their rounds of the Washington-Baltimore social scene and didn't meet until they had made their separate ways into the space program.

Both were single at the time but they never dated because Savage had been engaged to a pretty Boston girl whom he'd met and fallen in love with while at the university. She was a secretary in the Baltimore Orioles Baseball Club front office.

However, their plans to marry went awry after Savage settled down in his work on the Coast. The young woman apparently felt Floyd's dedication to space medicine was his first love and that she could never hope to magnetize his attention away from his work. Shortly before Christmas of 1986, she returned the ring and said goodbye.

Only then did he take serious notice of Veronica, who had just recently been reassigned to work in close proximity with Savage in Dr. Simms's space sciences laboratory on the UCLA campus.

Previously, she had been in bacteriological and germ studies at the immunization center on the college grounds. Though the two buildings were within a few hundred feet of each other, Floyd's and Veronica's paths seldom crossed.

When they did, they exchanged polite greetings, hardly anything more.

But after she was shifted to the space sciences lab's staff, Savage not only took notice of Veronica, he began dating her. By the time Dr. Simms had made his decision to stage Operation WAMIS, Floyd and Veronica were looking into each others big blue eyes with something more profound than platonic fascination.

The professor was cognizant of the endearing close relationship the young doctor and nurse were sharing. In his own mind, Simms, the bachelor, looked upon the couple's attachment as a definite plus. And so he selected them for the mission—and with considerable eagerness, for he knew of no others more qualified to fill those critical roles assigned to Savage and Trees on the mission

"Everyone follow me," Simms called out after the last of the passengers had stepped off the copter.

With a bounce in his walk, Simms led his group around the northeast corner of the Hillman headquarters mining complex building.

As the students rounded the bend in clusters of twos, threes, and fours, following closely on the heels of Dr. Simms, Dr. Savage, and Nurse Trees, a chorus of cheers cracked the silence, which until then had been broken only by the crunch of footsteps on the frozen coal dust.

The horizontal adit to the mine shaft loomed dead ahead.

"This is it," Simms said quickly, drawing a swift, decisive breath.

There really wasn't any need for that.

Everyone who'd seen the mine entrance had no difficulty recognizing it.

As they approached the opening, Simms asked the group to gather around him. "We're going down in three relays, because the car only has a capacity for ten. So let's have the first nine of you come into the shaft . . ."

Floyd Savage and Veronica Trees, who were standing alongside Dr. Simms when he trumpeted his instructions, trailed him into the shaft and boarded the workers' electric car. They were followed by Rita Logeman, Elaine Pernick, Jack Kelly, Frank Waller, Linda Renson, Sandra Sheiler, and Mervin Kotler.

"I'll be back to pick up the rest of you in about twenty-five minutes," Simms announced briskly. "Please don't stray."

The professor flicked on the headlight, then shifted the motorman's control with a motion that looked practiced.

It *was* practiced, for Simms had piloted the car up and down the three-mile 45-degree incline no fewer than 200 times since construction at the bottom of the mine was begun. He was never away for more than a few hours all during the eight months that Plandome Construction's crews were preparing the mine for Operation WAMIS.

As the car left the siding and entered the main shaft, the passengers suddenly broke into a refrain of excited exclamations.

"Ooh, wow!" cried Rita Logeman. "This is almost like Disney World's roller coaster . . ."

"It's more like a toboggan slide to Dante's Inferno," Elaine Pernick said ponderously.

Jack Kelly was up to the occasion as the man with the every-ready remark. "I was told I was on the road to Hell, but I had no idea it was such a short ride . . ."

As the transporter approached its last mile, the headlight over the front bumper, which had been illuminating the way along the blackened tunnel, suddenly seemed to be performing a useless service. For ahead, at the end of the shaft, a brilliant glow was shining up the tunnel that canceled out all the luminosity the headlight was beaconing.

Mervin Kotler was the first to notice the brilliant light ahead in the tunnel. But only one person on the car—Dr. Simms—knew what the source of the light at the end of the shaft represented. It was a high-intensity beam produced by the atomic generator installed in the life-support systems room at the bottom of the shaft.

"Good God!" exclaimed Kotler. "If this is Hell, it certainly is a well-lighted place!"

"And there isn't a single fire burning," chortled his girlfriend from the Super Bowl embarrassment, Sandra Sheiler.

Professor Simms brought the car to an abrupt halt at the end of the tunnel. The tracks came to an end against a railroad like bumper. It had been installed there to prevent the possibility of a runaway car crashing into the life support systems room at the end of the line and the septic tank complex that lay beyond the room.

"This is the end of the line, you wonderful people," Simms said with glee as he braked the car to a stop at the bottom of the shaft. The large metal double doors closing off the vault living quarters from the shaft were wide open.

The view of the interior was a colorful tapestry of antiseptic, but comfortable warmth. While it may not have been exactly furnishings and decor by the best of American interior decorators, the setting certainly posed a stark contrast with the bleak three miles of tunnel approach and the first-impressions the visitors were experiencing as they cast their eyes on the surrounding harsh countryside and dilapidated structures.

A chorus of *oohs* and *ahs* greeted the sight of the arrivals' home for the next year.

"Hey, this is beautiful!" cried Sandra in delight.

"Good heavens, I don't believe my eyes!" Mervin Kotler exclaimed. He turned sharply to Dr. Simms.

"How on earth did you fashion such an exquisite layout way down here? It's incredible!"

Smiling with delight that the room met such instant approval from his subjects of experimentation, Simms shot his arms over his head and made Winston Churchill victory signs with his index and middle fingers.

"You have no idea how thrilled I am that you like your new surroundings," Simms said in a pleased voice that was ever so slightly edged with impatience. "I tried to think of everything for your comfort and health. Now, if you'll make yourselves at home—your bedrooms have your names on them—I want to get back upstairs and bring the others down here. Please excuse me for a while . . ."

Simms returned to the transport car and guided it on its tedious uphill course to the top of the tunnel. For the second run to the bottom, the professor signaled nine more passengers onto the vehicle.

As they got aboard, he checked off their names on his roster:

Hank Weddle, 22, junior, Covina, California.
Cy Michelmore, 21, sophomore, San Francisco.
A. Gerald Mahar, 22, junior, Reno, Nevada.
Paul Day, 22, junior, Ames, Iowa.
Randolph Hughes, 21, sophomore, Tuscon, Arizona.
Rosalyn Johnson, 23, junior, Richland, South Dakota.
William Garth, 22, sophomore, Richmond Heights, Virginia.

Ellen Roiso, 22, junior, Paulsboro, New Jersey.

Maryjane Frost, 23, junior, New Orleans.

When they had reached their destination at the end of the three-mile hegira, the students exploded with the same excitement and enthusiasm as the first group had demonstrated. They all knew the setting was to be their lodging for a full round of the seasons.

Twenty minutes after having deposited that group of students at their lair of isolation, Simms was back at the top counting the last eight heads before going below and bringing the official start to Operation WAMIS.

"Okay, folks, I'll log you as you climb on the car," Simms said in haste, eager now to get the final preparatory phase out of the way. The last cadre of students was checked:

Claire Narbonne, 21, a sophomore from Long Beach, California.

Jacob Marsh, 21, sophomore, Seattle.

Joan Myrtle, 22, junior, Mokelumne Hill, California.

Frances Littlejohn, 22, junior, Monitor, Oregon.

Nancy Civitelli, 21, sophomore, Denver.

Helmut Schlossburg, 24, junior, Milwaukee.

Victor Samson, 21, sophomore, LaPlatte, Nebraska.

Ruth Sherry, 22, sophomore, Hamilton Park, Pennsylvania.

Their arrival below generated still another round of accolades for the surrroundings that were to be their home for the next 365 days.

When the cheering subsided and these last eight students had inspected their bedrooms, the bathrooms, kitchen, and laboratory, they settled back in the comfortable upholstered couches, armchairs, and chaise longues in the living room area where the earlier arrivals had already been seated.

Dr. Simms had a few final words to offer. There was no need for a lengthy speech or last-minute instructions. The students had been thoroughly briefed in the many months of preparation that led to this "moment of truth," as the professor again called it as he spoke to the group.

"There is nothing I can add to what has already been said," Simms stated somberly. "You have been completely oriented for this period of isolation and I don't believe there's anything more to say. I have complete confidence in each of you—that you will carry out your duties here like the staunch and able soldiers I believe each of you is. If I didn't feel this way, I wouldn't have let you reach this stage of our historic journey."

His voice had begun to choke and then suddenly it trailed off. To most of his listeners it appeared that the professor had been overtaken by emotion.

And that was precisely what he wanted them to believe.

"Well, now," he started again in languid

tones, "I'm going to leave you. Good luck and God bless all of you . . . I shall see you again on Monday, January 2 of next year . . . the year of our Lord, 1989 . . ."

Simms glanced at his wristwatch.

"It's two-twenty P.M.," he said, turning and walking to the car. As he mounted the vehicle and took hold of its controls, he flicked the switch and the quiet murmur of the motor was heard.

"It'll be exactly two-nineteen P.M. when I see you again one year from today. Goodbye . . ."

With one hand guiding the controls and the other waving, Dr. Gordon Lyle Simms and the car disappeared from view.

The twenty-six human guinea pigs were on their own finally and at last, ostensibly for that year in isolation . . .

When Dr. Simms had reached the top of the mine and switched the car onto the siding, he quickly went through a series of motions that hadn't been detailed or even drafted in the elaborate step-by-step plans and prospectuses that had been reviewed and finally approved by NASA and UCLA. Those were the strict guidelines and standards of safety, which the government agency and university had stamped their respective seals of approval.

Oddly, there'd been no provision. in the contract with Plandome Construction for the installation of heavy steel doors at the mouth of the tunnel. Yet, such doors had been erected—not by Plandome but by the Ajax Safe and Vault Company, Inc., in Mobile, Alabama.

Simms paid for the $2,485 installation out of his own pocket. The work was done after Plandome had completed its commitment on the construction and its crews had cleared out.

Now as he left the transporter car, Simms took quick, urgent steps toward the mouth of the tunnel. The doors had been placed just at the apex of the sloping shaft.

They had been designed to be flush with the floor of the shaft. Yet the Ajax people who installed the doors found it curious that Simms had wanted them fabricated as they had been.

It didn't make sense that the doors couldn't close. The trackbed prevented the doors from coming together.

But Simms had a ready explanation. "This mine is going to be shut tight eventually. When it is, a section of the track will be removed so the doors can be closed."

And that was precisely what Dr. Simms embarked on doing now. . . . With a lug wrench and other tools he had stored in the Hillman Coal Company's offices, he proceeded to dismantle the two eight-foot sections of rail, which had posed the obstruction to the door's closing.

It was a simple task. Two lag bolts held each end of a rail to the track plate. Approximately eight turns of the lug wrench was all the effort required to remove each bolt—sixty-four turns for all eight bolts. Timewise, it was no longer than twelve minutes.

The rails weighed ninety pounds each. Even

for a man of Dr. Simms's age and limited strength, the task of sliding the steel rails even for a few feet along the ties was hardly a challenge. Once that step was out of the way, Dr. Simms jammed a crowbar under three ties and pried them loose from their coal-caked floorbed. Then he lifted them on end, one at a time, and toppled them into the shaft.

Now Dr. Simms began sealing the vault. But as he swung the doors toward each other, bits and pieces of coal embedded in the ground caused the doors to jam. Simms met that obstacle with a pickaxe and shovel, which he had had the foresight to bring.

The professor hadn't overlooked a single detail in his plan to make the mine as securely isolated as he wanted. Thus, he was able to shut the steel doors as tightly as he intended them to close.

When he brought them together, finally, he clamped the bolt in place, turned the lock, and put the key in his pocket. Then he took the shovel again and banked earth against the bottom of the door. He tamped the dirt until it was a solid airtight mass.

He carried the tools to the office but returned once more, a caulking gun in hand now. He applied the point of the sealant tube along first one side of the door jamb, then the other. Finally he caulked whatever spaces he detected between the tops of the doors and the roof.

Simms had made certain that no air from the outside filtered through those doors. It was indispensable requirement of his plan to keep untreated air from seeping into the tunnel. The only air from the atmosphere entering the mine was that which was being sucked through the five-inch plastic conduit by the oxygen-generating equipment in the life-support room.

That air hose, which had been rerouted below ground for a short distance at the place where the steel doors were installed, was feeding air into a nuclear-powered temperature moderator. That unit was programmed to convert sixty cubic feet per second of the coldest or hottest air from the outside into the comfortable 70-degree atmosphere that the oxygen generator was designed to pump through the ventilation registers in the underground vault.

His attention to detail was exacted even upon his very last need to complete his commitment to the launching of Operation WAMIS.

The Air Force helicopter that had flown the group from Louisville to Ravenna had returned to Fort Knox after landing the passengers. But Dr. Simms wasn't stranded in the old mining community, because he had brought a rented car to Ravenna on an earlier occasion.

And now the time for his departure had come. He got behind the wheel of the sedan and began tooling his way toward Louisville. Suddenly a wide grin of satisfaction creased his face. He lit a cigar and smoked it with fast erratic puffs until he felt relaxed and the tensions of the past several hours began to disappear.

Dr. Simms always had supreme confidence in himself in whatever undertaking he tackled. But even for one with such enormous ego, he found it somewhat difficult to believe that his plan—up to this stage—had come off without a hitch.

He felt free.

Free to pursue the second phase of the venture he had conceived . . .

CHAPTER VI

A Detour to Long Island

Eastern Airlines's Flight 637 was given control tower clearance for takeoff from Standiford Field in Louisville at 6:29 P.M. on Monday, January 4, 1988.

The giant Globescanner Mach III jetliner flew to Republic Airport in Farmingdale on New York's Long Island in a shade under twenty-two minutes. Dr. Simms's hop was a detour in the itinerary he had pre-filed with NASA before leaving the UCLA campus to settle his group in the mine and get Operation WAMIS under way.

He was to have departed Ravenna in the helicopter, which had flown the students there from Louisville. But he altered the schedule the night before, shortly after checking in at the Holiday Inn. The professor phoned Maitland Thurber, NASA's administrator, in Houston to apologize that he couldn't meet the space chief in Cape Canaveral on Sunday in accordance with arrangements made weeks beforehand.

Simms was to perform an extensive series of

tests on the life support systems aboard the Galactic I, the ten-passenger space shuttle orbiter that was to be launched in July for the spectacular manned landing on Mars.

By this time the voyagers to the Red Planet had been selected: four astronauts—three males and one female—, three women physicists, a male astronomer, a woman physician, and a male geologist. This group was ordered to report to the Cape on that Sunday to begin learning everything about their space transporter that was to take them on their fifty-nine-day journey, land them on the red-tinged rock-strewn Martian soil, serve as their shelter until their portable, inflatable bubble-top laboratory was erected, and then, after six months of intensive exploration, this magnificent flying machine would bring them back to earth.

The shuttle orbiter itself, the second generation of reusable spacecraft that made its debut in 1987, was designed and built by North American Rockwell as a descendant of the series of space shuttle orbiters that came off the production line beginning in 1977, with the first of the vehicles named Enterprise.

In the years since, more than two dozen identical space shuttles were produced and sent on repeated missions in both earth and lunar heavens. Their principal function was lofting hardware and people into space to establish, first, orbiting stations around the world, then similar fully manned outposts circling the moon.

The space shuttles had convoyed hundreds of

scientists, chemists, geologists, physicists, astronomers, and other space investigators to the orbiting stations in the half-dozen years since 1982 that the explorations were performed by NASA.

Even now, in 1988, some ninety space researchers were girdling the earth in eleven stations and another thirty were aboard three observatories circling the moon. In the latter missions, small crews periodically descended to the lunar surface and conducted tests on soil and rock samples and other investigations that the Apollo astronauts of 1969 and the 1970s could not perform as effectively as the explorers of the 1980s. The latter benefitted greatly by the advantages of close-at-hand life-support systems of the orbiting labs.

Landings and takeoffs were accomplished in those ungainly, insectlike lunar landers known as LMs. There were three such craft left over from the Apollo program after tight money and widespread criticism aborted the series of manned lunar explorations in 1972, after the Apollo 17 team of Eugene Cernan, Ronald Evans, and Harrison Schmitt splashed down in the Pacific on December 19.

The two story-high, 33,000 pound surplus LMs, which had been designed and built by the Grumman Aerospace Corporation, were lofted into a lunar orbit by Saturn rockets. Once the LMs circled the moon in tandem with orbiting laboratories, their function as landing craft assumed far more remarkable levels of efficiency than their predecessors.

Instead of getting one-time usage out of the LMs as the Apollo astronauts had, the people in the space stations used the lunar modules constantly for shuttling between their laboratories and the lunar surfaces they chose to drop down on. This greatly increased performance was made possible by refueling with liquid hydrogen and oxygen stores hauled from earth by the space shuttle orbiters.

The initial landings of the three LMs in the mid-1980s were identical to the way Neil A. Armstrong and Edwin E. Aldrin, Jr., guided their Eagle to a landing on the Sea of Tranquility on that historic Sunday, July 20, 1969.

The moon modules put down on three widely separated locales, which enabled the scientists in the orbiting laboratories to study highly contrasting lunar landscapes.

Of course, in the 1980s space laboratory era, the 4,800-pound ascent stage wasn't sent crashing to the moon's surface as it had after Armstrong and Aldrin docked to Apollo II and rejoined Michael Collins aboard the spacecraft.

In the latest epoch of space conquests, the LM cabin—once it docked with the orbiting lab and was refueled—could return to the moon with another pair of explorers. Yet, in the early months of those missions, the "taxi," as the upper stage was called, could only put down on the "launch pad" of its lower stage. To have landed on the rock-strewn lunar surface would have been disastrous, for the floor of the cabin would surely have been punctured and the occupants killed instantly.

Nevertheless, it still was a highly precarious feat putting down the upper stage on the lower-section lander. It took precise, pinpoint maneuvering. Grumman had strongly challenged NASA's decision to play such hairpin games with space hardware—but especially with lives.

Yet, NASA ignored the protests.

Meanwhile Grumman's engineers—still reflecting the fierce pride they all had shared on that memorable July 20, 1969, and all through each of the subsequent moon landings, when their LMs always performed flawlessly—took matters into their own hands.

They designed and built three sets of tripod landing legs for the upper stages. Then the legs were delivered by space shuttle and installed with clamps and bolts to the bodies of the three modules while poised atop the landers.

When those installations were completed, the lower sections were abandoned and the "taxis" went on performing a multitude of missions with inordinate versatility. They landed anywhere their passengers wanted them to on the lunar turf. Thus, exploration of virtually every inch of the moon's landscape was made possible by those three surplus—supposedly obsolete—LMs.

Despite those spectacular achievements in America's space program, that first generation of shuttles had neither the range nor the necessary life-support systems to sustain any sort of travel into deep space. Their capacity was strictly limited to a range of 200,000 miles—

the vicinity of the moon. Nothing further than that.

But the engineers at North American Rockwell didn't rest on their laurels. They went back to the drawing boards and designed a space shuttle vehicle with the capacity for deep-space travel.

As drafted in its original concept, the ship, named Galactic I, was to have been driven by far more powerful engines than those that guided the first-generation space shuttles in earth orbits and landings. However, the rocket system of the new spacecraft would still derive its thrust from liquid fuels, such as hydrogen and oxygen in the vacuum of space, then kerosene and oxygen in the atmosphere when the vehicle came in for landings.

While the new power plant was designed to propel the new ships into deep space, it still had relatively limited performance qualities. It would again be lofted into orbit by a rocket—a larger, more powerful one than Saturn and which was also being designed at the time. And while it could reach the twenty-six million miles to Venus or even thirty-five million miles to Mars, it would only orbit the planets with its four-man crews, not land, and then return to Earth and put down like a plane.

But before North American Rockwell went into production with Galactic I, the designers frantically returned to their drawing boards. Suddenly the atomic engine figured as the new power source for Galactic I.

The engine was a spinoff of the very power

plant Dr. Simms had furnished for the life-support systems in Ravenna. Of course the nuclear engine developed for the space shuttle was much larger, and it was designed and built by General Electric.

Hailed as a spectacular breakthrough, the engine was an unqualified engineering marvel. No larger than just one of the prototype F-I engines clustered beneath the Saturn 5's first-stage rocket, this totally new creation in propulsion systems energized an unprecedented 15.6 million pounds of thrust—more than twice as much as all five engines in Saturn's first stage.

But even more remarkable in that technological breakthrough was the elimination of monstrous, weighty kerosene and liquid oxygen and hydrogen tanks. Aside from a few feet taken up by the engines on each of the three stages of the 278-foot Saturn 5, the fuel tanks occupied virtually the entire body of the rocket.

Ten feet and five inches long, forty-five inches in diameter, the Aere Perennius—as GE named this magnificent atomic engine after the Latin for immortal "—power plant was approximately a thirtieth the size of Saturn—but spectacularly more efficient.

It had a core of uranium that could literally burn, not for the two million or so years that was the life expectancy of the nuclear-powered engine Dr. Simms helped develop for his Operation WAMIS life-support systems, but ten times that capacity—twenty million years.

That certainly was the greatest advance toward immortality that any man-made object had ever come, up to that period approaching the twenty-first-century.

The Aere Perennius all at once changed all concepts at North American Rockwell about Galactic I's capacities and capabilities.

In dropping provisions for fuel tanks aboard, a total of 3,000 cubic feet of space was gained. That additional area was converted to crew quarters, enlarging the ship's accommodations from the original four to ten persons.

Yet the most remarkable advance in the advent of the nuclear-powered Aere Perennius was the overnight obsolescence it brought to the cumbersome and costly Son of Saturn program, which was to have been undertaken jointly by The Boeing Company and McDonnell Douglas Astronautics Company.

There was no need anymore for a new generation rocket to launch the Galactic I—not when it had its own power source of infinitely greater capability.

Generating its own 15.6 million pounds of thrust, Galactic I now could easily lift itself into space like a conventional plane. Then it could course through the vacuum of the universe for distances heretofore undreamed of even in the recent past when man was preparing to orbit Mars in a four-passenger Galactic I.

Now not four but ten explorers were to be taken to the Red Planet, not only to circle it but to land, to investigate its surface for half a year, and finally return to earth in the same three months it was to have taken them to fly there.

A year in space—and it was to be only the beginning!

"Thanks to General Electric for Aere Perennius and to North American Rockwell for Galactic I, we can now explore space to its farthest reaches," Maitland Thurber declared in his announcement about the historic development of the GE engine and the redesigning of the space shuttle into that new configuration, which suddenly raised the big question: How long can humans live in space?

Until that time, those hundreds who had served in earth and lunar orbiting laboratories actually—yet puzzlingly—had spent only relatively short periods of time in space. The usual tour of duty was three months, sometimes less, occasionally longer. But no effort was ever made to test human endurance and tolerance aboard those laboratories for extended periods—such as the time it would take for a round trip to Mars.

Members of the President's Scientific Advisory Committee had expressed confidence long before that the voyage of Galactic I—the earlier model designed to fly to Mars, orbit the planet a few brief days, and return home—would bear no undue hardship on its four astronauts.

"We are convinced," the advisory panel's statement read in early 1986, when the program was made known, "that the manned flight to Mars two years hence will pose no difficulties for the crew. From all indications, the astronauts will find it relatively effortless to adapt to that environment for the six months of their journey. They should experience no extended period of discomfort, certainly no hardships—unless they should encounter serious illness."

The scientists, however, carefully skirted the issue of what might be done in the event one or more of the crew became gravely ill. The implied understanding was that the mission would be aborted if a dire emergency arose, and the ship would return to earth.

But there was virtually no discussion about emergency medical care for an astronaut who came down with something like acute appendicitis while Galactic I was going into orbit around Mars. While the ship had adequate space aboard to install medical equipment and facilities where such an operation could be performed, no provision had been made to place someone on the craft who could perform such surgery. Not one of the four astronauts scheduled for the flight was a medical doctor.

Then, however, when the liquid-fueled Galactic I space shuttle program was scrubbed after the advent of the atomic Aere Perennius engine, an inordinate concentration of interest was focused suddenly on the well-being of the ten-member crew that was to embark on the Mars mission aboard the redesigned nuclear-powered spaceship.

It was at that point that Dr. Simms, who'd worked on the life-support systems not only on the two Galactic I shuttles, but earlier spacecraft as well, came forward with his suggestion to conduct the experiment with the twenty-four students in a year's total isolation.

Since the President's Scientific Advisory Committee then belatedly realized its laxness in conducting survival tests of long-range duration, it gave its immediate and unqualified approval to Simms's proposal.

NASA then directed Simms to proceed with his plan for Operation WAMIS.

What had brought Dr. Simms to Long Island that night of January 4, 1988, was a matter that he had discussed with Maitland Thurber well in advance of his departure for Ravenna from Los Angeles. The professor was to meet with the developer of a stunning machine that was installed aboard Galactic I and that had two roles to play in life support. Simms was to receive some up-to-date briefings and instructions on the unit's operations.

That get-together was scheduled for Sunday, January 3. And Simms was to have flown to Cape Canaveral immediately afterward. But when he phoned Thurber from the Holiday Inn in Louisville, Simms begged for another twenty-four hours, explaining that some extremely urgent personal matter had come up and needed his immediate attention.

The NASA boss did not ask the professor what that matter was. Thurber merely wanted

Simms's assurance that he'd show up on Monday, for his presence at the Cape was imperative in the orientation of the ten-member Mars exploration team. Simms and only Simms knew every facet of the spaceship's intricate and extensive life-support equipment, and only he could best acclimate the crew to the functions of Galactic I's highly sophisticated systems.

In fact, understanding and operating those systems was far more involved than twisting and turning dials for the computer-programmed automated takeoff, the flight to Mars, the landing on the planet, and the return through the blackness of space to the safety of Earth. A Rhesus monkey with ten minutes of orientation could fly Galactic I to Mars and back.

Dr. Simms directed the cab driver at Republic Airport to take him to the Kings Grant Motor Inn six miles away, on Sunnyside Boulevard just off Exit 46 on the Long Island Expressway in Plainview.

When the cab pulled up in front of the motel, he paid his eight-dollar fare with a ten-dollar bill and let the driver keep the change. As he stepped out of the taxi, Simms found himself surrounded by a scene of wild confusion.

A blinding glow of klieg lights illuminated the landscape into near high-noon brilliance. Cameras were whirring from three widely spaced locations, all focused on a handsome black-haired man escorting a reddish-blonde beauty into the motel lobby.

"Cut!" shouted the director, who was obviously pleased with the way the couple's entrance was captured by the cameras.

"No retake this time . . . it's right on!"

No one could have harbored any doubts that this was shooting for a movie, even at that late hour at the King's Grant. However, Dr. Gordon Lyle Simms had no idea what it was all about until he asked the young clerk at the registration desk.

"They're finally shooting the Alice Crimmins case," the clerk said matter-of-factly.

"What's that about? Seems I vaguely remember hearing about it a long while back," Simms mused.

"I wasn't even born then, but I remember hearing my parents talking about it when I was growing up. A very pretty redhead was supposed to have killed her two young children, a boy of four, a girl of five. She was finally arrested, tried, and convicted. But she served almost no time in prison because her conviction had been reversed.

"Then she was prosecuted and convicted again . . . but she got into one of those work-release programs and she lived the life of a foot-loose floosie. She finally married the lover who'd stood by her all the many years of her ordeal."

"Sounds like a soap opera," chuckled Simms. "Was the actor I saw walking in with the actress that lover?"

85

"No way," the desk clerk volunteered. "The guy you saw bringing her into the motel was another of her lovers. He was the one who took the stand and swore that Alice confessed to him she killed her kids."

"What I don't understand," Simms said to the clerk, "is what all the excitement out there has to do with the motel. Why are they shooting scenes at the Kings Grant?"

"Oh, that's no problem, sir," the clerk replied. "Alice Crimmins and that lover spent a lot of nights making love here."

Simms wanted to know what significance that had with the case.

"Well, as I understand it, sir," the clerk responded, "Mrs. Crimmins confessed to her beau in one of our rooms that she either killed her children or had help in doing so . . ."

"And they're making a movie out of that?" exclaimed Simms in a voice edged with incredulity.

"Yes, sir. The confession in room one-fourteen was the basis for Alice Crimmins's conviction at both her trials—in 1968 and again in 1971. So, that's why they're shooting the scenes here tonight."

"What a weird world we're living in," Simms rasped as he filled out his registration card and signed it. After that, he was given his key and went to his room.

Dr. Simms started the next day, Tuesday, January 5, with a light breakfast in the Kings Grant dining room. Then he went to the lobby and found himself caught up once more in the frenetic activities of the movie company. Now they were shooting interior scenes for the Crimmins film!

Simms glanced at his wristwatch. He had a few minutes to kill. The rental car he had requested at the desk the night before was being driven to the motel by a yellow-jacketed auto jockey from Hertz on Jericho Turnpike in Huntington Station, some five miles away. The professor wanted the car at 11:30 A.M.; it was only 11:15 now.

He bent into an upholstered leather armchair next to a potted palm and observed the filming activity with bored tolerance.

Although his eyes followed the action being recorded by the cameras, Simms couldn't concentrate on the goings-on. His mind was elsewhere. He was thinking about his noon appointment with Boyce McMorrow, chief engineer for Aerospace Research at Grumman in neighboring Bethpage.

McMorrow was a key force in the development of the revolutionary particle accelerator, a nuclear-powered machine designed to produce a vacuum automatically over an airless celestial body, such as a planet, moon, or asteroid. The principle underlying this concept hadn't yet been tested in space, but would soon be when Operation Mars got under way.

The vacuum phenomenon would put into discard the localized oxygen-filled shelters, such as the many that had proliferated as land-based laboratories on the moon after Grumman modified the upper stages of the three LMs into versatile landers. Once all the moon's surface had become readily accessible to the crews in the orbiting laboratories, launching scientific explorers to any destinations on the lunar crust posed no problem. For when they put down now, they brought their own portable-inflatable domes to establish laboratories and conduct extended tests without cumbersome spacesuits.

The particle accelerator was programmed to spin or weave an invisible yet truly existent cover or dome over the planet, at an altitude at first of no more than a mile. In that vacuum, biochemists could energize a primitive, but breathable, life-sustaining atmosphere by releasing the enormous wealth of oxygen which is locked under the crusts of all celestial bodies in the solar system.

In time, as vegetation and forests were cultivated and became full grown, and settlements also spread across the landscapes, the once-hostile planets, moons, and asteroids inevitably would acquire their own atmospheres to sustain all life as readily and comfortably as on earth.

Dr. Simms was completely aware of the design and capability of Grumman's particle accelerator. In fact, the professor had helped install it aboard Galactic I in late September after the ship was delivered to Cape Canaveral by North Amercian Rockwell's chief test pilot, Roger Firmy, who had personally put the craft through exacting tests in the atmosphere as well as in space before turning it over to NASA.

But there'd been a strange development when the particle accelerator was shipped to Canaveral. It disturbed Simms greatly . . .

For two years, the professor was kept informed about the progress in the machine's development and fabrication virtually every step of the way. He was also given to understand the particle accelerator could perform a vital secondary function: generate heat from its atomic power plant and produce a colloidal suspension of black particles in space.

In an airless environment, these particles coagulate instantaneously and form a remarkable sheet, very much like plastic. The sheet is impervious to both heat and light. Moreover, as more particles are emitted from the accelerator's jet spouts, the larger the plasticized screen becomes.

Early information hinted there may be no limit to the size of screen the machine can fabricate while spewing its black particles from an external mount on the Galactic I. But no further details were furnished.

Meanwhile, colloidal suspension was accepted as the ultimate solution to the problem of landing on solar bodies such as Venus, whose 800-degree Fahrenheit temperatures would literally incinerate space travelers from Earth long before they even neared the planet.

But with a plastic screen shading the spaceship on its approach, weaving a canopy of protective shade over the landing site, manned flights to Venus and explorations of the surface were deemed entirely within the realm of practicality now. Indeed, a preliminary flight plan was already being charted for such a mission in a Galactic I spaceship for the early 1990s.

Since Simms was given to understand the particle accelerator not only produced a vacuum but a plastic screen as well, he couldn't understand why the machine had been shipped to Canaveral with a forty-five-page specifications instructions manual, which made no mention of colloidal suspension. The booklet dwelled exclusively on how to operate the machine for its vacuum phase.

Simms confronted Maitland Thurber with that inexplicable omission. He was not too surprised with the NASA administrator's response since the professor already knew Operation Mars's flight plan intimately. He was aware that there was no call in the program for the use of colloidal suspension. The planet's distance from the sun—greater than earth's—obviated the need for a plastic screen to blot out the sun.

"Would you think of spinning collodial suspension over Miami, Dr. Simms?" Thurber asked airily.

"Not unless I wanted it to snow there," the professor smiled with an honest response.

"Well, we certainly have no need to shield our landing party from the sun on Mars," Thurber said firmly. "Not when the temperature range is between fifty and one hundred degrees."

Simms shook his head in disagreement.

"Maitland, we'll do a grave disservice to this crew if we send them to Mars without at least an instruction manual on how to run the particle accelerator for colloidal suspension."

Thurber looked at Simms with a frown shaped by bewilderment. "What are you talking about, Gordon?"

"Let us assume they're able to establish a habitable environment on Mars with the particle accelerator, then begin their explorations," Simms said with deliberation. "My biggest fear at that stage is the peril of radiation that will confront them. In that thin atmosphere, it will be considerable. The sun's rays may be more damaging than we're able to foresee, despite all the studies we've made."

Thurber threw up his hands. "You win again, Gordon. I'm not convinced you're right. But I go along with you. They should have the option of being able to put up that screen. And besides, what'll it cost us? Really nothing. All we need is a pamphlet of instructions. So, why don't you arrange to get your hands on one? Call them at Grumman. Then when you come down to the Cape to orient the team on life-support systems in January, you'll be able to brief them about colloidal suspension as well."

Simms phoned Grumman Aerospace and spoke to Boyce McMorrow, the genius behind the particle accelerator's development. The professor wasn't communicating with a stranger.

Simms and McMorrow had known each other for thirty-five years—since their days at James Monroe High School in the Bronx.

Simms had grown up in the Hunts Point section, McMorrow in the Parkchester area.

After graduation, Simms and McMorrow both pursued engineering studies, but in separate directions. McMorrow earned his B.A. and Masters degrees at Harvard, Simms at UCLA, where he also took his Doctorate studies.

After college, McMorrow took a job at Grumman and stayed for all the years since. Simms went to a teaching post at UCLA and remained there, advancing in reputation as one of the world's foremost space scientists.

In the years since they went their separate ways, Simms and McMorrow saw each other infrequently. Yet they kept in touch constantly. They were involved in the same space projects repeatedly. However, circumstances had not drawn them together in many years. The last time time they saw each other was in 1972 at Cape Canaveral on the Apollo 17 launch, the last lunar flight of that early space program.

When Simms spoke with his old friend in September, and told him Thurber wanted the crew briefed on the operation of the particle accelerator for colloidal suspension, McMorrow was dismayed.

"This isn't something we can prepare overnight," he said defensively. "It'll take a few months . . ."

"Can you have it ready by early January?" Simms wanted to know.

"Yes, I'm quite certain we can," McMorrow replied.

They then agreed to meet on that Sunday, January 3 on Long Island . . .

Simms looked at his watch again after waiting patiently for a short take of the Alice Crimmins movie to be concluded at the front desk where Joseph Rorech, the lover, signed the register for Room 234.

The professor rose from his chair and walked to the front desk. A clerk approached with a smile.

"The name is Simms and I reserved a car . . ."

"Oh, yes, sir," the clerk said smartly. "We just rang your room but there was no response. The car is here and these are the keys."

Simms signed the rental agreement and took the keys. He fought his way through the confusion of movie-makers and onlookers once more and went outside. He found the 1988 two-door hatchback Ford Airflow where the clerk said it would be in the parking lot.

He got behind the wheel, drove eastbound on the Long Island expressway to Exit 49-S and, following directions McMorrow provided, drove along Route 110 for approximately two miles.

Simms sucked in a deep breath of satisfaction after he spotted a sign reading MARCPIERRE. That was the landmark restaurant McMorrow had proposed for their rendezvous.

Simms parked, the walked into the restaurant.

"Ah, *oui, monsieur* . . . may I have the playzure of escorting you to your table?"

The words had come from the smiling lips of a tuxedoed, balding host with gold-framed glasses. The professor shrugged with suspicion. He was about to say that he had an appointment to meet someone, yet found it unecessary to utter a word.

"No, no, no, Dr. Simms, please do not say a word, I know exactly where to take you. But first, allow me . . ."

The greeter with the French accent was Al Haas, the owner of the restaurant who was really of German descent and born in the South Bronx. He had picked up his Gallic accent in the corridors of the same James Monroe High that Simms and McMorrow had attended. Only Haas had preceded the professor and Grumman engineer to the Boynton Avenue school by some seventeen years.

Haas helped Simms off with his overcoat and handed it to the hatcheck girl.

"And now, *Docteur*, eef you weel follow me, please, I weel show you to Monsieur McMorrow's table . . ."

Haas led Simms over the plushly carpeted foyer toward the brick archway that opened to the main dining room. As he walked in, Simms at once caught sight of his old friend. McMorrow was seated at a table in the far corner.

"Monsieur McMorrow," the jolly restaurateur persisted in his put-on accent, "allow me to introduce Docteur Simms."

By now McMorrow was on his feet and half-expecting that byplay by Haas, an incurable kibitzer. McMorrow was one of the Marcpierre's oldest and steadiest patrons. Actually, he was one of a score of top engineers at Grumman who'd made the restaurant their favorite dining and drinking oasis since it opened in 1960 under Haas's stewardship.

As Simms and McMorrow shook hands and exchanged greetings in warm, animated tones, Haas stepped away discreetly, leaving the two men to themselves.

They sat at the table and an instant later McMorrow narrowed his gaze and screwed his face into a pretended scornful pose.

Simms looked at his friend with bafflement. "What's wrong, Boyce?" Simms wanted to know.

"You have a hell of a nerve, Gordy," McMorrow said scoldingly.

"Why . . . what have I done?" Simms said in sober astonishment.

"Every since you spoke with me on the phone," McMorrow rasped, "I've worked on the manual for colloidal suspension you asked for. But that was no problem at all. It just took time to prepare. But what has been bugging me all this time is, what in hell are you going to do with colloidal suspension on Mars?"

Simms smiled and made a gesture with his arms.

"You just don't know to what ends we're going to provide our Mars exploration team with every life-support system possible," the professor said.

"Well, all I've got to say," McMorrow murmured, "it seems to me this whole program to land people on Mars is way out . . ."

"I'm sure you're kidding, Boyce," Simms said somberly.

McMorrow looked out over the dining room and signaled the maître d'. Then he turned to Simms.

"Gordy, I know you very well," McMorrow said softly. "You're a stickler for details. You don't overlook a thing. In fact, you're a backbreaker." McMorrow broke into a wide grin. "Don't be dismayed, old pal," the Grumman engineer snorted. "I've prepared a whole pamphlet on how to run the show with colloidal suspension. But I want to talk to you about it first."

The professor leaned back in his chair and chuckled.

"I'm delighted to hear you say that, Boyce. I didn't come all this way just to pick up a pamphlet. I'm looking for answers to the many questions I have about keeping those people on Mars in greatest safety through any contingency . . ."

"That's a fat order, Gordy," McMorrow snorted. "But I'll try to help out. And what I want to say right now is that I'm not faulting you for pressing like you have. It's merely that I want you to know I consider you a damned backbreaker. But I'm happy that you are. You've got a mighty big responsibility with so many lives in your hands ..."

McMorrow looked up at the maître d' who had arrived at the table with a wide grin.

"Come on, Gordy," McMorrow said, "Let's order a drink ..."

CHAPTER VII

A Space Program Coverup: Genetic Perils

For the first few sips of their Bloody Marys, Simms and McMorrow were content with an exchange of small talk. But the professor soon channeled the conversation to the topic that had brought the two men together.

"I see you have some papers, Boyce," Simms smiled thinly. He nodded toward a large brown folder that was on the chair beside McMorrow.

"I do, that's for sure," McMorrow said, blowing a plume of smoke from his cigarette toward the ceiling. "But there's more to be said about colloidal suspension than we've put into the manual. That's why I said I wanted to talk to you about it."

Simms shifted in his chair. He felt the least bit on edge. He had waited a long time for this moment—when the brain behind the development of the particle accelerator would perhaps provide the answers about the machine's optimum operation, something the professor himself had calculated in theory if not in practice. He was confident of his conclusions, yet he wanted to be certain. And what better way than checking with McMorrow?

"Without breaking out the manual, Gordy," McMorrow said with a sigh, "I think I can explain the essential operating principles. But what I want you to understand above all else is the kind of machine that you have in the particle accelerator."

McMorrow took two quick sips of his drink.

"Unquestionably, you're thoroughly familiar with the way the accelerator creates a vacuum, so I'm not going to dwell on that. But the colloidal suspension is simply an incredible adjunct to the vacuum. Between you and me, I think it's even more remarkable—and certainly a far more significant safety measure in space exploration."

Simms shook his head quickly. "I agree. Because in my view corpuscular radiation is a perilous biological hazard. Until now there's been no foolproof defense against the penetrating killing protons and electrons through the walls of spacecraft hulls . . ."

McMorrow was tapping his fingers on the table in obvious impatience.

"Let me interrupt you, Gordy. That's precisely why I was so annoyed when you called me in September and said you wanted a brochure on how to operate the accelerator for colloidal suspension. Do you know that it was our intention at Grumman as far back as two years ago to prepare instructions for both uses? But somebody down at NASA said that wouldn't be necessary."

100

"Who said that, do you know?" Simms asked in a concerned tone. "I sure would like to know who that jackass was."

"No idea," McMorrow said flatly. "But that certainly was a stupid decision."

"Did you try to get that order rescinded?"

"No, because when it came down to me it had an element of finality from upstairs, which I didn't believe should be questioned."

McMorrow emptied his glass and called for another round of drinks.

"But that was good thinking on your part, Gordy," McMorrow said positively. "The order of importance that I've always attached to priorities in any exploration of a planet we've never visited in person before is, one, throw a solar curtain around the ship. In fact, this is what they should be doing for the space stations and the moon colonies. Of course, that wasn't possible before we developed the particle accelerator. But now that it's here, a reality, there's no reason to delay that application. It's a sound safety measure. Damn it, you know what cosmic primaries can do when they bounce against metal hulls."

Simms drummed his fingertips on the tablecloth.

"All too well," he shook his head knowingly. "Once that happens, you have more than a spaceship. What you have additionally is a gigantic X-ray machine."

"And then what happens to the living cells from the radiation?" McMorrow said sharply.

Simms looked up at the ceiling. His face was a mask of consternation.

"I think you know what I'm talking about, Gordy. Am I correct in that assumption?"

"Boyce, I know what the space program has done to procreative capacities of every living being who's ever been rocketed just even out of our atmosphere."

"I've been keeping a pretty accurate score, Gordy," McMorrow said abruptly. He reached into the inside pocket of his jacket and pulled out a leatherbound memo pad.

"It begins with Sputnik I, although I have that date and event listed, October 4, 1957, only because it was the beginning of this tragic and foolhardy oversight."

"Let me interrupt you, Boyce," the professor said heavily. "Not oversight. I call it an outright unconscionable dereliction of responsibility and trust. They've known what's been happening for more than thirty years, ever since the Russians sent up that dog ... what's his name ... ?"

"Right here," McMorrow cut in quickly, looking in his book. "The name was Laika and it was November 3, 1957 ... but it gets very serious after that because they saw what happened to the dog and then to the mouse that we sent up. But even the monkeys and the cats weren't enough to ask, 'Hey, what the Hell's going on up there?' "

"Well, the Kremlin said it first, 'So what?' and sent Yuri Gagarin into orbit," Simms said. "I don't have the date on my fingertips but I know Gagarin stayed up for only one orbit—yet, even that was too much."

"Actually, Gordy, even Alan Shepard's and Virgil Grissom's one hundred seventeen-mile-high sub-orbital joyrides were a bit much, I found, and yet their studies didn't deter them from continuing the madness."

McMorrow put his hand up and signaled the maître d' again. "Either this subject or the drinks has worked up my appetite," he said forcefully.

A rugged 200-pounder who carried his weight on a 5-foot-8 frame, McMorrow not only gave the appearance of being fat, which he was, but liking it. At the Marcpierre they knew him as an eager and very large eater.

The maître d' brought the menus.

"Come back in a while, John," McMorrow said in a polite but dismissing tone. The tuxedoed maître d' responded smartly with a "Yes, sir, Mr. McMorrow."

Then he turned and strode away.

The Grumman space chief looked over the celery and olives and hot midget bread loaves the busboy had put down in the center of the table. McMorrow narrowed his gaze at the professor.

"Gordy, I won't belabor the point," he said solemnly. "But I'll just skim over my list to assure you I've had people safety at heart through all my years in the space program, just as I know you have."

McMorrow peered at his book again and read more names: "Gherman Titov, John

Glenn, Scott Carpenter, Andrian Nikolayev, Pavel Popovich, Walter Schirra, Gordon Cooper . . ."

He stopped the recitation at that juncture. "It's getting monotonous," he said. "But let me just wind it up like this . . ."

He flipped page after page and finally came to the place in the memo pad that he was looking for.

"Now we're into 1988," he said running his finger down that page. "We're only three days into the new year and I'm not aware of any shuttle orbiter flights in this period because I've been away from work for the holidays. But in my rundown for 1987 . . . let's see . . . Gellerbach, Fay, Ramsey, Toller . . . oh, God . . . a hundred and twenty-five Americans were up in space during last year alone . . . Do you know what they're doing to those people?"

Simms put the menu he'd been holding down on the place setting in front of him and wrung his hands. "The same thing that they've done to those others they've sent into space since Shepard and Grissom."

McMorrow snorted heavily and pointed a scolding finger at his companion, not out of anger but for emphasis.

"The list of people who've been in space, by my count, is two thousand eight hundred and forty-one. Ninety-two were women in that bunch. And it doesn't begin with Al and Gus, as you just mentioned, but with Gagarin . . ."

Then McMorrow quickly shook his head in

disagreement with his own assertion. "Actually it begins with the dog and the mouse."

"They became aware of what was happening to life in space from almost the beginning," Simms said. "But they never took proper precautions."

"But they always took refuge in the argument that, genetically speaking, no discernible changes had ever occurred in either animals or humans in space," said McMorrow with no tolerance in his voice. "Yet, they lied through their teeth. I'm convinced of that. I've kept a record and there hasn't been a single instance in which anyone who ventured out of our atmosphere ever returned to procreate or reproduce."

Then he fell silent for a moment to let his words echo for effect. He broke the silence by bringing a clenched fist down on the table. "Not even one meaningful pregnancy that we've ever heard about," McMorrow said sharply.

"What amazes me all the more," Simms said with bitterness in his tone, "is the total gullibility of the press. I remember being in Houston sometime around 1979 or 1980 and a science writer from the *Los Angeles Times* went snooping for the story around the people in Space Medicine. But he got such a snow job that he never wrote a line. Those medical mongers sluffed him off with barefaced lies. One of their most vapid defenses was, 'Oh, our people who went in space all had their families set. They had children already and didn't want anymore . . .' "

But as the years passed and increasing numbers of space ventures were carried out—not only by the United States but the Soviet Union, France, England, China, and other countries— no man or woman who ever rode out of earth's atmosphere, even for relatively brief periods, came back to father or bear a child.

Yet, only a relative handful of science and medical writers ever wondered about that or harbored enough suspicion to ask why such a strange phenomenon was occuring. However, they were always conned out of doing stories by NASA's medical teams, which wanted to conceal that disturbing, if not terrifying, manifestation linked with space travel.

The discussion was interrupted when the maître d' returned to the table for the order. As a steady and longtime patron, McMorrow knew the specialties of the house. He recommended *duck flambé* and Simms agreed to join his dining companion in that main dish. After the waiter left, McMorrow turned to Simms with a quizzical expression.

"All right, Gordy, I've spouted enough with what I think is wrong with the space program. I know you traveled all these miles to get the lowdown on colloidal suspension. Nevertheless, I'm sure you'll forgive my detour, because what this system is all about may just be the solution to the corpuscular radiation that we fear has caused genetic damage to our space fliers."

Simms broke out in a wide smile.

"Boyce, you certainly came up with some very revealing thoughts. And I'm certainly heartened to know there's someone else in the space program who shares my views and apprehensions."

McMorrow nodded and smiled drearily. "Swell, Gordy, so I've an ally who sees eye to eye with me," he said with a rush. "But that's not why we're here. You came all the way to Long Island to get an instant education in colloidal suspension. And, believe it or not, I'm going to give you one beginning from this moment . . ."

Simms smiled with a deep underlying pleasure. "You've got both my ears, Boyce."

CHAPTER VIII

A Lesson on How To Blot out the Sun

The waiter brought the luncheon guests their appetizers and walked away as McMorrow picked up a spoon and wiggled it over his fruit cocktail for a thoughtful moment.

"Before we begin digging into colloidal suspension, Gordy, there's just one more thing I want to say. I'm deeply impressed with your deep dedication to safety in space. You're not one to play games with people's lives. But there's one thing that puzzles me . . ."

Simms gazed at his friend with an apprehensive smile. "What stumps you, Boyce?"

"It has to do with Operation WAMIS," McMorrow muttered while forcing a smile betraying his uneasiness.

"What don't you understand about it?" Simms said stiffly, all at once perturbed.

"Hold on, Gordy," McMorrow came back swiftly. "I'm not looking to knock you down . . . I'm merely trying to find out why the newsmen have been so unkind. Why, *The New York Times* hasn't stopped rapping you."

The professor put a spoonful of fruit salad into his mouth and chewed it hurriedly. "What concerns me," he said gulping, "is what second thoughts you have about the isolation experiment."

McMorrow grimaced in protest. "I have no second thoughts, Gordy. The only question in my mind is why you went to such a hell of a lot of trouble to put those people that far down . . . what was it, three miles? . . ."

Before Simms could reply, McMorrow began laughing. "All I want to know, Gordy, is what you were thinking of when you picked that spot?"

Simms shifted in his chair. He felt uneasy whenever anyone asked that question, and this was no different than all the other times.

"I chose that mine," the professor said in a measured tempo, "because it was the farthest place from earth's natural environment I could find. I didn't want those students in a building or other surface structure, because it might be susceptible to possible interference, intrusion, or influence by outside forces. But down in that shaft in Ravenna, they are in total isolation. It's as near as one can come to a Mars environment on Earth."

McMorrow moved his head up and down.

"Of course it is. And I'm in accord with your choice. But let me say one thing about that . . ."

"What's that?" Simms asked, his composure now returned.

"Well Gordy," McMorrow quipped, "you won't have to worry about that bunch where you've put them. They're down so far that, I guess, even if Hell freezes over they wouldn't feel a chill."

Simms was jolted by the crack but he tried to hide his feelings. His eyes had opened wide and he grimaced uncomfortably for a brief moment. But before McMorrow could get a reading on the professor's inexplicable reaction to an obviously innocuous remark, the professor all at once broke into a sly grin.

"They'll be a heck of a lot warmer than the team that lands on Mars," Simms winked. "That colloidal suspension screen will make it a lot colder than they'd be without it."

The temperature on the Red Planet averages minus 70 degrees Centigrade and McMorrow made a hasty calculation on a piece of scrap paper.

"By my reckonings, the cover will not reduce the sun's heat appreciably," he said. "In our operating instructions, we recommend only limited unraveling of the screen over any area. What I'm saying is that you shade only the general sector inhabited and worked by space explorers. You don't unfurl it too far beyond. In that way, the sun still provides heat around the perimeter of the protected area."

"But it's safe heat," Simms observed correctly. "There's no radiation in the shade."

"Absolutely none," McMorrow concurred. He put his spoon down into his now-empty fruit cocktail dish as the waiter brought the main course to the table on a wheeled serving cart. "Let me tell you a few significant things about the particle accelerator. You didn't receive this information in the early literature, but I'm sure you're aware of it. The power plant is fed not by plutonium 238, as we originally designed it, but by uranium 235."

Simms nodded his awareness. "I know. Thurber let me in on the switch in design back when you made the change."

"And I assume you know what the difference is," McMorrow said matter-of-factly.

"I certainly do. You're talking about a decay rate of seventy-one million years before only half of the nuclear battery burns out."

"Do you think we'll be around to watch that event?" McMorrow asked sardonically.

Simms leaned back automatically as the waiter placed the serving of duck in front of him on the table.

"What has me somewhat confused is the methodology behind this concept of colloidal suspension. I think I understand it, yet I'm not sure that even the brochure you've prepared will make it altogether clear to me."

"That's why I suggested this get-together before you read the pamphlet," McMorrow said crisply. "Now, if you'll pay attention, I'll give you the whole lowdown."

McMorrow took a mouthful of food, chewed it, cleared his throat, and turned an attentive eye to Simms.

"Gordy, the thing you must remember above all else is that heat generated by atomic fusion causes colloidal suspension of the black particles that you distribute in space. The black carbon element supplies an infinite stock-pile of those particles."

Simms was impressed. He also understood the principle. "The black carbon element is the nutrient that feeds the the nuclear power plant that produces the black particles in suspension, right?" Simms said.

"Exactly," McMorrow acknowledged. "And the carbon element has a virtually limitless capacity. We estimate the foot-long element we've put into the particle accelerator's colloidal suspension feeder compartment might have almost the same lifespan as the nuclear battery. A miserly pinch of element is enough to form a canopy from here to forever."

"Incredible!" exclaimed Simms. "That means colloidal suspension theoretically can spin out plasticized solar protection screens for millions of square miles."

"More probably in the billions," McMorrow corrected grandly. "Enough to cover our solar system plus the entire Milky Way and the hundred million stars in it."

"It's unbelievable!" Simms rasped with renewed astonishment. "The whole universe!"

McMorrow drew in a deep breath. He seemed to enjoy the professor's startled reaction.

"Gordy, I'm going to let you in on a little secret," McMorrow grinned with pleasure. "We've done our homework with this machine. It's the greatest advance ever in life-support systems. With the particle accelerator we can land on any planet in the solar system and create a completely safe environment for our space explorers."

"There's little question that this machine puts us on the threshold of colonizing the moon and planets," Simms said animatedly.

"It certainly does," McMorrow agreed. "This old earth of ours may find the answer for what to do with overpopulation sooner than anyone expected."

"That's heartening indeed, Boyce," the professor said quickly, yet at the same time trying to conceal his impatience. He wanted to hear more about the technical workings of the machine producing colloidal suspension. "What miracle have you shaped that holds those particles together and makes them form a screen? I know the trouble people in zero gravity have just trying to drink water because it separates in droplets..."

"Okay, that's the bottom line," McMorrow said after drinking from his water goblet and chasing down a mouthful of food. "I know you're aware from studying our early schematics to NASA that the spinoff from the accelerator's jetsprouts produces a high-pressure flow resembling the sort of vapor jetstream conventional aircraft leave behind in atmospheric flight."

Simms nodded. That much he understood. But what he wasn't certain of was how wide the stream of particles would spread or expand in space.

"That depends on the amount of rpm's you turn up while running the machine," McMorrow went on. "The control has eight different swath settings. It can disperse a screen as narrow as fifty miles on the lowest swath. That setting is recommended nominally to give ships in flight protection against cosmic radiation. But keep in mind the swath settings are in uneven gradations. They go to the second setting, which is a hundred miles, then to two hundred, five hundred . . ."

"What's the maximum width the accelerator can screen in one pass over a given area?" Simms wanted to know. "Is it still nine hundred?"

"No," McMorrow shook his head. "We made some improvements in the design over the early specs. So now we have a max of a thousand miles—"

"A thousand!" exclaimed Simms with surprise. "That's pretty good."

"I don't see why that excites you so much, Gordy," McMorrow frowned. "You're not going to be using anything as big as that until you begin colonizing up there. For low-key explorations like we're doing on Mars this year, I'd say a hundred-mile screen is more than adequate. After all, as I told you before, you don't want to hide too much sun. Otherwise, you'll put those people on the mission in a deep freeze."

"I certainly am not aiming to do that," Simms said laconically. "But I'm still wondering to be using anything as big as that until still haven't spelled out how the particles get together to form a solid screen."

"When the particles spew from the jetport,

they are microscopic in size. But they undergo an immediate and remarkable metamorphosis. Upon their entry into the vacuum of space and contact with the cosmic primaries, there's an instantaneous interaction, which produces a swift and steady expansion of the particles. That expansion—and that's what's so remarkable about the process—is accompanied by a very rapid buildup of molecular structure in the emitted particles. These expand and regenerate with such rapidity that in split seconds the screen is formed."

"And it's just as you described in your early advisories," Simms interrupted, now with considerable anxiety. "Is it really like a polyethylene screen?"

"Exactly," McMorrow smiled. "While it has different chemical properties, it nevertheless has an equivalent number of applications as polyethylene or Kapton do in space."

The space program had adopted Kapton seven years earlier, in 1981, in the construction of an unmanned solar sailing ship that rendezvoused with Halley's Comet in February, 1986, during its once-every-seventy-five-year appearance. The sail, resembling a square kite, whose sides were a half-mile broad, carried a 2,500-pound instrumented spacecraft, which rocketed itself in orbit around the comet once the solar sail had been wafted by the solar winds to the vicinity of the hurtling mini-planet.

The whole package was designed by an engineering team at the Jet Propulsion Laboratory in Pasadena. But since no life-support systems were required for the Yankee Clipper, as the ship was dubbed, Simms was not associated with the project.

Yet, he went through a great deal of red tape in NASA to obtain the old sketches for the solar sail. Simms had taken a curious interest in the steering mechanism of the solar sail, actually "steering sails"—small vanes attached at the four tips of the sail and operated by remote control radio imulses from earth.

"Why the hell do you want to find out how the vanes work?" NASA Director Thurber asked when Simms came to him in dismay after lower echelon space officials had refused to release the drawings to the professor. That was in early 1987, after the Yankee Clipper's successful rendezvous with Halley's Comet and just when Simms became aware of Grumman's startling progress in development of the particle accelerator.

The professor convinced Thurber that the request to examine the Yankee Clipper plans was entirely reasonable.

"When we employ colloidal suspension in space to protect people from solar radiation," Simms argued, "we've got to adopt controls for the canopies similar to what the solar sail had. There may be occasions when the plastic shield must be moved to a new location. But if the shuttle orbiter has gone off on a mission somewhere, how will those remaining behind on the surface shift the screen when they must carry their explorations and studies to an unprotected area of the planet?"

Just as he had succeeded in his arguments so many times in the past, Dr. Simms once more maneuvered Thurber into capitulation. The NASA boss had the highest regard and respect for Dr. Simms, and if Simms crossed verbal swords with Thurber long enough, he could get virtually anything he wanted. Thurber trusted Simms completely and was convinced his dedication to the space program was greater than anyone else's.

"Say, Gordy," McMorrow said finally after coffee was poured. "I want to let you in on a secret."

Simms looked with renewed interest at his friend. "What's that, Boyce?"

"You know more about the particle accelerator and colloidal suspension system than anyone on this God's earth—only with the possible exception of myself. And, to be perfectly frank with you, I have a feeling you may know even more about it than I do now."

Simms roared with sudden laughter and McMorrow joined in.

"What do you say, Gordy," McMorrow asked. "Would you like to pay the check so we can get out of here?"

"Good idea, Boyce," Simms chuckled. "And let me say thanks for all you've done."

"My pleasure," McMorrow smiled. "Just apply your newfound knowledge well."

Simms shook his head complacently.

"Believe me, Boyce, I certainly will apply it well . . ."

CHAPTER IX

Countdown to Blastoff

Simms was in excellent spirits as he drove back to the Kings Grant Motor Inn from his mission to the Marcpierre Restaurant. The information he elicited from Boyce McMorrow buoyed the professor.

Much of the knowledge wasn't all that new. Simms had been aware of many of the particle accelerator's mechanical characteristics for some time. Yet, the additional details his friend had furnished gave the professor the margin of comfort he wanted to have before returning to Cape Canaveral for the Operation Mars briefings.

When he arrived at the motel, the doctor was relieved to find the movie company had departed. The clock on the wall behind the desk read 4:45. Too early for dinner, especially since he'd just lunched.

Simms went to his room, removed his overcoat and suit jacket with great relief, then plopped back shirtsleeved into the upholstered arm chair. He knew precisely how to spend the next few hours—studying McMorrow's thirty-two-page brochure.

Turning to the first page, Simms began reading with a deep, absorbing interest. He hadn't taken an Evelyn Wood speed-reading course, but even if he had he wouldn't have thumbed through the text speedily. The professor was determined to read and digest every word about colloidal suspension in the pamphlet.

After more than an hour of riveted concentration on the booklet, Simms closed the covers and put it down on the lamp table beside the chair. Then he stood and stretched lazily to chase the stiffness from his leg muscles.

He checked his watch. It was 5:55. Simms picked up the motel TV guide and went to the video set. He switched it on and checked the program listings. It took a few seconds to find what interested him: the news on CBS. He turned the dial to Channel 2, then went back the armchair and settled comfortably in it.

Chris Borgen, the newscaster on the six o'clock Evening News, appeared on the screen and rattled off the day's happenings.

First came world news: China and the Soviet Union had another border skirmish without casualties, but Moscow sent a note just the same to the Chinese Embassy in Moscow protesting "hostile conduct by your troops"; happier news originated from the Middle East where Israel and the United Arab Republic of Egypt held joint celebrations in Tel Aviv and Cairo marking the ninth anniversary of the signing of their permanent peace accord, and from Paris came word that structural defects caused by rust and corrosion had forced the closing of the Eiffel Tower for repairs, to be completed by early 1989 and in time to mark its first century celebration.

On the domestic scene, Borgen reported: "Warning signals are flashing as Congress prepares to take up the Mondale Administration's wide-ranging proposals to keep the economy humming through the coming fiscal year. Even before getting their first briefing on the President's tax program, the Republicans have begun sniping at the package calling for one hundred billion dollars in cuts as a gimmick to help him get reelected in November..."

The big local news was Mayor Carol Bellamy's exclusive interview in the New York *Post* in which she told editor Steve Dunleavy that New York City had decided to hold a 1989-90 World's Fair, thus keeping up with the tradition started in 1939 of staging expositions every twenty-five years.

None of these news items excited Simms as much as the lead story in sports: "The fiasco over the 28-28 Super Bowl tie between the Tampa Bay Buccaneers and the Seattle Seahawks continues to confound the office of Football Commissioner Pete Rozelle. As you may recall, Sunday's game was suspended on account of darkness after the sixth period of play because the Rose Bowl has no lights. The NFL is trying to decide whether to let the tie stand and divide the prize money evenly among both teams, toss a coin to select a winner, or play the game over in the Superdome. As uncertain as Rozelle may seem to be, there's one thing he's decided not to do. That is have the team go into a seventh period of sudden-death play. His view is that if the teams suit up again, it'll be for a full-fledged game played before another capacity crowd and an ample supply of candlepower such as is available in New Orleans . . ."

A smile crinkled Dr. Simms's face as he listened to that sports item. Without waiting to hear the balance of the broadcast, Simmons got up from the chair and faded Chris Borgen and CBS Evening News from the screen.

"I wonder whether I shouldn't drop Sandy Sheiler and Merv Kotler a note about these late developments in Super Bowl XXII?" the professor asked in a voice that he suddenly realized had been uttered not under his breath but out loud. He shook his head. "I've got to stop talking to myself," he said, "Just because I'm doing so well winding up preparations for my mission, I ought not lose my foolish head. I've simply got to learn to shut my mouth . . ."

Dr. Gordon Lyle Simms yawned. He had been seated at the desk in his room at the King's Grant for more than three hours since returning from dinner in the motor inn's Camelot Room. It was just past midnight as he checked the time.

He flipped over the pages of his legal-size

yellow pad. Neatly scrawled blue-inked script filled eighteen pages of the pad. Simms had been scribbling at a furious pace since returning from dinner.

It'd been a long, tedious, yet very productive day. A sense of satisfaction coursed through Simms as he looked back on all that he had achieved on this Tuesday.

Now looming ahead was the dawn of a new day and the professor's flight to Cape Canaveral for the training countdown of the ten-member space team of the Operation Mars mission.

Simms rose from the desk and fetched his attaché case from the closet floor. He opened it on the desk and carefully placed the eighteen-page memorandum inside, as well as the Grumman brochure on the operation and maintenance of the particle accelerator's colloidal suspension system.

Again the professor checked his watch. It was 12:30 A.M. Wakeup call. Then he undressed and went to bed.

In the morning, Simms needed no ring from the desk to rouse him. He had opened his eyes into excited full wakefulness a minute or so after seven. For an hour he had lain in bed just gazing up at the ceiling and studying the slow-moving reflected shadows formed by the sun filtering through the cracks in the blinds.

His thoughts were on the day's active schedule, which was to take him to Cape Canaveral by mid-afternoon. He had reservations on Eastern Airlines Flight 456, departing

Republic Airport at 1 P.M. and due in Titusville at 1:35 P.M. Maitland Thurber had arranged to have the professor helicoptered the last thirty miles from the airport on the Florida mainland to the NASA complex on the Cape.

But before he could leave Long Island, Simms had an urgent errand to perform and the sudden jangle of the telephone startled him out of his daydream. He thanked the operator for the call, returned the receiver to its cradle, and swung his bare feet to the floor. He rose yawning lazily, stretched his arms horizontally for a full fifteen seconds, and then sucked in a deep, decisive breath.

Yes, he told himself, he'd take a shower.

He opened his carry-all suitcase on the canvas luggage rest and carefully selected a change of underwear, socks, and shirt. After flipping the flap to get to the suit compartment, he also picked a plain brown tweed sports jacket and tan slacks. Then he packed away the clothes he'd worn up from Louisville and went into the shower.

It was 9:30 A.M. now. The professor stood before the dresser mirror giving his face and attire a final going-over. Then he stepped back with a smug smile. He heartily approved of the way he looked—and he was ready.

Simms took the carry-all suitcase in his left hand, tucked the attaché case under the same arm, opened and shut the motel room door with his right hand, then gripped the handle of the attaché case with his free hand. Finally, he walked surefootedly toward the front desk.

The cashier had Dr. Simms's bill ready but hadn't included the charges for the Hertz car rental. The professor still needed the use of the car for an errand he was about to embark on. He'd turn in the car at the airport.

Once more Dr. Simms drove onto the Long Island Expressway and exited at the same off-ramp as he'd taken the previous day in going to his rendezvous with Boyce McMorrow at the Marcpierre. But now, instead of turning south on Route 110, he crossed the highway and drove on the expressway's service road a short distance. Then he turned into the first drive-way after the corner. It led to the parking lot of a four-story office building.

Simms's destination was the Chase-Manhattan Bank branch fronting busy Route 110, also called Broad Hollow Road in that sector of Melville. The bank occupied a prominent street-level portion of the building, a 10,000-square-foot area at the northeast corner.

After parking in a stall, the professor grabbed his attaché case, locked the car, and walked with brisk quick steps into the bank. He approached the section where the manager and assistant manager had their desks. A re-ceptionist, whose desk was positioned as a buffer between the customers and the bank offi-cials, smiled dutifully at Simms and asked how she could assist him.

"I'd like to rent a safe deposit box, ma'am," he said very businesslike.

"Certainly, sir," she replied, reaching into the right-hand top drawer and pulling out an application card.

"If you'll fill this out, sir, I'll get you a box immediately," she said pleasantly. The young woman handed Simms the card and a pen.

Simms jotted down the brief information required for the bank's records and handed the signed card to the receptionist.

"Now there is just one more thing to resolve," the young woman said. "What size box would you like?"

"I don't need too much room," Simms replied.

"Then I believe our smallest box, which rents for twenty-four dollars a year, should suit you."

"Simms quickly wrote a check for the amount and handed it to the woman.

"If you'll follow me, please, I'll get your box," she said, rising from her desk and signaling Simms to follow her.

She walked about fifteen feet and opened a door in a glass-enclosed room. Simms looked at the room with eyes staring in astonishment.

"Is this where your safe deposit vault is?" he asked in a languid voice.

"Why, yes," the receptionist answered quickly. "Is something wrong with that?"

"You mean to say it isn't downstairs, below the first-floor level?" the professor said with a trace of disturbance in his voice that he was unable to conceal.

The woman looked at Simms with puzzlement. "Why, no, sir, our safe deposit boxes are in this room. Does that make a difference to you?"

Simms shook his head. "No, not at all. Now, may I have my key?..."

"Do you want me to get your box?" the woman wanted to know.

"No, not just yet," Simms responded quickly. "I'm not prepared to put in anything now. But you can let me have the key. I must leave now."

The receptionist handed Simms the key with a look of bewilderment. She had never before handled a customer who was quite so eccentric as this one.

The professor walked out of the bank mumbling under his breath. *Damn it,* he told himself, *I had to find a bank with safe deposit boxes on street level. Well, I'll have to look for one that has its safe deposit boxes downstairs.*

Simms drove out of the parking lot and turned north on Broad Hollow Road. He crossed over the Long Island Expressway after the light turned green and tooled his car a half mile further. Suddenly ahead loomed the large blue-black-white lettering of a Chemical Bank branch just north of the Pinelawn Road Intersection.

Simms went into the parking lot behind the four-story building whose upper floors housed Chemical's corporate headquarters for its Long

Island operations. Again lugging the attaché case, he entered the bank and looked about. It was a huge facility, more than twice as large as the other bank he'd been to. But the professor wasn't interested in physical dimensions, merely the location of the safe deposit vault.

His eyes searched carefully all around the first floor level, which was actually four steps above street grade. He half-smiled as he spotted a sign that read, TO SAFE DEPOSIT BOXES. An arrow pointed to the down staircase. *This is more like it,* the professor told himself. He walked to a desk where a pretty middle-aged receptionist smiled pleasantly and asked if she could help him.

He was guided through a routine at this bank slightly different than the other. The receptionist directed him to a grouping of desks on the far end of the floor.

"Please ask for Mrs. Mary Spanacopito," the receptionist said. "She will arrange for your safe deposit rental."

Simms found Mrs. Spanacopito solicitous to the extreme. Instead of having the applicant fill out the card for the box, she asked questions and wrote the information down.

"Now, if you'll please sign here, Dr. Simms, I'll take you downstairs to our vault."

Simms scrawled his name on the card and paid for the box with a check in the same amount as the rental for the box at Chase-Manhattan.

"Oh!" Mrs. Spanacopito exclaimed as she

looked at the check, "your account is in California."

"Yes," Simms replied stiffly, "should that make a difference?"

"Certainly not," the bank employee said with a trace of embarrassment in her voice. "It's just that you've aroused my curiosity. I'm wondering why a depositor with the Bank of America comes all the way to Long Island to rent a safe deposit box."

Simms smiled tightly. "For a very good reason, my good lady," he said heavily. "I happen to do business on both coasts. And that's why I want a safe deposit box at this end of the country."

The professor narrowed his gaze at Mrs. Spanacopito. "Now, do I get that box or do I take my business somewhere else?" His tone was jocular and Mrs. Spanacopito sensed his mood at once. Her face crinkled in a smile.

"Come with me, Dr. Simms, and I'll get you squared away," she said pleasantly.

The professor followed her to the staircase. They walked down to the lower level where the professor's escort approached a woman at the desk leading to the vault. On looking up and seeing Mrs. Spanacopito, the keeper of the vault pressed a button and the sliding steel-barred door slid open.

"Do you have the keys for HOOO423?" Mrs. Spanacopito asked.

"Let me see," the keeper of the vault said with an air of importance almost bordering on impudence. "I'll check just as soon as I see the application card. Do you have one made out?"

The woman from upstairs was cognizant of the vault lady's obnoxiousness. She handed her the card and waited with practiced patience for the keys.

"Everything seems in order," the keeper of the safe deposit boxes said, reaching into a drawer for the keys and handing them to Mrs. Spanacopito.

"Thank you, Anita," Mrs. Spanacopito said as she took the keys and put them into Simms's hand. "There you are, sir," she said smartly. "You now have a safe deposit box."

"Thank you," Simms grinned. "I'd like to put something into my box now."

"Just come this way," the woman at the desk said, escorting him into the main safe deposit box vault. She inserted the bank key into Box HOOO423, then turned to Simms.

"May I have your key, please?" she asked in a businesslike tone.

Simms handed over one of the two keys he'd received for the box. The woman turned the lock, pulled out the box, and handed it to Simms with a prudent smile. Then she led him to a private cubicle.

"When you are finished using the box, sir," the vault keeper said quickly, "just open the door and bring the box to me." The door shut automatically and Simms was left alone at a small shelflike desk with his empty safe deposit box and attaché case. He opened the attaché case and removed the eighteen-page memo that

130

he'd written the night before. He took a pen from his pocket and wrote a hasty addendum to the memo. It had to do with why he spurned the Chase-Manhattan safe deposit box for the one at the Chemical Bank.

When he was finished writing, Simms folded the eighteen-page memo, put it into a business envelope, sealed the flap, then scribbled on the envelope, "To be opened only upon my death, as per instructions in my will, which shall have been found in the Bank of America's Century City branch."

After completing the deposit of the memo into the box, Simms closed the cover, got to his feet, opened the door, and walked into the forward vertibule of the safe deposit box vault where the woman in charge was seated behind her desk.

"Will you put this away, please, ma'am?" Simms asked, handing the safe deposit box to the vault keeper.

"Of course, sir," the woman replied. She got up from her desk and went into the vault. She took the box from Simms and returned it to its place in the wall. Then she handed his key to Simms with a proper smile.

Simms smiled back, thanked the woman for her assistance, walked upstairs, and left the bank. He got behind the wheel of his rented car and drove to Republic Airport, six miles down Route 110. He turned in his Hertz car and paid for the privilege of its rental with his American Express credit card. Then he boarded the plane bound for Titusville ...

131

The NASA helicopter was waiting on the taxiway just beside the Eastern Airlines terminal. As Simms stepped off the airliner at Titusville, a smiling, broad-shouldered man in a gray pinstriped suit approached.

"Mr. Simms?" he asked.

"Yes, I'm Simms."

"I'm Captain Fred Farnsworth," he replied smartly. "I'm with NASA and I was instructed by Mr. Thurber to escort you to Cape Canaveral. Will you come with me, sir?"

Simms beamed broadly. "Of course you may," he said grandly. "Please lead the way."

Eight minutes later, the helicopter put down at Cape Canaveral and Simms descended the ramp with eager steps.

"Well, Gordy, it's about damned time you got down here," a voice greeted the professor as he planted his feet on the tarmac.

"Maity, you son of a gun!" exclaimed Simms. "It's so good to see you again."

Gordon Lyle Simms and Maitland Thurber shook hands and embraced warmly.

"We've been waiting for you, Gordy," the NASA chief rasped. "Now that you're here, we can get under way."

"To where?" Simms asked in pretended ignorance.

Thurber looked at the professor with bewilderment. But just as quickly he sensed that Simms was joshing. The NASA boss drew in a deep breath of relief when he realized that Simms was merely trying to make light of the situation.

132

Of course, Simms knew very well what his presence in Cape Canaveral was all about. Indeed, he was there to prepare the ten-man team in Operation Mars for the countdown to the July 4 blastoff . . .

CHAPTER X

Danger in Space

Gordon Lyle Simms settled into his room at the Ramada Inn at Cocoa Beach, which NASA had reserved for him. According to the arrangements made long beforehand, the professor would remain at Cape Canaveral throughout the critical preparations for the countdown of Operation Mars, then after the launch stay on at the spaceport all through the year-long flight.

He was committed totally to perform a virtual one-man mission on the pad—monitoring the critical life-support systems aboard the Galactic I and directing the fine adjustments from the base to keep the machinery on the craft at peak efficiency.

While his anxiety was at nerve-frazzling edge to check out the atomic-powered space shuttle and see whether the particle accelerator was everything Boyce McMorrow told him it was, Dr. Simms applied a rein on his emotions. It was late afternoon and darkness was

135

settling over the Cape. Tomorrow would have to be soon enough.

That evening, Simms went to dinner with Maitland Thurber, who phoned after the professor had checked in. Something had come up and it couldn't wait for tomorrow.

During cocktails in the motel dining room, the NASA boss first exhibited an immediate and inordinate curiosity in the outcome of Dr. Simms's journey to Long Island and his meeting with Boyce McMorrow.

"Did you get everything you were looking for?" Thurber asked with an uncharacteristic intensity. "Can colloidal suspension be made to work on this mission?"

Simms was taken aback, indeed almost stunned by the question. He shook his head vigorously.

"Without a peradventure of a doubt," he smiled. "Boyce not only provides us with a superb instructional manual but he has also briefed me extensively on the functions of the particle accelerator in both phases, for vacuum operation and for weaving a plastic screen to protect our space missions from radiation hazards."

Thurber raised his glass in a toast to Simms. The gesture was done with such enthusiasm it startled the professor, who was already wondering what had generated such a sudden interest in colloidal suspension, a factor that had never figured in the flight plans for Operation Mars—until Simms himself insisted on it. And then when Thurber yielded to the doctor's insistence that it be made operational on the spaceship to the Red Planet, the concession he thought was merely a way of humoring him. But now Simms began to wonder. What was Thurber driving at? What had come up that couldn't wait for tomorrow?

"I must express my deep gratitude to you, Gordy," the NASA boss said with unusual sincerity as he drank to Simms's good health. "Everyone in the space program owes you a generous vote of thanks for the abiding interest you've taken in your work. I know of no one with your dedication and perseverance in the interest of safety for our people in space. Your efforts will be remembered for a very long time . . ."

A lump formed in Simms's throat. It was the first time in what seemed like ages that he'd been moved like this by emotion.

"I'm deeply grateful for your very kind words, Maity," Simms said, swallowing hard. "But many of the goals I've managed to reach wouldn't have been attained if it hadn't been for your understanding and indulgence in my objectives."

As the main course was served—two New York cut sirloin steaks, both rare—Thurber narrowed his concentration on the immediacy of preparations for the July launch.

"We may have six months left before we send the Galactic I to Mars," Thurber said in a somber tone. "But that isn't as much time as I would like to have. Yet, neither of us has a choice or even a voice in the schedule. We must put that ship in the air on July Fourth—or Congress will decimate our appropriations. And that's why, starting tomorrow, you and I must proceed in the preparations just as though it were a crash program."

Simms stared at Thurber with puzzlement suddenly shading his face. "I'm bewildered by what you've just said, Maity," the professor exhaled heavily. "Are you telling me now that we're running behind schedule in the program?"

"No," Thurber frowned. "I'm not saying that. But there've been some disturbing developments in the past week that you can't possibly be aware of. And they are a cause for some concern . . . to be very truthful, a great deal of concern. . . ."

Thurber sliced a generous portion of steak, impaled it on the end of his fork, then held it suspended in front of his lips. He was about to speak but deferred to his gastronomic instincts. He shoveled the meat into his mouth and chewed it rapidly.

Simms regarded Thurber with a measured, riveted gaze. The professor was stunned by the director's ominous tone.

Thurber all at once sensed the professor's dismay and grappled for the right words to express the thought he wanted to convey.

"I may have been overly alarming, Gordy, and I'm genuinely sorry if I've upset you, especially during dinner. Yet, I must level with you because it's a situation you must face first thing tomorrow when you begin preparing the crew for the mission."

That didn't soften the harsh expression of wonderment on the professor's face. If anything, he was even more deeply puzzled now.

"What are you trying to tell me, Maity?" Simms rasped. "Is there some problem? . . ."

His voice trailed off briefly. Before Thurber could respond, Simms spoke again. "I'm confident you're going to fill me in, Maity, but when? You've got me worried. What is this all about?"

"Okay, Gordy . . . I'm truly sorry for being so mysterious. But this thing has really thrown me for a loss. . . . Can you remember what the British scientist J.B.S. Haldane said about our cosmos?"

Simms's forehead creased in furrows. "Yes, I do . . . in fact, I repeat it constantly to my classes. Haldane said, 'The universe is not only queerer than we suppose, but queerer than we *can* suppose.' But what has that to do with with. . . ?"

"Okay, I'm going to let you in on this just exactly in the strange and fantastic way it came to me from Dr. Furth Koenig at the Kitt Peak National Observatory."

Thurber placed the knife and fork on his plate, reached into his inside jacket pocket, pulled out an envelope, and removed a letter.

"Dear Maity," Thurber began to read. "I am profoundly troubled about an observation we have made in the region of Mars and I feel it is incumbent upon me to inform you of this de-

139

velopment since you are preparing for a mid-year manned flight to that planet.

"I am not trying to undo what Edwin Hubble contributed to astronomy. I don't have to dwell on his celebrated discoveries that some of the fuzzy nebulosities on his photographic plates were not nearby clouds of gas, as most of his contemporaries who sat in the prime-focus cage of their telescopes assumed.

"But allow me to astonish you with a startling discovery in this year of 1988. It occurred January 1 at exactly 2251 hours.

"Our one hundred fifty-eight-inch Mayal telescope was focused on a rim of the Milky Way and we had made a series of plates in that position. In developing the plates taken from 2251 to 2310 hours, a series of eighteen, we discovered that the fuzzy clouds, which almost always since Hubble's time at the dawn of the twentieth century were determined to be distant galaxies, were not that at all.

"Not this time, Maity. This time we established that a segment of a mysterious spiral nebulae was not several million light years away, but a mere thirty-four million miles distant. Indeed—on the very orbital path of Mars!

"Now, Maity, this should not disrupt the mission if you are in a position to provide substantial protection for the Galactic I."

Thurber paused in his reading and turned the page. He looked at Simms through narrowed eyelids for a moment, then focused his attention on the letter again.

140

"We have not determined precisely the origin of this cloud but we know it carries high-frequency, high-energy radiations of ultraviolet, gamma, and X-rays. It is almost as though a piece of the Van Allen belt were shaken loose by last year's Uranus phenomenon. As you know, the planet's spin axis and magnetic field axis were pointed then, as they are every eighty-four years or so, directly at the sun and at the solar winds that feed those radiation particles into the belt. I have no other explanation for this disturbance in the periphery of Mars.

"It is also a possibility, however, that the cloud might be a remnant of some stellar explosion, a runaway bubble of debris from such an event. But we're not certain which it might be.

"In any event, it should not interfere with your Operation Mars or Mission to Mars, whichever label applies—I've been seeing it used both ways. But what I want to alert you to is this danger we've just discovered. In sending you this information, I'm responding to your request to keep you advised of all changes in our observations of the immediate solar system, which could have any possible influence on your flight.

"I will merely add that you must take extreme precautions to guard the crew from the hazards posed by this cloud. Under weightlessness, radiation has markedly greater effects on living matter. Therefore I cannot stress too greatly that a shield such as you have spoken of in the past is certainly indicated for this flight . . ."

Thurber folded the letter, stuffed it into the envelope, returned it to his pocket, and went back to his meal. He wanted Dr. Simms's reaction and stared rigidly at him while digging into the steak at the same time.

The professor gave himself a moment to digest the stunning news from the astronomer whose observations were conducted with one of the world's most powerful telescopes, located on the outskirts of Tucson. It certainly was disturbing to hear about that radioactive cloud—but what had Simms been trumpeting all along about safety in space?

Who had made such an outcry for colloidal suspension on the Mars mission? It was Simms, of course. If he hadn't raised a stink back in October for the optional set of operating instructions for the particle accelerator, there'd have been no manual now—and the July 4 launch day for Operation Mars would surely have to have been scrubbed.

Simms appeared distressed by the message from the observatory, yet he didn't seem as shaken as Thurber had expected him to be.

How odd, Thurber told himself. It was clear that Simms was more perturbed in those earlier moments at the table by the anticipation of hearing from the space boss what exactly had gone wrong in the program to explore Mars, than the problem itself, which, at least in Thurber's mind, was something that should have reflected far greater concern on the professor's part.

Simms appeared now to be buying himself extra moments to think before responding to Dr. Koenig's spectacular discovery. But when he finally tried to speak he was interrupted.

"Gordy," Thurber blurted impatiently, "I almost have the feeling that Furth's letter amused you. Is there something about this radiation peril that tells you it can be taken lightly?"

Simms took a few quick sips from his water glass.

"Did I say that?" he gulped. "Please don't put words in my mouth. Of course it's a disturbing development. But haven't we already taken all the necessary precautions to guarantee the crew's safety through every possible radiation hazard the universe can hurl at us?"

Thurber blinked. He was taken aback by the confidence with which Simms responded. He was a tower of strength and the chief of America's space program had a sudden thought about that. The professor had won his argument about putting hardware aboard Galactic I that would provide a plastic shield against radiation. Was this Simms's way now of saying to Thurber, "See, I told you so. It's a damned good thing I got my way"?

Yet now they were confronted by a totally different form of radiation peril. Simms had demanded the particle accelerator's operation in colloidal suspension for protection against the direct rays of the sun. But the radiation discovered at Kitt Peak wasn't the same as a beam of sunlight.

The newly discovered peril was oozing out of a thick, gaseous cloud in the direct flight path to Mars.

"Am I to understand that you believe the crew can employ that same plastic shield to penetrate this contamination without harm?" Thurber asked in a pained voice.

"I certainly do mean to say that," Simms said forcefully. "There is no better protection against radiation in space than the plastic that the colloidal suspension system produces. Believe me, Maity, that radioactive cloud will have no effect on our mission."

Thurber wiped his lips with his napkin after chewing the last morsels of food in his plate. He looked across the table at Simms's plate, which had a few forkfuls of food left in it.

"Aren't you going to finish?" Thurber asked wonderingly. "I thought the meal was quite good."

"It was," the professor smiled. "But I've had it."

With an air of put-on disdain, he dropped his knife and fork onto the plate and pushed it away from his place setting.

"I can go for some coffee," Simms beamed. "And then I'd like to hit the hay. There's a lot to do in the morning. Oh, by the way, what time do we punch in?"

"If you set your alarm for seven, you won't have much trouble getting to the base by eight-thirty. I'll have a Jeep Roadrunner outside the door for you in the morning. There'll be a driver behind the wheel but that's only so he can show you the way to the Galactic's launch complex. After that you'll do your own driving. When Bob Katz drops you off at the Administration Building, you'll find me on the second floor. I'll take you to the ship and introduce you to the crew."

Thurber shook his finger at Simms in a playful gesture.

"It's a lot different in these parts since you were here the last time, Gordy. No longer do the rockets stand poised against the sky, flexing their massive muscles from their gantries on the launching pads."

"I know," Simms agreed. "Those once-awesome symbols of man's impatience to leave his planet no longer signal that goal, do they?"

"You're so right, Gordy. Now we just scoot down the runway and take off like a big bird to reach unconquered space. How prosaic!"

As the waiter poured the coffee, Simms confronted Thurber with a thought that would not have come up if Dr. Koenig hadn't discovered the radioactive cloud close to Mars.

"In light of this situation, Maity, I would suggest very strongly that we schedule a test run or two for Galactic I."

"For what?" Thurber almost choked on his coffee. "That's not part of the preparation at all . . ."

"But it should be in light of what you've just told me," Simms said, straightening up in his chair.

Thurber tightened his lips and gritted his teeth momentarily. "I'm not quite certain I understand you, Gordy. What does the news from the observatory have to do with testing the craft?"

"It's not the craft I'm anxious to test," Simms said suddenly, his eyes narrowing. "It's the particle accelerator that I want to check out. I'm very anxious to see how well it functions on the colloidal suspension circuit."

Confusion was written all over Thurber's face. "Are you saying we've got to put the particle accelerator through a test run in the air?"

"Not in the air," Simms corrected gruffly. "In space is where that test must be run."

Thurber appeared shaken. "You mean you want to send Galactic I through an actual space flight merely to test the particle accelerator?" he asked stiffly.

"That's precisely what I mean," Simms said. "How do you expect to put the particle accelerator to a test for colloidal suspension if you don't do it in the vacuum of space? How do we know it'll do what we're told its proficiency is?"

"But we never contemplated launching Galactic I until the actual flight to Mars," protested Thurber.

"Of course you didn't," the professor said impatiently. "But neither had anyone contemplated the intrusion of a radioactive cloud on our flight path. I say to you, Maity, it's imperative that we take the ship up for a test as soon as it can be readied for the flight."

Thurber sipped some coffee and began smiling at Simms. It was an admiring smile.

"By golly, Gordy, you're a tiger. I must hand it to you, you really are a headstrong buzzard."

Simms felt triumphant now. He looked across the table with a broad smile and sighed comfortably. "How soon do we take her up, Maity?"

"Well, I'm not in a position to give you a flight plan right this moment," Thurber said thoughtfully. "But I assure you that I'll certainly do everything possible to expedite one."

Simms put his coffee cup down and wrung his hands briskly. Thurber studied the gesture with a suspicious eye. He sensed that the professor was angling for one more request.

"Anything else on your mind, Gordy?" Thurber pressed bluntly.

Simms nodded. "As a matter of fact there is," he smiled blandly. "Inasmuch as the Galactic I will go through a dress rehearsal, I feel it is incumbent upon me to go along and ride herd on the particle accelerator."

Thurber's face crinkled as he broke into a wide grin. "I never expected you wouldn't ask," the NASA chief said crisply. "Of course, the answer is yes. And to tell you how I feel personally, I would just as soon have you on the voyage to Mars, too. But, of course, you are needed much more desperately down here."

Then as an afterthought, Thurber mused,

147

"Besides, what the hell will happen to those people you stuck down in that mine?"

"Oh, you don't have to concern yourself about them," Simms said in a confident tone. "They'll be in perfectly fine straits for as long as we hold them down. But you happen to be perfectly right. My place is on the pad . . ."

Thurber called for the check. Then he smiled at Simms. "You'd better be out there bright and early tomorrow morning, my friend . . ."

CHAPTER XI

Dr. Simms Meets the Crew

It'd been four years since Dr. Gordon Lyle Simms had last been in Cape Canaveral. That was during a five-week spell in mid-Summer of 1984, when he served as overseer of the life-support systems aboard the inaugural flight of Space Shuttle Gulliver to lunar orbit, which established the first moon-girdling laboratory.

Many dramatic advances had transpired since that era, not the least of which was the surface changes at the Cape. In the beginning, the early days of the space shuttle, NASA had constructed a 15,000-foot-long, 300-foot-wide, 16-inch-thick runway on the low-lying scrub palmetto and sawgrass terrain near the Atlantic coast.

The width and length of the runway for the first space shuttle craft was much larger than those at commercial jetports. That was required for the eighty-three-ton spaceships returning to earth at a 15- to 20-degree angle at speeds of 160 knots—with only one opportunity to land. The craft had only small on-board engines for maneuvering and very little fuel capacity.

The thickness of the concrete was dictated not by the landing speed of the delta-winged shuttle but by a weight factor, which didn't apply to the space vehicle alone. For when the shuttles were delivered to the Cape, they didn't arrive by barge nor fly there on their own. They came piggyback from the West Coast atop converted jumbo jets, such as the military C-5A built by Lockheed and the Boeing 747, the world's largest passenger-transport planes of the 1970s and early 1980s.

The jumbo jet and its freeloader space shuttle thus had to have that sixteen inches of concrete to withstand the enormous weight of the twin flying machines.

The early space shuttles couldn't get off the ground by themselves but relied on recoverable solid fuel booster rockets for liftoff. To the shuttle itself was attached an external liquid fuel tank, which fed the craft's engines after separation from the rockets. This tank was jettisoned just before the shuttle went into orbit, eight minutes after liftoff, and burned in the earth's atmosphere on reentry.

For the most part, in those early and mid-1980s, however, Cape Canaveral still looked like Cape Kennedy, as it was called after President John F. Kennedy's assassination in 1963 and for some nine years afterward, until the Cape's citizenry overruled the House of Representatives in Washington and had the name revert to its ancient Spanish origin.

It wasn't until the advent of the Galactic I that the face of Cape Canaveral underwent its most sweeping change. Until then the great rockets and boosters for the Mercury, Gemini, and Apollo programs, and the ones that followed for the more than 1,000 shuttle flights into space over the first seven years of that undertaking, had been the chief attention-getters on that exposed, sun-beaten stretch of Florida. They had stood poised against the sky, massive in their multi-story heights, awesome symbols of man's conquest of that once uncharted no-man's domain called space.

But now, in 1988, when Dr. Simms was returning to the scene of his many earlier triumphs, the alterations etched on the landscape were almost incomprehensible. That thin strip of land between the Indian River and Atlantic Ocean—so narrow that even a middle-aged man like Simms could throw a pebble from one body of water to the other—had undergone vast changes.

Aside from the obvious differences—the disappearance of the great rockets and their gantries and the concrete blockhouses where the countdown and monitoring operations were centered beside the pads—the Cape was hardly anything like it was the last time Simms had seen it.

A rush of new economic life had caused an upheaval on Space Coast, as it was called. Twice in the short span of a generation, the Cape had fallen victim to congressional fickleness, which almost destroyed the peninsula each time. The first disastrous turnback occurred in the early 1970s, when the U. S. space effort was virtually put into mothballs after the Apollo moon landings were aborted.

Then, after a five-year hiatus, new economic life stirred along central Florida's famed Cape when the nearly three-mile runway was built for the space shuttles. The once bustling plants, offices, hangars, and motels, which had stood empty during the depressed post-Apollo years, suddenly came to life again. Aerospace employment, peaking at 25,000 during the early 1970s, had plummeted to 8,500 just before the resurgence that came with the space shuttle program.

Then in the early 1980s, the working force was revitalized to a healthy 30,000.

Still, that was not comparable to the greater heights reached by industrial and commercial development, as well as employment, by this year of 1988. Now the work force, according to the Bravard Economic Development Council's most recent figures, exceeded 56,000 and the unemployment rate was 0.3, unheard of not only in Cape Canaveral's precincts but virtually anywhere in the country.

What had helped bring about that happy and healthy circumstance of economic well-being was the influx of such giants of industry and commerce as the Harris Corporation, a major electronics firm; Dictaphone, the recording pioneer; Rockwell International, the parent company of North American Rockwell, builders of the space shuttle; Chrysler Corporation, the auto builder; and scores of other top-rated firms.

And on that new Cape Canaveral landscape came such other boom-day installations as new motels, new restaurants, new taverns, and new businesses of every sort that dealt in clothing and condiments, appliances and appurtenances, photography and phonography, and many other trades.

Insofar as the spaceport itself went, Simms would find the runway built for the Space shuttle had been lengthened from 15,000 to 26,500 feet, just a bit longer than five miles—more than three times the length of any runway for conventionally flown planes.

And for good reason, too. The new breed of space shuttle, now parked on the runway at Cape Canaveral, not only had almost the combined weight of the eighty-three-ton space shuttle and Boeing 747, which flew in tandem in landings at the Cape in years gone by, but also needed that distance, not for landings, but takeoffs—done without the aid of booster rockets and other liftoff gimmickry of the past.

The Galactic I had an atomic power plant and a limitless capacity for both speed and duration of flight in space. Yet, there was one requirement on landing and takeoff. The ship had to have an inordinately long runway, because a nuclear-energized space vehicle with its weighty power plant was extremely heavy. Thus, that weight added considerably to the ponderosity of the ship on both takeoff and landing.

That, then, was the Cape Canaveral to which Dr. Gordon Lyle Simms was returned on Wednesday, January 20, 1978.

Simms awakened shortly before 7 o'clock in the morning. He was out of the shower, shaved, dressed, and finished with breakfast in the motel dining room by a minute past eight. He was palpably nervous as he signed the check and rose from his chair. His state of agitation wasn't generated wholly by anticipation of getting the preparation routine for the Galactic I crew under way.

What made the normally placid professor so excited was the imminent prospect of his first visit to the Galactic I. As close as Simms had been to the space program, his participation in all the earlier preparations for Operation Mars had been strictly from long range. He had not seen the Galactic I as a finished product, although he had had a first-hand look at the new breed of space shuttle as it was being assembled at the North American Rockwell plant.

Simms felt as though he knew the ship inside out, even though he had not seen it all put together. He had been furnished with the detailed specifications and blueprints so that he could design the various life-support systems that were built into Galactic I. Thus, he knew almost everything there was to know about this marvelous flying machine. Yet, that wasn't the same as setting eyes upon the ship in flight-ready state, dressed in its virtually indestructible thermal layer of nickel-chrome alloys and coated insulation of compacted fibers of shimmering quartz and silicon, the coat that will enable the shuttle to reenter the atmosphere at 17,000 miles per hour and withstand the buildup of a fiery 3,000-degree surface temperature. And now he was on the verge of seeing the Galactic I in readiness for its inaugural flight...

Inhaling the cool Florida morning air with a long, deep breath as he stepped out of the Ramada Inn lobby, Simms's eyes searched sharply along the busy highway for a sign of the jeep that Maitland Thurber was sending for him.

The morning rush was well under way by now and traffic on the highway had built up to a bumper-to-bumper frenzy. Almost all the vehicles were heading in one direction, northeast to the Cape Canaveral space complex.

Suddenly, Simms caught sight of a jeep barreling down the nearly deserted southwest-bound lanes. When the vehicle turned into the motel driveway, the doctor sucked in another deep nervous breath. When the jeep was braked to a stop, Simms stepped toward the passenger compartment and smiled at the driver.

"Dr. Simms?" asked the man behind the wheel.

"Yes," the professor said, and without waiting to be invited stepped in and plopped down in the seat.

The jeep was driven from the motel grounds

and fell into the stream of traffic bound for the spaceport. Despite the crowded road conditions, the drive took a mere ten minutes.

"We're here, sir," the driver smiled as he pulled to a stop in front of an aluminum and smoke-glassed two-story office structure at the edge of a concrete runway. "You'll find Mr. Thurber on the second floor. The security officer inside will guide you . . . oh, by the way, sir, I was instructed to give you these . . ."

The driver handed Dr. Simms the jeep keys. "It's yours now, sir," the man chuckled. "You'll find everything in order . . . full up on oil, water, brake fluid, and, oh yes, all gassed up, too."

"I'm very much obliged to you," Simms said politely, taking the keys and hopping out of the car. He made his way into the building and paused as he reached the foyer. A blue-uniformed guard behind a reception desk stood up. Simms identified himself and the guard recognized the name without even consulting his roster of scheduled visitors who'd been given prior security clearance.

"You'll find Mr. Thurber's office just up at the head of the stairs, Dr. Simms. Go right on up, sir."

Alerted by a call from the guard, a shapely, honey-haired secretary greeted the professor as he reached the second floor. Her welcome was a syrupy "Good morning" followed by a "Please follow me, sir." She escorted Simms directly into the NASA chief's enormous mahogany-paneled office.

156

Thurber was in a cheerful mood and was already on his feet when Simms strode into the room.

"Good morning, Gordy," the space boss smiled. His mood was tranquil but he seemed in a rush to get under way.

"Are you all set to meet the crew?" he asked quickly. "They're all down in the ready room and I'm certain quite anxious to hear you tell them how they're going to survive the trip to Mars."

Simms laughed but didn't say anything. His attention was drawn to the wall at the right of the door. It was covered almost from floor to ceiling with neatly framed, glass-covered testimonials and awards that had been presented to Thurber during his twenty-five years with the space program.

"That's fantastic," said Simms admiringly. He was glancing at a sequence of letters that were written on White House stationery and that occupied a prominent section of the wall.

"Are you impressed?" Thurber asked with a sigh of boredom.

"I can't help but be." Simms face lit up as he read of the signatures in a loud, animated voice: "Eisenhower, Kennedy, Johnson, Nixon, Ford, Carter, Mondale . . ."

Thurber took in a deep breath and exhaled slowly. He snickered and shook his head. "Never was on a first-name basis with any of those Presidents," he chuckled. "What a shame."

He moved toward Simms and gripped his

arm. "Come on, Gordy, this is no way to prepare for that landing on Mars," Thurber said. "Let's get out of here."

Simms wasn't certain which way to go when he was ushered out of the office. Thurber took the lead down the stairs. They walked past the receptionist and the uniformed guard, who opened the front door to allow the men to leave the building.

"It's just a short walk to the compound," Thurber said as he led the way around the northeast corner of the building. The path wound around a carefully manicured grassy mall landscaped with rows of uniformly spaced palm trees and neatly trimmed beds of horsetails and clubmosses.

Simms didn't have to be told they had reached their destination. The sign with the black-bordered red lettering on a white background, proclaiming MANNED SPACECRAFT CENTER, made it a dead giveaway. The sign was planted on a pair of wooden posts on the lawn of a windowless green stuccoed building that was a study in architectural simplicity, if not drabness. It looked like it might have been transplanted there from one of the back lots of the Twentieth-Century Fox or Metro-Goldwyn-Mayer studios in Hollywood before the movie companies succumbed to the downfall of the star system and the "progress" of the 1980s urban sprawl, which raised condominiums and shopping centers to the importance and esteem once accorded the art of film-making.

The Manned Spacecraft Center was a relatively new structure and Simms recognized it as such. It had been put up in the time since the doctor's last tour of duty at the Cape in 1984. No such facility had existed at Canaveral at that time because all the training for space flight in prior years had been conducted at the facility in Houston.

But with the rapid growth of the space shuttle program and its attendant increased demands for trained crews and technicians to man the orbiting earth and lunar space stations, the need for a training center in proximity to the shuttle launch and landing site at the Cape was mandated. Thus the "green giant," as it was tabbed, was erected on the Canaveral peninsula.

While it didn't merit any architectural awards even for its design simplicity, the building was nevertheless an imposing giant. It was a little more than fifty feet high or as tall as a five-story building, and it occupied 40,000 square feet, or approximately an acre.

But its exterior was of no consequence to those who made pilgrimages there to avail themselves of the marvelous facilities in the interior for training space crews. For astronauts as well as scientists, chemists, geologists, astronomers, and all others who were prepared for their journeys into space, it was the mecca, the pinnacle of the astronautic sciences.

By 8:40 that Wednesday morning when Thurber escorted Simms past the guarded entranceway and took him into the building, the training activities were already underway at a serious and hectic pace in almost every sector—except one.

That was in the auditoriumlike ready room situated a few short steps beyond the entry lounge. In contrast to the rest of the hustle and bustle in the Manned Spacecraft Center, the ready room was a scene of standing serenity. Even the presence of the ten people waiting to begin their preparations for Operation Mars under Dr. Simms's guidance did not present anything more than a resonance of hushed whispers.

Maitland Thurber preceded Professor Simms into the ready room and led the way along the narrow sloping aisle to the foot-high platform that was the stage on which lecturers delivered their perorations to the trainees.

The people in the room fell into a respectful silence when they sensed Thurber's entrance. They didn't know the professor but they couldn't have had any doubt who was following Thurber down the aisle, since they were expecting him to be presented by the NASA chief.

Thurber stepped upon the foot-high stage and went to the lectern. He tapped the mike and discovered it was dead.

That didn't faze him. He sucked in a deep breath, looked out over the gathering and smiled pleasantly.

"For the past two days since you people arrived at the Cape, we've seen each other almost constantly," he said airily. "Well, the time has come to stop that."

He turned and nodded toward Dr. Simms, who was standing to the left of the lectern on the auditorium floor.

"Will you come up here, Dr. Simms, and greet your pupils," Thurber said jovially.

Simms stepped up to the platform and looked out at the crew as Thurber walked to the section where they were seated.

"I'll introduce these nice people to you," the space boss offered, placing his hand first on the shoulder of an attractive salt-and-pepper-haired woman with a round, pixylike face.

"This is Rebecca Cooper and she is a geologist from Tempe," said Thurber, eyeing her with a smile, which she promptly returned. She rose slowly to her feet to acknowledge the professor's soft-spoken "How do you do . . . very pleased to meet you."

Thurber added a brief few additional remarks to his introduction about the lady earth scientist. "Dr. Cooper is teaching and research professor at Arizona State University. And as you get to know her better in the next few months, you'll respect her increasingly for her remarkable expertise in lunar rocks and soil . . ."

Dr. Cooper was the 1986 recipient of the Bancroft Geological Award after having spent two months on the lunar surface conducting experiments on soil and rock samples. Among her more outstanding discoveries during drilling in the Sea of Tranquillity sub-soil were finds of bauxite, molybdenum, tungsten, and nickel. While it would still be many years before those ores were mined on the moon, the mere fact that such earthly treasures existed on the supposedly barren moon was in itself a remarkable development.

"I know about you, Dr. Cooper," Simms said in a respectful tone. "Please sit. I have the deepest admiration for both your credentials as well as your achievements."

He looked at the others who were about to be introduced by Thurber and addressed them in a plaintive voice. "I wish you'd remain seated when the introductions are made. I don't command such reverence. Certainly not this early in the day."

The remark prompted some giggles in the gathering.

"And this is Captain Randolph Stuart of the Air Force," Thurber started again, putting a finger on a rugged-looking, wide-shouldered man in blue uniform. The silver wings on his chest denoted his pilot's status. The name itself conjured up an immediate recognition in Dr. Simms.

"You need no introduction, Captain," Simms said in a crisp, respectful tone. "It's a pleasure to know the man who's going to fly this crew to Mars and back."

Stuart was a veteran of five prior missions in shuttles with a total space flight experience of 350 hours, most of it in lunar activity. That was in addition to the 5,600 hours of aircraft flight time this thirty-eight-year-old nineteen-year veteran of the Air Force had logged before being assigned to the space program.

He'd been selected to serve as chief pilot on Operation Mars and the publicity about him in numerous newspaper and magazine stories had not eluded Professor Simms.

Thurber went along with the introductions from Stuart to the third and fourth members of the cabin crew, Astronauts Rigby Deems and Frank Perlman, both twenty-nine years of age, both first lieutenants, and both also from the Air Force. Their combined experience in space flight amounted to two missions apiece, with Deems holding about forty more hours of time over Perlman, who had logged a hundred hours.

Next to make Simms's acquaintance was thirty-three-year-old Phoebe Swedlow, a Naval commander and flier. Holding a commander's rank, this personable, cheery-faced astronette had been in the space program for two years, had flown only one brief mission in a shuttle resupplying an earth-orbit space station. But she had superb credentials that were established on the ground.

She had supervised crew training for the shuttle flights the past five years at the Manned Spacecraft Center in Houston. As chief of the Flight Crew Support Division, Commander Swedlow indoctrinated some four score astronauts in the uses of on-board sextants and telescopes for aligning the spacecraft navigation systems with the stars, landmarks, or the horizon; for each mission phase such as launch, mid-course navigation, earth or moon orbit, rendezvouses with space platforms and stations, linkup, and a multitude of other vital functions, Phoebe Swedlow indoctrinated the crews with an exactitude and precision regarded superior to the output of most other instructors at the base.

Her role on the mission was to operate the Martian Module, the descent-ascent four-passenger vehicle transporter that would bring the crew and supplies down to the planet and up to the shuttle that would remain in orbit around Mars for the six-month exploration period.

Although Galactic I had capability to land on Mars or any other planet for that matter, it could not do so in this year of 1988—because there were no landing strips yet. They would be built in a year or two. Any attempt to land the shuttle on its pioneering venture to the Red Planet would be disastrous, for the landing gear could never put down safely on the rock-strewn, pockmarked surface.

Thurber introduced the three women physicists next. They were Dr. Anita Browsey from Dartmouth College, Dr. Henrietta Jordan from the University of Chicago, and Dr. Danielle Savage who was administrator for space sciences and applications at NASA.

The ninth member of the exploration team was the astronomer, Philip Santangelo, and he was introduced to Simms with a humorous aside whose jocularity eluded everyone but Simms. "Dr. Santangelo has the distinction of having spent the last fifteen years looking at our universe through the world's largest telescope," Thurber said with an extravagant tone. "And of course that has its advantages—as well as disadvantages. I will not belabor how a smaller eyepiece enabled Dr. Santangelo's colleague, Dr. Furth Koenig at Kitt Peak to make startling discovery . . ."

Thurber smiled and turned to Simms. "Of course, Gordy, I'm certain you want me to leave that explanation to you to describe, am I right?"

Simms nodded, half-smiling. The comment and exchange eluded everyone, including Dr. Santangelo.

"And now may I present Dr. Lenore Shivard whose mission on this mission will be to keep everyone hale, hearty, and healthy." Thurber introduced the tenth and final member of the exploration team. Her credentials were impeccable—she was the medical director at Walter Reed Army Hospital in Washington, D. C., and a recipient in 1985 of the Nobel Peace Prize for Medicine for having established the genetic cause of cancer and having synthesized a fully functional bacterial gene that proved effective in destroying more than 95 percent of all carcinogens.

With that last introduction out of the way, Thurber glanced at Simms and nodded. "Take it over, Gordy," he smiled. "It's all yours now."

Simms folded his arms across his chest and leaned forward so his elbows rested on the lectern. He seemed comfortable and at ease as he addressed the group, trying to eye each crew member in turn. He had prepared his introductory talk and delivered it with confidence.

"This mission is not any different than any flown before," began the professor, examining the faces with a probing eye to detect the slightest suggestion of boredom, inattention, or momentary flight of interest.

"I need not stress how vital it is that you people assimilate the technical knowledge about the many life-support systems we have aboard the Galactic I. It is imperative that you absorb every bit of information about those systems."

Simms nodded in the direction of the four astronauts who were seated together in the front row.

"You gentlemen and lady have already completed your training for flying the ship. You have acquired, I am confident, all the knowledge about spacecraft controls, the use of on-board sextants and telescopes, and certainly you have been thoroughly briefed to fly not only the planned mission but also several possible alternate missions in the event that abnormal conditions are encountered on the journey."

Simms lifted his head, tilted it back, and peered out at the other crew members. He frowned at them and again studied every face for reaction to what he was about to say.

"The rest of you . . ." he curled his lips in a slight smile, looking at Dr. Cooper, whose face he suddenly thought appeared more attractive than when he first set eyes on her. "I'm going to warn you right now, this is not a joyride. Your responsibilities on this flight will be just as numerous and as important as the four pilots who will be flying this mission. Life-support—and I lay great stress on those words. Let me repeat them—life support. They mean your life. Please realize this . . . you will be on this mission for virtually an entire year, three hundred and sixty-five days.

"At one point in this mission you will have reached a distance of thirty-five million miles from earth. That's roughly eighty-eight days from home. Sickness, injury, or any debilitating episode must be dealt with out there . . ."

Simms straightened up suddenly and shot a pointing finger into the air.

"Will you be able to handle it?" he asked in a gruff, demanding voice that was out of character for someone as soft-spoken as Simms. His audience sensed the change and accepted it, just as the professor felt no awkwardness over his brassiness, which was a put-on for effect. It worked because he sensed his listeners had been intimidated and were now according him total attention.

"Let me assure each of you," Simms said in a grave but confident tone, "you will be able to handle it—and you will come back as safe and sound as you are at this moment sitting before me. I will make certain of that from now and until the instant your ship leaves on its mission on July Fourth."

He studied the faces again and was heartened to detect a sense of relief in most. Only a couple—Dr. Cooper and Captain Stuart—failed to give Simms a reading. They betrayed no reaction, just the same steady, stony stare that was fixed on their faces from the instant the professor began cataloguing the potential perils on the year-long journey to that strange planet.

Very quickly now Simms zeroed in on the gaseous cloud that was photographed by the observatory in Arizona and alluded to in a playful but veiled reference earlier by Thurber when introducing Dr. Santangelo, the astronomer from Palomar.

The professor turned to Thurber, who'd taken a seat in the front row on Captain Stuart's right.

"May I have that letter from Dr. Koenig, please?" Simms asked.

Thurber pulled the envelope out of his pocket, removed the letter, leaned forward in his chair, and offered it to Simms, who took it with his outstretched hand.

"What I'll read now is a very lucid, very frank, and a most significant development," he said with deliberation. "I want you to listen closely. But please don't be alarmed and don't be overly concerned, although you must keep this matter in your awareness at all times."

Simms then began reading the astronomer's letter about the gaseous, radioactive cloud in the orbital path of Mars. After every sentence, the professor paused, glanced at the group with a studied expression to gauge their reac-

168

tion. The faces responded to the news exactly as he had hoped they would—with astonishment and bewilderment.

"That, then, is the story," Simms said as he finished reading the letter and handed it back to Thurber. "I expected you to be taken aback by this unexpected development, just as I was when Maity read the contents to me last night. But I want you to know that this is no longer a problem. Thanks to some heady and heavy preparations and extremely sophisticated protective devices, we're going to weather the situation as though it didn't exist."

He looked at Thurber and frowned.

"Maity, how soon can we have the ship ready for that trial run?" he asked.

Heads in the seating section spun around and glared at each other. The faces all at once had become animated, mirroring a variety of expressions ranging from surprise to astonishment and from glee to a seemingly mild trepidation, at least on the face of Dr. Shivard, the Nobel laureate cancer expert responsible for the health and well-being of the crew on Operation Mars.

Thurber responded in a quiet, matter-of-fact tone. "She's ready to fly at a moment's notice. All we need is a target date and we'll have the ship cleared for takeoff."

Simms looked back at the crew and tapped the fingers of both hands on the top of the lectern.

"We will have a test flight, as you just heard me say," he announced with a neutral expression. "It will be held just as soon as indoctrination on the machinery and components aboard the craft can be accomplished."

A hand went up in the front row and it interrupted Simms.

"Yes, Captain," the professor said, addressing himself to Stuart.

"A very elemental question, Dr. Simms," Stuart said almost apologetically. "I assume you are speaking of an orbital run . . . is that correct, sir?"

"Of course," Simms replied quickly and flatly. "Our concern is that gaseous, radiactive cloud. On board, we have a magnificent machine called the particle accelerator. I'm certain all of you were briefed about its primary function—to create a vacuum in which an atmosphere can be manufactured."

He inhaled deeply and allowed his lips to turn into a slight smile. "Yet, that particle accelerator has another function that you are not aware of . . ."

Simms then lectured at some length on the principles of colloidal suspension, and why it was imperative at this juncture to test the machine in space—the only environment in which it can perform that phase of its output.

Amazement was clearly written on several faces, but no one was more astounded by the revelation that the machine can spin an endless sheet of black plastic in space than Dr. Jordan, the physicist from the University of Chicago. She was also a specialist of note in many chemical experimentations, particularly in the field of plastics. At one time she had supervised the development of plastics at Dow Chemical, but then her interests turned to the fields of heat, light, and sound, and even to some extent to the study of magnetism and radiation. That was when she went to the University of Chicago.

"Dr. Simms," Dr. Jordan said sharply. "I have been aware of the properties embodying colloidal suspension for some time. In fact we had worked with them for several years in the laboratory when I was doing specialty work in that field," she said, her voice almost breathless from the disclosures Simms just made. "But . . . but . . . you are speaking, sir, of a most improbable invention . . . at least, to me it is . . . I'm overwhelmed that such a machine has been developed."

Dr. Jordan paused and shook her head.

"Yes, Doctor," Simms moved his own head with an up and down motion, "no one was more astonished than I to learn that this machine had been developed. But let me also add to that, ma'am . . . nor was anyone more thrilled and overjoyed than I that such a marvelous advance as colloidal suspension had been developed."

Simms rubbed his hands together. "Not only developed, Dr. Jordan, but fabricated and installed in Galactic I. It was a stroke of fate, nothing less."

Simms eased away from the lectern and took a few short steps that brought him to the edge of the stage. He stuffed his hands in his trouser pockets and smiled.

"Now, will you all join me in visiting the ship? I think it's time we got acquainted with that space buggy."

Simms stepped off the stage as the crew left their seats and filed into the aisle behind Thurber, who had risen and walked part-way toward the exit.

"If you'll follow me," he said briskly, "I'll introduce you to your, er . . . space buggy."

Everyone chuckled and fell in behind Thurber.

CHAPTER XII

Test Flight

The cylindrical-shaped, gleaming aluminum-alloy Galactic I looked like a futuristic flying machine that might have rocketed right out of the pages of a Buck Rogers saga. The spaceship evoked a cacophonous outpouring of *oohs* and *ahs* from the crew that was to ride this fantastic vehicle to Mars and back.

Even Dr. Simms was overwhelmed by the ship's size and sleekness. It was almost twice the dimensions of its predecessor first-generation spaceplane shuttles. Although similar in some respects to the first series of ships launched in 1979, which revolutionized space travel, the Galactic I contained a far greater number of differences.

It was two hundred feet long and thirty feet wide compared with the sixty-foot length and fifteen-foot width of the first shuttles. Its load capacity was exactly three times the 65,000 pounds that the early models were capable of orbiting, and its delta-shaped wingspan of one hundred and eighty feet was exactly one hundred and two feet greater than the Enterprise series that were still being launched into space, with their solid rocket boosters and huge fuel tanks but only from Vandenberg Air Force Base in California.

"What a beauty, what a gorgeous hunk of space machine!" exclaimed Simms as he followed Thurber to the stair ramp leading to the crew compartment. The hatch was located in the forward section of the cargo bay, some twenty-five feet above the concrete pad on which Galactic I was standing.

Thurber led the way up the ramp with Simms close on his heels, followed by the others who climbed the steps in close single file.

When they reached the interior of the spaceship, they found a huge three-tiered monstrosity whose upper two levels could be reached either by stairs or a service elevator.

"Here on this lower level is the cargo bay," Thurber began, pointing to a cavernous compartment that seemed even larger than that of a conventional late 1980s jet transport. "There are eight thousand cubic feet of room here," the space boss explained. "And if you're having difficulty figuring how much cargo will fit in that space, then just imagine what eleven freight cars can hold and you'll have a fairly accurate picture of the capacity."

Thurber pressed the elevator button and the doors glided open. The lift wasn't very large and it drew a raspy comment from the NASA administrator. "They didn't expect too many passengers would want to ride up and down at any one time, so they gave us a modest-sized elevator," he said chuckling.

Then he pointed to the stairs. "Let's walk up," he said lazily. "It's good exercise."

The second deck was a glistening configuration of anodized aluminum walls, red carpeted floor, and recessed lighting. The area was compartmentalized with low-level partitions into a half-dozen sections in which the Martian voyagers could conduct different experiments during the flight and their six-month occupation and exploration of the Red Planet.

After taking the group on a tour of the third deck—the sleeping quarters and lavatory and shower facilities—Thurber escorted them downstairs to the flight control cabin. This was a huge installation comprising an elaborate sprawl of instrumentation and gadgetry on a multitude of wall panels, consoles, and ceiling and floor units.

"As Captain Stuart and the rest of the astronautic team who trained on the simulator in Palmdale will tell you," Thurber began, "this is the living end so far as controls go on a space vehicle. I've been assured by the biggest engineering brains in the space program that the computerized navigation system aboard this craft cannot be further improved for at least ten years—that's how advanced everything is. We're really set for the twenty-first century."

Since Captain Stuart, Lieutenants Deems and Perlman, and Commander Swedlow had spent the better part of six months at Palmdale "flying" the simulator, which was an exact replica of the cabin on Galactic I, they didn't mirror the immense admiration and, indeed, astonishment of the geologist, the astronomer, the physicists, and Dr. Shivard, the physician, who had never been inside the ship before.

But the most interested of all those on this inspection tour of Galactic I was Professor Simms. His greatest attention was magnetized by the visit to the control cabin, which he had not seen finished when he had been to North American Rockwell's assembly line.

Although the flight compartment had not been fully outfitted on the ship at that time, the doctor had acquired an intimate acquaintanceship with its design, since he'd studied the blueprints and specifications closely.

In listening now to Thurber's briefing about the simplicity of piloting and operating the ship, Simms encountered nothing new or surprising. He was aware of precisely how the Galactic I was engineered—to fly with push-button ease. But he listened with respectful silence as the space boss went through the exercise of outlining the key features of the flying ship.

"One of the more sophisticated aspects of this beautiful spacecraft is its digital fly-by-wire capability," Thurber said. "I'm speaking here of the printed circuit variety of wire. Everything that has to do with flight control is channeled through computers. There are no control cables, no push-pull rods, no levers, no mechanical systems of any sort. The ship is totally controlled by electronic robots, which offers far greater flexibility and safety in flight."

Thurber looked at Simms. "Well, Gordy," he said amiably, "I guess I'll leave things in your hands now. You know where the life-support systems are and certainly you are well acquainted with them. Therefore I'll not even attempt to speak about them."

Turning to the others, he said, "Well, people, if you'll excuse me now I shall be off. But you can count on seeing me around."

He glanced at Simms and smiled. "I'm going to stick around just to make certain Gordy does his best in getting you guys ready for your great adventure."

Everyone laughed but Simms seemed to enjoy the moment of light gabble most of all. He was still chuckling after Thurber had left the flight cabin and gone down the ramp on the way back to his office.

Simms quickly confronted the astronaut who was to be the chief pilot on Operation Mars. "Captain Stuart," the doctor said edgily, "how soon do you estimate the ship can be readied for a test flight?"

Stuart frowned in contemplation for a long moment. He turned and cast a meditative glance at the main control panel. Then he looked at Simms with a grimace.

"I think this baby is ready to spread her wings whenever the tower can give us clearance," Stuart said. "Of course, I'm quite certain that you're aware of the fact that it'll take approximately forty-eight hours in any event after the go-ahead before we can become airborne."

"That's for the countdown, right?" Simms said, knowing full well what the answer was.

Stuart nodded affirmatively.

"Do you foresee any hitch preparing for the start of a countdown by, say, tomorrow or the day after?" Simms inquired.

"So soon, Dr. Simms?" exclaimed Stuart in a surprised voice. "Is there any reason for such a precipitate speedup in flight plans? It was my understanding that the crew would undergo reasonably lengthy onboard training . . . in fact, it wasn't even in the cards to fly a test mission until you informed us about it this morning."

During that exchange, the others stepped away from Simms and Stuart and politely busied themselves in examining other areas of the flight control section.

The professor stiffened at the captain's seeming resistance to the proposal for an early test flight. He was highly irritated but tried to hide his reaction.

"I'm not so sure you were as impressed—nor indeed alarmed—by Dr. Koenig's report about the radioactive clouds as I was," Simms said with a put-on sigh of impatience.

"Oh, no, Doctor," the captain said sharply, now seemingly at a disadvantage because he'd been put on the defensive. "I regard this peril with considerable concern. However, you've attempted to assure us that the particle accelerator will provide more than adequate protection. . . . Isn't that what you said, sir?"

Simms liked that. Stuart's lips were dripping respect. The professor liked that very much because he now sensed that the captain was not only on the defensive, but also was in retreat.

"Let me be brutally frank, Randy," Simms said with a sudden smile. "I hope you don't mind the familiarity . . . but I do believe we'll all get along with a greater spirit of camaraderie if we work on a first-name basis. Do you agree with that assessment?"

"I certainly do, Dr. S . . . er, Gordy," Stuart stammered with a shy but widening grin.

"That's better," Simms said in a pleased tone. He'd won the first round, but now he felt Stuart must be convinced fully that the test flight was absolutely necessary, and should be undertaken at the earliest opportunity.

"You see, Randy, the man who developed the particle accelerator is, in my personal view, an engineering genius. I've known Boyce McMorrow for many, many years—long before he went to Grumman. Indeed, we went to school together. And, I need not press the point, I trust him implicitly. Yet, I wouldn't want to risk your life nor the lives of the other nine persons on this ship by conceding that the particle accelerator will perform as touted."

Simms placed his hand on Stuart's forearm and tugged him gently toward the starboard bulkhead. "Come over here, Randy, I want you to look at this piece of machinery."

Simms took the astronaut to the particle accelerator, a coppertoned, shoulder-high rectangular unit with four large barrel-like cylinders and an array of color-coded red, green, blue, and yellow tubes of a quarter-inch diameter, each leading from an adjacent unit that obviously was the power plant, into the individual cylinders of matching color.

An assembly of numbered and lettered push-buttons in a console atop the machine comprised all the controls required to operate the unit in both vacuum phase as well as colloidal suspension.

"This is the baby," Simms said to Stuart. "Boyce McMorrow delivered her into the world and she's a wondrous piece of machinery. Yet . . ."

Simms let the words drift away. He looked sharply at the captain, who seemed overwrought by anxiety to hear what the professor was driving at.

"You and I agreed back in the ready room that this machine cannot function in the atmosphere, that it must be in the vacuum of space to perform, right?" the doctor said, pursing his lips and making a low staccato whistling sound.

"Well, I took your word, Gordy, and I certainly have no reason to doubt that you are completely accurate in your assessment," Stuart returned in a condescending tone.

"Fine, that's exactly what I half-expected you'd say," Simms smiled. "You took my word that this machine will work only in space, and I accepted my good friend Boyce's assurance that this particle accelerator works in space . . ."

All at once, Stuart began registering a glimmer of an awakening. His face creased in small, almost imperceptible folds as his lips curled into a smile reflecting traces of embarrassment.

"Have I gotten through to you yet?" Simms prodded quickly. He was determined now to put the recalcitrant astronaut into full route, but without inflicting denigration.

"I'm pretty sure I get your message," Stuart said in a low, submissive voice. "None of us knows for certain really . . ."

"Whether the damned thing will or will not work when we get it up there, right?" Simms interrupted in a voice so loud that several of the ship's complement who were inspecting the flight compartment turned around and stared at him with surprised looks.

"Now, Randy, suppose it doesn't function as it's supposed to," Simms continued hammering away at the captain. "How long will it take to correct the fault? A week? A month? Six months? Then what happens to our flight plan if we discover malfunctioning in the system when we are deep into our training program and time is against us? Can we afford a delay in launch—do you have any idea what Congress will do with our budget in 1989?"

Stuart shrugged his shoulders and moved his head up and down slowly. He didn't break his silence but that wasn't necessary. His gesture spoke volumes. It flashed a loud and clear message to Simms. The captain now full concurred

181

with the professor that the sooner the particle accelerator was put through its test in space, the sooner the questionable safety factor posed by the gaseous cloud will have been put to a resolution.

With Stuart's obstruction effectively removed, Simms cordially invited everyone to give him attention.

"Randy and I, as you undoubtedly overheard," he began, "have come to a meeting of the minds about the test flight I spoke about earlier. We both agree now it should come off as quickly as we can have a formal countdown started."

Simms looked at each of the crew, who returned his gaze with a mixed galaxy of emotions. They had heard the doctor say a test flight was indicated after discovery of the hazardous floating cloud near Mars. They also couldn't help but hear the telling exchange between Simms and Stuart in the flight control cabin where they were all standing now.

Yet, suddenly the time element had become a matter of prime concern to all, since it cropped up so suddenly and unexpectedly. None before that morning had been told what Thurber had known since receiving the letter from Dr. Koenig a week ago, and Simms who only learned about the dangerous element in space from the NASA chief over dinner the night before.

"Are you anticipating the test mission as something that may take place in a few days or so?" Dr. Swedlow, the flight surgeon, asked pointedly.

Simms looked toward Stuart questioningly, to make certain there was no impediment the head astronaut on the flight could foresee. "Anything to stand in the way if we worked on such short notice, Randy?" the professor asked.

"Not from the standpoint of flying the ship," Stuart said. "So far as I'm concerned, once we get clearance I'm ready for the countdown to begin."

Simms turned to the woman physician whose face was masked quite visibly now with a worrisome look. "Are you disturbed about anything, Doctor?" the professor asked.

"Yes, I'm puzzled about one thing, Dr. Simms," Dr. Shivard said hoarsely. Clearing her throat, she shook her head and pointed to the cabin door.

"When we traipsed through the laboratory out there a few moments ago, I saw none of the medical supplies that I had put on order for the flight. We certainly mustn't consider ourselves in a state of readiness for a countdown when the most vital components for our well-being in space haven't yet been brought aboard."

Simms rocked back and forth on his heels, his face dour and mirroring his own dismay at that news. "You're so right, doctor," he said sharply. "But of course none of us had anticipated a flight on such short notice. But this is a matter of the greatest concern to me and it will be attended to at once. I'm certain it will not take more than an hour or so to round up those supplies . . ."

"Oh, I know it won't, Dr. Simms," the flight surgeon said. "All of the supplies are in stock here on the Cape. They are standard medical kit contents on all spacecraft."

"And if I recall correctly, Simms put in with an air of professorial awareness and authoritativeness, "there are no added starters on the list for Operation Mars."

"No added starters, Dr. Simms," interjected Dr. Shivard with a smile. "Except, of course, the quantities differ vastly . . ."

"Oh, of course, I'm very cognizant of that," Simms countered in a pleasant, assuring tone. Then looking directly into the physician's eyes, he said, "You must get started at once, Doctor. Why don't you run over to supply right now and have them rush those medical items here as soon as possible?"

Then with a laugh, he quipped, "Or sooner . . ."

That brought a smile to Dr. Shivard's face again as she walked out of the cabin on her way to execute her errand.

Then Simms turned to the others. "Well, does anyone see any additional problems or may I proceed with a request for a clearance to a countdown?"

Simms looked around. A few heads shook negatively, others didn't react. All in all, no one voiced an objection. Simms had been given a mandate to proceed.

"Very well," he said, turning to Captain Stuart. "Let me see . . . this is Thursday, January the twenty-first." The professor pushed a button on his digital wristwatch and narrowed his gaze.

"What if we were to request the countdown for eight A.M. Friday?" he said in a tone that sounded more like an order than a solicitation for an opinion. He turned his head and looked from one member to the other for a response. No one had anything to offer.

"Let me assure you all that this isn't how thinly your various interests will be catered to when I have finally prepared you for the flight to Mars in July," Simms said with a ring of sincerity in his voice. "Each of you who is going on this journey has a vested interest in your particular specialty, such as astronomy, geology, radiation, or whatever. And I will make certain by then that all of your needs on the trip are met, that all your equipment and supplies are on board. However . . ."

Simms wrung his hands as he paused and looked around at the faces for a reading on how much attention he was receiving. He judged that everyone was listening intently.

". . . as I said, your needs will be met. But not on the test flight. We're only going to fly a brief orbital mission to shake down the particle accelerator. We must determine whether the machine will manufacture the plastic sheeting that we'll need for protection against radiation."

Phoebe Swedlow suddenly distracted the professor when her face screwed in seeming puzzlement.

"Did I say something that you don't understand, Commander?" Simms smiled at the astronette.

"Well, it's just that I believe we all would like to know how much of a test flight this will be . . . how long are we going to be in orbit?" Phoebe said. "I'm not protesting, it's just that it's a detail we ought to know pretty soon."

Simms nodded agreement. "Of course," he said. "The point is well taken. And I can answer that with, I believe, some fair amount of accuracy."

He pulled a calculator out of the inside pocket of his jacket and made some hasty computations.

"Not long at all," he said quickly. "I'm certain that three, at most four, orbits are all we'll require to put the particle accelerator to a full test. All that I'm anxious to see is a plastic screen formed in space. If that happens, the machine will have passed muster. If it doesn't, then we've got problems . . . and something will have to be done immediately to correct the fault."

Now Dr. Santangelo, the astronomer, had a question. "I'm looking forward to the flight with eagerness, so please don't get the impression that I'm trying to take a raincheck," he said in an apologetic tone. "But what I want to know is whether you'll expect the laboratory force to go through the motions of a working flight, or are we just going along for the ride?"

Simms took a deep breath and exhaled with

a relieved sigh. "Let's say this'll be an educational flight," he smiled. "It would be ludicrous to expect any of you to perform scientific experiments in two or three orbits. Moreover, what could we learn up there in such a short time that a thousand other space voyagers haven't already learned over the years?"

The professor glanced around at the faces once more.

"Any other questions?" he asked.

There were none.

"In that event," he said turning toward the portal, "let's break for lunch."

"One minute and five seconds and counting..."

Monday, January 25, 1988.

The time was 8:42 A.M. and the Galactic I was sitting on the edge of the south runway, poised for takeoff. Dr. Simms was scurrying through the ship, from the laboratory seating section, where the six scientists were comfortably belted down in their safety lounge chairs, to the control cabin, where the astronauts were similarly buckled in.

"All set?" he asked earnestly as he stuck his head into the laboratory in the final seconds.

"Yes, we're ready and holding our breaths," laughed Anita Browsey, the Dartmouth physicist. She was in a frivolous and giddy mood, as were several of the others alongside her. The excitement of going on their first space flight had numbed their sensibilities. They were reacting as though on a drug-in-

187

duced high, which they were not. While stimulants and depressants, such as Dexedrine and Darvon, were included among the twenty-six items in every medical kit aboard, they were never administered prior to liftoff and entry into space or before effects of weightlessness had been felt and each individual had a chance to react to that strange no-gravity environment.

"Exactly one minute." The voice came from the tower over the Galactic's intercom.

"Hey, Dr. Simms," Captain Stuart called from the control cabin. "Get in here and strap yourself down . . . please hurry."

"Just relax and stay cool," Simms advised everyone in the laboratory with an extraordinary calm. "There'll be very little discomfort in this takeoff. It'll get to you for only about a minute, then you'll be out of those G-gravity blues just as soon as the captain points our nose toward the line of flight."

The professor's message was drowned out once again by the tower controller's voice.

"Twenty-five seconds and counting . . ."

Simms threw his hands over his head suddenly in a pose of surrender.

"This is it," he croaked. "I'd better strap in."

He surged out of the laboratory area and barged into the control cabin.

"Where the hell have you been, Gordy?" cried Stuart. "We're ready to blast off. If you don't get yourself secured you're gonna be flattened against the bulkhead . . ."

Simms hopped onto the fifth and only unoccupied safety lounge chair in the control cabin and strapped himself down.

"Nine seconds and counting . . ."

Suddenly, the voice from the tower broke the rhythmic, monotonous cadence of the countdown and said alertingly, "Prepare for takeoff . . . five seconds and counting . . ."

Some three minutes earlier the Galactic I's atomic engine had been turned on. It had been humming in almost total silence, which was so deceiving for a power plant of such vast capability, not only for lifting the 550,000-pound vehicle into space but also in hurtling it through the universe at heretofore unattainable speeds.

The flight plan for Operation Mars, however, called for a very modest speed in traveling both directions. There were several hard and fast reasons for that decision despite the fact that the incredible Aere Perennius engine developed by General Electric during a late stage of the Galactic I program had heretofore unimagined greater speed proficiency than the liquid oxygen power plant that initially had been designed for the ship.

Those earlier model specifications called for the required 25,022 mph escape velocity that was to be achieved with a boost from the Son of Saturn rocket, then a free-flight through space. Thus Galactic I would have followed a path much the same as the Apollo modules and their successor space shuttles of the late 1970s and 1980s.

That meant the average rate of speed for Galactic I enroute to Mars and back would have been approximately 16,000 mph, or considerably faster than the 7,500 mph on flights to the Moon, where Earth's gravitational tugging exerts greater influences than in the far-out reaches of space.

With the atomic-energized Aere Perennius powering Galactic I, the potential rate of speed grew to a virtually limitless mph ceiling. And though the engine hadn't been tested in space, hardly any propulsion expert doubted the engine could drive a space vehicle close to the speed of light—186,282 miles per second—and attain a theoretical rendezvous with Mars in a mind-boggling three and a half minutes.

But NASA ruled out such a flight because of too many uncertainties, not the least of which were the yet untested theories about time and space developed by Albert Einstein. Go beyond the speed of light and you go backward in time, the early twentieth-century scientist had formulated. But that was a paper theory. No one had yet attempted to prove it in space. And NASA wasn't about to cut any new pathways into the unknown during Operation Mars.

Thus, it was decided not to average more than 16,000 mph on the journey to the Red Planet—a speed no greater, nor any slower, than would have been achieved in the free-flight of Galactic I had it been launched with a conventional liquid hydrogen power plant.

That meant Galactic I and the space voyagers would take ninety days, or 2,166 hours, to journey the thirty-five million miles. And there was no particular objection to that schedule inasmuch as the flight, many years in planning, had a full itinerary of experiments for the on-board scientists during the three months to Mars and the three months for the return trip.

But the decision to fly at "normal" speed to Mars and back didn't preclude a plan to subject another Galactic I shuttle craft to a high-speed shakedown flight in the not-too-distant future. A tentative target date of November or December of that year had been selected for such a test. NASA had already begun preparing a crew of astronauts for that flight, which was to achieve a speed of about 50,000 mph, or twice the velocity for escaping earth's gravity.

The flight plan for Galactic I in Operation Mars called for a cut-off of power once the vehicle fell into its free-fall flight path to Mars. It would course to its destination just as all prior manned flights to the Moon had done, as well as the numerous unmanned vehicles such as the Mariner and their successor Centurian series in landings on Mars and photographic fly-bys of Jupiter and Saturn.

But on this test flight to put the particle accelerator through its operating phases in colloidal suspension, a speed of only 18,500 mph was required—just enough to put Galactic I into pre-charted elliptical orbit of approximately one hundred and fifty miles in its perigee, or lowest point, and two hundred and forty miles at it apogee, or greatest distance from earth's center.

"You are clear for takeoff!" exclaimed the voice from the tower with expected, yet startling suddenness.

All at once Galactic I's after-burner exploded with a brilliant flash of red-blue flames and a swirling plume of gray-black smoke. The gleaming ship responded to the thrust of 15.6 million pounds of relentless, unyielding, virtually limitless power generated by the core of uranium feeding energy into the Aere Perennius engine.

With acceleration unlike any spacecraft had ever shown, Galactic I shot along the runway with a low-moaning swooshing sound that suddenly grew deafeningly loud as Captain Stuart gunned the engine for liftoff.

"What a magnificent sight!" exclaimed Maitland Thurber in the tower observatory as the ship climbed rapidly into the sky at an angle that soon grew into a near-perpendicular one.

"It looks faster than a Saturn," remarked the control master, Rich Woolsey, who was sitting at the monitoring channels.

His voice all at once was drowned out by the ground-shaking, ear-splitting din of the sonic boom that Galactic I caused a mere ten seconds after liftoff—that's how fast the acceleration went from zero speed to the breaking of the sound barrier at 740 mph.

"It not only looks faster, it *is* faster," Thurber said excitedly as the Galactic I very quickly now shrunk into a pinhead in the sky, discernible to the naked eye only by the contrail shaped by the hot engine gases in the frigid stratosphere.

Aboard the Galactic I, Captain Stuart and Lieutenant Perlman were busily engaged in communicating voice reports to Mission Control in the tower at Cape Canaveral as well as Mission Monitoring Trackers at Houston Space Center, where some of the finite telemetry and evaluation systems were keeping a check on the flight.

"All vibration from takeoff now past," reported Stuart on his radio. "Sky has changed now. We are in total blackness. All power off . . ."

"Everything looking good from here," Houston crackled back. "You are on target in your orbit . . ."

"Roger, we read you," Perlman responded.

"Your flight duration is calculated at four hours and fifty-six minutes for three orbits, Galactic I," the tower at Canaveral advised the ship. "Your ETA [estimated time of arrival] on return after three orbits is one-seventeen P.M. . . . Calculating now for additional orbits . . . that will be one hour and thirty-nine minutes for one extra turn . . . three hours and eighteen minutes for two. . . . Advise not to exceed five orbits . . . that will put your

ETA for touchdown at four-thirty-five P.M.
. . . must remind you problem of landing in
dusk . . ."

"Roger, no sweat," responded Stuart. "We
shall abort on fifth orbit if mission is not accomplished . . . over."

Stuart then turned to the others in the cabin.
"Well, what're you waiting for?" he said in a
buoyant tone. "Unstrap and start doing something useful up here!"

Simms removed his restraints and floated
out of his lounge. He grabbed a handrail and
managed to put his feet on the floor where
now, with his magnetized soles touching the
metallic deck, he was able to maintain control
over his movements without drifting in the
cabin.

Stuart and the other members of the flight
crew did the same, but with far greater ease
and efficiency that the professor. After all,
they were all veterans of space travel while for
Simms this was a pioneering venture even
though he'd been with the program more than
half his lifetime.

His first concern was the scientific team in
the laboratory. To his surprise they had all responded to the strange onset of weightlessness
as though it were a welcome and pleasant experience. Dr. Shivard, the ship's physician, and
Dr. Santangelo, the astronomer, had already
unbuckled their straps and seemed to be adjust-
ing to their first minutes in space with widely
disparate responses.

Dr. Shivard was floating about the laboratory in semi-helplessness. She had not gained her bearings and thus couldn't implant her boot magnets to the deck. But Dr. Santangelo was way ahead of everyone, and when Simms entered the laboratory he found the astronomer peering out the space observatory porthole and experiencing paroxysms of ecstasy at the sight of the heavens he'd never seen from such an altitude.

"The incredible universe!" he exclaimed over and over. "Man has marveled at heavens from earliest times," he waxed rhapsodically. "I've known them intimately as an astronomer peering through telescopes . . . but never did I dream they could look like this. Yes, I've seen pictures and I've listened to descriptions and read what was written by those who've been up here before . . . but seeing the universe firsthand, this galaxy-filled universe . . . it's so different. So thrilling . . ."

"I'm delighted to encounter such outpourings of enthusiasm from you, Dr. Santangelo," Simms said with a lilt in his voice. He looked around at the other four who were still buckled in their safety lounges.

"Are you going to stay buckled in or don't you want to experience the weightlessness we're in?" Simms asked pointedly . "Come on! Off your butts, everyone! . . ."

One by one, they began unstrapping themselves and undergoing the same floating sensations that Simms and their colleagues, Santangelo and Shivard, were experiencing.

By now Dr. Shivard had found her bearings and stood upright, feet fixed firmly to the deck. Soon after the others all managed to regain their postures in the gravityless spaceship. And then there was unanimity among all— weightlessness is a heady, enjoyable feeling.

"I don't think any of us will mind the trip to Mars the least bit," the flight surgeon said. "Indeed, I believe we're going to find it a very pleasant change from our Earth-bound environment."

Simms shook his head. "I agree with you, Doctor," he said. "I'm only sorry I'm not going with you. So I'd better take advantage of this brief tour in space afforded me by doing what I came up here to do. If you'll excuse me, folks, I'll proceed to the particle accelerator . . ."

He left the laboratory and returned to the flight control cabin.

"All set to manufacture a few yards of plastic out there, Gordy?" Stuart asked in a light-hearted voice.

"A few miles of plastic, yes, Randy," Simms replied. "But not before I get this darned accelerator turned on and programmed for production."

Simms now was in a highly-charged emotional state. The moment of truth had come at last and Dr. Gordon Lyle Simms wanted more than anything in the world to test the machine.

More than anything he wanted to see a sheet of plastic formed in the vacuum of space from the process of colloidal suspension—the black particles emitted from the carbon element as it is heated by atomic fusion.

It's got to work . . . it's got to work, Simms said to himself again and again as he approached the control console and prepared for the fateful engine firing.

CHAPTER XIII

It Works!

The console and its keyboard of twenty-six square black keys were no mystery to Dr. Simms. He had studied the instructional booklet Boyce McMorrow had prepared for the flight and memorized every step that must be followed to set the particle accelerator in motion for colloidal suspension.

Punching the keys in the proper sequence—5-R-2-P-Q-5-6-D-B—programmed the appropriate combination of electronic signals to generate the particle acceleration process inside the multi-colored suction thrusters of the tubing on the front of the machine. These extracted energizing matter out of the red, green, blue, and yellow cylinders in proportionate quantities pre-programmed into the machine's computerized brain, which had been sealed into the unit at Grumman.

A flashing display on the screen above the keyboard console was the only guidance the machine's operator required to determine whether the feed-in of energizing elements was in proper ratio for the .002-inch gauge plastic that was recommended for deployment on the Martian flight. A greater thickness—.005 inches—was prescribed for areas of space closer to the sun, such as the vicinity of Venus, and thicker yet for the time in the distant future when man might dare venture to the caloric environs of Mercury.

His initial excitement about the impending test reached a nerve-fraying edge for Simms as he scanned the screen for confirmation of the feed-in ratio.

The screen lit up and the numbers and letters came on in red on the opaque glass—5-R-2-P-Q-5-6-D-B.

"Bingo!" Simms almost shouted. "It's reacting perfectly!"

The astronauts applauded politely. However, the most significant phase still lay ahead, just moments from now. Will the jetspouts eject the black particles into space to form the plastic?

Before that could happen, the machine needed one more nudge—the thruster had to be depressed. That was a push-button control, which generates the flow of heat into the carbon element.

Stuart and Perlman moved toward the control cabin's observation window and peered out anxiously for a sign of activity from the jetspouts. Suddenly Perlman gulped and made a gurgling sound. "Golly!" he gasped. "It's happening!"

Perlman stood away to give Stuart an unobstructed view of the phenomenon of a plastic screen actually forming before their eyes.

"This is not to be believed," Stuart rasped, obviously overwhelmed by the sight. "Hey, Gordy . . . come here and cast a look!"

Simms's face was twisted by a broad, anticipatory grin. He looked the machine over hastily to make certain it was functioning properly and needed no further attention for the moment. When he satisfied himself that he could leave, he hurried over to the observation window. In the freedom of space, each step he took was a quantum leap. Had it not been for the magnetic soles on his boots, he would have undoubtedly bounded into the overhang, if not through it.

"Oh, good heavens, it's really working!" he shouted in glee. "Why, it's beautiful . . . it's fantastic . . ."

Out in the blackness of space, the plastic screen was not clearly discernible at first glance. Yet it was a highly visible presence because the relentless, ever-present light of the sun was being reflected on the shiny surface of the ever-widening, rapidly expanding plastic sheet.

"How marvelous," Simms went on with an enthusiastic lilt in his voice. He stared transfixed out the window at the lengthening plastic sheet, which the machine was manufacturing at an inordinate speed.

"It must be a hundred miles long already," a thin, high-pitched voice exclaimed suddenly. Phoebe Swedlow had moved to the aft observation window and was gazing out in amazement at the screen, which had already blotted out the view of the earth from the back of Galactic I.

By now the scientific team had grown accustomed to their new environment of weightlessness and, having been astonished by the plastic screen they'd spotted from the space observatory porthole, came in a body into the control cabin to bestow their felicitations upon Simms for making the particle accelerator function successfully.

"It is indeed thrilling," exulted the professor. "Just look at that screen . . ."

He went back to the machine and punched another series of commands on the squared keys of the console. This time the sequence was 7-A-2-P-Q-4-7-D-B. It was for a one hundred-mile swath of plastic spinout. That sheet that was first formed was on the first, or lowest, swath setting of fifty miles.

As the numerals and letters lit up the opaque glass again with the new combination, a slightly louder hum was heard from the particle accelerator's low-droning atomic power plant.

"Why, that's unbelievable!" cried out Danielle Lemage, the Space Science and Application administrator from NASA. "Look at the size of the screen now! It's covering the earth!"

Indeed it wasn't covering the earth but hiding it from the eyes of those aboard Galactic I. Of course, Dr. Lemage was speaking in the figurative sense. Nevertheless, the plastic shield extended now for several hundred miles and was growing steadily larger.

By this time Dr. Simms resolved that the particle accelerator had passed its test. He returned to the control panel and disengaged the push-button thruster, which was supplying the high-intensity heat to the carbon element. Instantly that ceased the flow of particles in space, which had been coagulating into plastic.

"Is that the extent of your test, Gordy?" ventured a curious Captain Stuart. He looked at the plastic sheet that obliterated all view of earth from the back of the ship and shook his head in awe.

"That's the end of the test, yes," answered Simms in a pleased voice.

"But . . . but," Stuart asked puzzled, "what do we do with that?"

He pointed a finger toward the screen from the observation port. "We can't leave it floating like that . . . it's a hazard to navigation."

"Oh, don't worry about it," Simms said in a dismissing tone. "When we reenter the atmosphere, Randy, that'll incinerate faster than you can bat an eye."

"Good heavens, Gordy," the captain said with a studious, gape-mouthed expression. "That never occurred to me. You mean we just pull it along with us when we go downstairs?"

"Of course," smiled Simms with a bright wide-eyed look at the captain. He then turned and studied the other faces. Each reflected an overwhelmed reaction to the professor's instant solution of a problem that none had anticipated, let alone foreseeing a way of doing away with it.

"It's amazing how you thought of that, professor," Dr. Shivard said admiringly. "You certainly are a genius."

"Thank you, Doctor," responded Simms with a proud smile.

The professor turned to Stuart and the other members of the flight crew. "You will want to know what buttons to push on this machine," he said casually. "But I don't think this is the time to orient you on the operation of the particle accelerator. We can do that on the ground when there's a lot of time and at a leisurely pace."

Heads nodded agreeingly.

Simms shifted his attention back to the machine while the crew and scientific team turned away to other interests. As the professor disengaged the controls on the console and unscrambled the coded orders for the one hundred-mile-wide screen, no one questioned Simms about why he had formed the .005-inch guage plastic screen in space.

That wasn't the guage that had been recommended for Mars but, rather, for use in the more intense heat that a space ship would encounter in flying to the orbital vicinity of Venus.

No one, of course, was aware of the thickness of the plastic that Simms had spun outside the ship. And no one except the professor himself was to know that it wasn't the .002-gauge, for after two more orbits the Galactic I would re-enter Earth's atmosphere and the evidence of Professor Simms's inexplicable test of colloidal suspension under specifications for a flight the spaceship wasn't scheduled to make, would be ignited by the atmospheric friction and burn away.

Only the doctor knew why he had chosen to produce .005-inch gauge and not .002. And now, as he secured the particle accelerator, he turned and went to the aft observation window for another view of the plastic blanket the Galactic I was towing over the earth like a mammoth pennant. He couldn't see anything of the earth itself through that screen—not the clouds, not the definitions of continents, outlines of oceans, nor even the rivers that had been visible earlier before the plastic sheet was spun.

Simms smiled to himself and walked to another observation port in the forward part of the ship. He looked down again and regarded a sight that quickened his pulse.

He could see the earth now. But he also saw something else over the earth's topography that was the most meaningful moment of this orbital flight for Simms.

The giant plastic screen was creating a very definable jet black shadow over the earth, almost as night itself would cast.

Simms knew then and there that the plastic

indeed was capable not only of protecting space explorers from the dangers of solar radiation in space—but of even blotting out the sun over the earth . . .

CHAPTER XIV

Spacejack!

"That was a superb performance, Gordy," rhapsodized Maitland Thurber as he greeted Professor Simms off the Galactic I after the landing on the Cape Canaveral runway. "You can't imagine what a thrill it was to watch that experiment up there. Do you know, Gordy, that we received televised newscasts from Santa Barbara, Honolulu, and Tokyo of the shadows you had cast over the landscape . . . in fact, at one point there were reports from Yokohama and Kyushu that the sunrise there was actually eclipsed for about thirty seconds when you towed the plastic screen over that part of the earth."

Simms drew in a quick, excited breath and braced himself. He pulled his shoulders back and let his chin go limp. "Are you kidding?" he croaked. "They actually experienced an eclipse from that little plastic shield we spun over the earth?"

"That's the size of it, Gordy," Thurber said in a low mutter. "It was so remarkable, all of

207

it, that I can hardly allow myself to get aroused anymore. I've been through so much excitement the last few hours that I feel I should coast a bit in my present state of insensibility and numbness."

"I know what you mean, Maity," Simms said, understandingly quiet. "I almost feel as you do. I've been in a state of high agitation so long that I also want to go limp."

By now the entire family from the historic but as yet unheralded flight of Galactic I had debarked from the spaceship and were looking toward the professor for instructions.

Simms came forward slowly and faced the gathering of space fliers and scientists. He shoved his hands into his pants pockets and stared at the people in front of him with a condescending smile.

"It was a remarkable flight," he said gently. "All of you showed me you were totally compatible with the trip and I have no reason to doubt you'll not be just as successful in your much longer journey to Mars."

What else can I tell them at this point, he asked himself? *Perhaps it'd be best to dismiss them and suggest they reform in the ready room in the late morning. They've all been so very cooperative and responsive to the start of preparations for Operation Mars. Why drag out this bloody facade any longer?* Simms asked himself.

Bloody facade? What bloody facade. . . ?

Tuesday, January 26, 1988 . . .

208

A heavy dark layer of nimbo-stratus clouds hung low over Cape Canaveral and obscured the early morning sun, which had broken through a slit in the overcast for one brief moment before disappearing again for good. That left the horizon over the choppy Atlantic on this windswept morning glazed in dark purple shadow, auguring a stormy day.

The U. S. Meteorological Service space station over the Caribbean was keeping a watchful eye on a developing tropical depression. A similar pattern in late December generated into a full blown winter storm that swept up the East Coast and dumped varying amounts of snow from the Carolinas to Maine and struck its heaviest blow on Long Island, where the depths reached to eighteen inches.

Dr. Simms had taken steps the night before of preparing himself for an early awakening by setting the alarm on his clock radio and leaving a request with the switchboard operator for a 5:30 A.M. call. For many uneasy sleepless moments after getting under the covers that night, the professor wished he hadn't alerted the desk of his intention to rise early. He was disturbed by the operator's curiosity and unusual familiarity when she asked, "Why on earth, Dr. Simms, are you getting up that early?"

"To milk my cow," he snapped sarcastically and hung up.

Now at 5:50 A.M. Simms was out of the shower, dressed, and standing at the window glancing at the threatening sky, wondering if the weather was going to impede his mission. He turned after a long, searching look at the clouds with his mind made up.

Nothing, not even a storm will make me turn back now, he told himself.

On the floor near the door were the two leather suitcases, which he packed the night before. One was filled with papers, pamphlets, and manuals, including a complete set of instructions on the start-up, propulsion, and guidance of Galactic I. The other suitcase was crammed with a dozen sets of undershorts and T-shirts, some fifteen pairs of socks, handkerchiefs, as well as shaving gear.

Simms began breathing with quick, shallow gulps and his heart had started to race now. He was in a high state of excitement as he sensed the moment he set for his departure had arrived.

He wheeled around and took long, eager strides to the door. He opened it, leaned over, picked up the grips, carried them to his jeep, which was parked outside his room, put them on the floor in the back, then got behind the wheel, and drove off.

At six in the morning a motorist traveling the highway to the Cape Canaveral spaceport encounters as much vehicular traffic as a driver traversing that route at midnight—just about zero volume. And that was how Dr. Simms found road conditions that Tuesday morning as he tooled his jeep to the apron where the Galactic I was poised in nocturnal slumber.

But wide awake were the two Marine Corps

sentries who'd just taken over from their counterparts after the 4 to 6 A.M. tour. The guards doing the 6 to 8 A.M. watch on the twenty-four-hour security detail for the Galactic I were dutifully patroling the apron's perimeter with carbines slung over their shoulders when Simms drove up in the jeep.

The arms were snapped off the shoulders with quick, practiced motions and pointed perfunctorily at the intruder. The traditional, time-worn command, "Halt, who goes there?" was barked routinely by one of the Marines. Neither sentry had had trouble recognizing Simms since he'd been on and off the Galactic I innumerable times in the past week. Yet, it's part of the systematization of military watches to hoke up protocol with the inanities of the toy soldier.

No sooner had Dr. Simms identified himself than the khaki-clad Marines returned the carbines to their shoulders and resumed patrol. The professor was free to board the spaceship.

He carried the two suitcases up the ramp and disappeared inside. Simms left the suitcase with the documents on the deck outside the control cabin and lugged the one containing his wearing apparel into the elevator. He got off on the top or third deck, entered the living quarters in a hurry, and lashed the suitcase onto a luggage storage rack in one of the ten private sleeping compartments for the crew.

Then he returned to the main deck and went into the control cabin with the other suitcase, which he then opened in great haste. He removed the documents and placed all but one under the spring retainer clamps, on the wall counter, devised to hold important papers and records in place in the weightlessness of space.

After then stowing the empty suitcase in a flight cabin storage chamber, Simms returned to the wall counter and picked up the document titled "Sequential Flight Instructions," which had not been secured under a retainer clamp, and brought it into the forward control operations section where the chief pilot and his crew are strapped down during takeoff, or launch.

Simms reached under the No. 4 safety recliner lounge—the same one he had lain in the previous day on Galactic I's three-orbit mission for the successful particle accelerator test. He pulled out the magnetized sole space boots he'd worn yesterday and put them on his feet. Then he deposited his own shoes under the lounge chair's small compartment marked "Street Footwear Stow" and closed the lid.

No detail had been overlooked in the effort to make the Galactic I the most perfect spaceship of all time. Its predecessors—the earlier first-generation shuttles and the Apollo, Gemini, and Mercury capsules—had been neglected when it came to total design concepts.

Thus, astronauts who flew those ships repeatedly encountered difficulty, for example, with floating objects. Clothes and papers, as well as other distracting and dangerous flying missiles not only caused discomfiture but posed a peril on those missions. Simms carefully flipped the pages of the "Sequential Flight Instructions" booklet, which he was careful not to stow and came to a stop on page nine. He carried his finger down the page of runover printed matter from the preceding page and all at once became totally absorbed in the reading material under the heading he was searching for, "Start-Up and Takeoff."

He had read those instructions a hundred times if he read them once since receiving the manual from North American Rockwell. Getting that manual was not nearly as complicated as it had been when Simms asked to look at the design specification for the Yankee Clipper, the unmanned solar sailing ship which rendezvoused with Halley's Comet in 1986.

His connections with the Galactic I and the space survival training program qualified him instantly to be privy to the instructions on flying the spaceship.

Now in the privacy of the flight control cabin, Simms once again reviewed the start-up instructions for Galactic I's atomic power plant and the programming of its computerized control system for designated flight.

The computer was designed to propel the craft along the precise trajectory needed to perform any given mission. The push-button console on the flight panel, which the chief pilot, or astronaut, had under his control, beamed instructions for the guidance and control system on the spacecraft.

Each system had a miniature computer of its

own with an incredible amount of data in its memory bank, as well as an array of gyroscopes and accelerometers, called the inertial measurement unit. Together, they were programmed to calculate precisely where the spacecraft was between earth and whatever heavenly body it was traveling to or traversing.

Those devices worked automatically, yet they required human adjustment from time to time. The person serving in that capacity had to have extensive knowledge in navigation so as to give the computer instructions, to take sextant sightings, and to direct their overall operation.

Such devices had been developed and installed on some of the later Apollo spacecraft that flew to the moon. The equipment made it possible in those days to fly nearly a quarter-million miles through space, make only one tiny mid-course correction, and allow the Lunar Module to land within television range of the recovery ship, a mere thirty-five seconds of the time calculated many months before the flight.

On the Galactic I, there was no need for the fifty separate engines crammed into the Apollo spacecraft, nor for the half-dozen rocket-powered steering mechanisms on those space-shuttle vehicles designed for critical mid-course corrections to get the craft in and out of its trajectory.

All the work now was done by the single high-intensity, fully synchronized atomic-powered Aere Perennius engine. Every system was integrated through failsafe propellent vacuum tube and electronic circuitry feeders emanating from the unfailing source of nuclear power that the engine was capable of providing for twenty million years.

And only one person controlled all those systems—the chief pilot.

The chief pilot designated to sit at the controls and guide Galactic I in space was the man who'd taken the ship upon its three-orbital mission the day before, Captain Randolph Stuart.

But at 6:31 A.M. of that Tuesday, January 26, 1988—when the Aere Perennius engine suddenly broke the early morning stillness over the Cape and the blinding flash of red-blue flames spewed from the shuttle's rocket exhausts and lit the darkness of the overcast morning—Captain Stuart was not at the controls in Galactic I.

Not Captain Stuart nor any other member of the handpicked crew of astronauts and scientists for Operation Mars was aboard the spaceship that was to take them on the historic voyage to that planet.

Only Dr. Gordon Lyle Simms was inside Galactic I and only he was guiding the spaceship down the runway in an astonishing unscheduled and unprecedented takeoff that would do more than merely startle and stun those who heard the thunderous roar and sonic boom when, in a brief ten seconds after liftoff from the Canaveral runway, the Galactic I achieved Mach I or 740 m.p.h. speed.

But that was only in the first ten seconds. In the next five and a half seconds there was a second but less obtrusive thunder in the sky, then very quickly it was followed by a third explosion as the spaceship passed Mach II and Mach III and ascended into the stratosphere, then the ionosphere, and finally space itself.

Piloted by one man who wasn't even supposed to fly the spaceship. . . .

CHAPTER XV

Where Has Dr. Simms Disappeared?

Barely seconds after the second sonic boom crashed down upon Cape Kennedy through the dreary low-hanging clouds darkening the landscape, Maitland Thurber was barking orders into the phone at his bedside.

"I tell you this is insanity," he shouted in an uncharacteristic rage. "Get him down! Get him down!"

The tower duty officer tried to maintain an even voice despite the unfair lambasting he was getting.

Navy Ensign James Truman had been holding down the watch in the tower on the midnight to 8 A.M. tour along with Army Specialist First Class Armando Corazzo and Marine Corps Corporal Frank Edgemere. Their tour had been as uneventful as it had been since the Cape was converted to a spaceport—and until the stunning start-up of the Galactic I's engine and the ship's sudden and startling departure.

Truman had phoned to break the stunning

news to the space boss, only to receive a royal reaming for something he had nothing to do with nor could do anything about except file a report, as he was now doing.

"But, sir . . . it's gone . . . the whole ship . . . it's out of sight . . ." the ensign stammered. His voice was solemn, as if the episode of the disappearing spaceship was an occasion for mourning.

"Notify the Air Force!" shouted Thurber in a tone still dripping inelegance that was not his style. "Get them immediately . . . call me back as soon as you have something."

Thurber slammed the receiver down and scrambled out of bed. He flicked on the dresser lamp and peered at his face in the mirror. He stroked his chin. The stubble was there but he wasn't going to shave. This crisis called for a quick departure and he prepared himself with extravagant haste.

It took him fewer than three minutes to jump into his clothes—the very ones he'd taken off the night before. The space chief wasn't aiming to be a fashion plate in this utterly improbable emergency.

As he wrestled an arm into his suit jacket, he was tightened into a new frazzle by the jangle of the phone.

"Thurber here," he rasped impatiently. "What is it?"

The voice wasn't the scared, subservient stutter that had crawled through the line a few minutes earlier. There was authority in this caller's brisk, demanding tone. Thurber needed no introduction to Major General Eugene Crowley, the adjutant to General Calvin Thatcher, commander of the Air Force and the only military figure in the political hierarchy running the space program who carries more clout than the civilians. Thus his office in the Pentagon not only controls every piece of machinery that has wings and flies for Uncle Sam, but also exercises a significantly influential control over the space agency's activities.

Crowley wanted to know two things: What was that blip that was caught for a fleeting moment by radar trackers in Alamagordo, New Mexico, and again in Guam? And what in the heck is that jibberish about a hijacked spaceship—and a request for an Air Force fighter plane pursuit?

"Yes, General, that's true," came Thurber's response with a strained edge. "The Galactic I has just gone off on an unauthorized flight."

Unauthorized flight? By whom? To where? How can this happen? What was security doing? The General's questions weren't meant to elicit responses. They were fired too fast. Crowley was fully aware of Thurber's harrowed and uninformed state. But that's what generals who are adjutants are supposed to do—confuse and confound others when somebody is making waves.

"They just awakened me with the barest facts, General," Thurber responded vaguely. "Let me get to the scene and I'll have a full report for you just as soon as I can scrounge up more information."

"Sir, he drove up in his jeep at oh-five-fifty-five hours and we challenged him," one of the two Marine sentries said through vacant eyes. "We both recognized Dr. Simms and had no reason to bar him from boarding the ship. No one had instructed us to do otherwise..."

Thurber was hearing *who* the spacejacker was now for the first time and reacted with unfathomable disbelief. The call from Ensign Truman in the tower had merely conveyed word to the NASA boss at home that the Galactic I had mysteriously flown away. The officer in charge of the tower had no clue then as to who had stolen the spaceship.

In his own disembodied mind enroute to the spaceport, Thurber tried to single out the obvious culprit with the capability to have skyjacked the Galactic I—one of the astronauts who'd been trained to fly the ship. The possibility also occurred to him that Phoebe Swedlow, the astronette, might have piloted off in it. But Thurber dismissed the thought at once as being utterly too ludicrous to entertain.

Now Thurber had been rendered so speechless by the sentries' report about the theft that he simply stared with the most abstract expression, gazing back and forth at the two Marines and the tower duty officer, who by now were ringed solidly by some two dozen or more military personnel that had responded with riot guns, rifles, and sub-machine guns.

It was a typical armed services answer to a crisis—send combat-ready foot soldiers out to catch a spaceship winging its way through the universe at a speed so great that even the tracking stations, as they would soon report back, not only couldn't determine how fast the Galactic I was zinging along, but had lost it, it was going so fast!

"Private!" Thurber finally broke his silence with measured solemnity. "I am going to ask you once again—who boarded that ship?"

He looked frowningly at the Marine, identified as Jerome Barker, who had frozen Thurber speechless with the mention of Dr. Simms's name.

At the same time, the NASA boss raised his hand in a sort of benediction suggesting all would be forgiven if only the sentry uttered the right name, a person Thurber could accept as the conceivable culprit in history's first theft of a space vehicle.

"There's no mistake, sir," Private Barker said with sharp reverence. "I recognized Dr. Simms. It was he. It wasn't the first time I saw him. I know what the man looks like . . ."

As if still doubting the eyewitness despite his assurances, Thurber turned with disbelief still clearly etching his somber face and a look that seemed to be asking Private George Flowers to help allay the lingering incredulity that was still gripping him.

"That's right, sir," snapped the second Marine firmly. "It was Dr. Simms, the same person who had stepped off the Galactic I after it returned from its flight yesterday. I know I couldn't be mistaken, sir."

All at once Thurber exploded surprisingly with an incredulous laughter that only added heightened tension around the concrete apron where, instead of the Galactic I, now stood an assemblage of military and NASA personnel that was beginning to reach crowd proportions.

"How could he do such a thing!" blurted Thurber through clenched teeth that were trying to grind back his volcanic anger. "That crazy man will not only kill himself but he'll destroy a billion-dollar spaceship!"

Thurber turned to the two Marine sentries.

"How did it happen?" he swallowed hard and lapsed into a stance that seemed to beg relief from the cataclysmic crisis into which the space chief had been thrust. He wanted to hear some lucid explanation of why Dr. Simms stole off in the spaceship. In his heart, Thurber knew the two Marines could never offer an explanation that would be suitable to the brass in the Pentagon—or even Congress and the White House. But what else could he do but go through the motions?

"General Crowley, you'll never believe it but . . ."

That was the straightforward and simplistic approach that Thurber adopted in explaining to the adjutant that the Galactic I had been hijacked by Dr. Simms.

"What the hell is Simms up to?" Crowley came back after several long moments of silence to convalesce from the shocking news that a scientist had stolen the spaceship. The

222

military bigwig on the phone from Washington sounded like—and he was—a very profound man of very few words, with a personality that demanded instant and explicit explanations.

"There's nothing yet that I can put my finger on, General," Thurber said immediately.

"Is there any speculation you can offer right now on what that ass is up to in making off with the ship?" Crowley shot back demandingly.

"Not at the moment, General," Thurber said with an effort. "But you know, sir, this is just the first twenty-five minutes of the episode . . ."

Thurber was trying to buy time. He wanted to investigate, and to begin by questioning everyone in the Operation Mars crew who flew with Simms the previous day.

"Perhaps he betrayed himself on the flight in some way, through some movement or act," Thurber suggested offhandedly. "Let me talk to those on yesterday's test run and see what I come up with. Then, I'll get back to you at once."

Crowley's voice bounced back gruff, almost arrogant.

"I hope you can," he snapped. "General Thatcher will be on my back for an explanation the instant I shock him with this blockbuster, Maitland. So come up with something before you-know-what hits the fan . . ."

Thurber returned the receiver to the cradle with annoyance after a loud click at the end of the line in the capital.

By now, Captain Stuart, Lieutenants Rigby

Deems and Frank Perlman, and Commander Swedlow had been roused from their beds in the officers' quarters by a messenger dispatched by Thurber, and they had arrived at the apron.

They looked around with probing stares for a glimpse of the missing Galactic I. When they couldn't see it anywhere, they became infected with wonderment. They hadn't yet learned that the spaceship was taken on an unauthorized voyage into the unknown.

Thurber's voice struggled for firmness as he turned to the astronautics team. "If you're wondering where Galactic I is," he said, his voice shaky despite his effort to steady it, "just look for it up there."

He pointed toward the dark clouds still lingering over the Cape with a finger that trembled from the effort he was exerting to control his distress. "Up there," he repeated laconically.

His pause now afforded the space fliers a breather to gather their thoughts, and at the same time to take Thurber up on his ludicrous invitation. Like automatons they followed his finger with their eyes dutifully in the upward direction it was pointing. As their pupils met the thick cloud barrier, they sensed all at once the utter irrationality of the space chief's invitation.

Thurber pulled down his uplifted finger and spoke again to the team, with a more genial and relaxed, but distinctly inquisitive tenor.

"If someone can please tell me what, if anything, Gordon Simms did or said on that flight yesterday, or anytime since I introduced him to you, I want you to speak up," Thurber said insistently. "Anything . . . anything at all . . ."

The response was a deafening silence. The flight crew's eyes met and stared at one another, then looked off into space, and finally turned with puzzled gazes to Thurber.

It wasn't necessary for them to say anything. Their collective expressions spoke volumes for Thurber—and each page of each volume was a complete blank.

"Let me ask you this," Thurber then said to them in an even less demanding tone. "Did Gordon express any interest in the controls . . . did he ask how to fly the ship . . . anything like that?"

"In my opinion he didn't even seem to be aware of any set of controls in the flight cabin except one," Stuart said quickly. "All he cared about, as far as I could see, was that particle accelerator. He seemed thoroughly acquainted with every control on the console. He spun that screen on the first shot. It was as though he'd been working with that machine half a lifetime."

"Yes . . . now that you mention it . . ." interrupted Deems in a halting voice, "it was so unreal to see Simms come to grips with a piece of machinery he'd never seen before, and to operate it with such finesse and expertise."

Phoebe Swedlow and Frank Perlman voiced identical views. Their observations of Simms at the controls of the particle accelerator left them with the distinct impression that he had

225

to be an absolute whiz to come up against the machine for the first time and exercise such disciplined mastery over it.

By this time the rest of the team comprising the half dozen scientists had responded to Thurber's early morning call. They had arrived at different intervals but within a span of only several minutes and had huddled about the apron where everyone else was gathered, straining to hear the exchange between Thurber and the people he was questioning.

However, when it came their turn to answer the NASA boss's anxious queries, none could provide a clue as to what incentive or motive might have galvanized Simms into embarking on his spectacular space act.

Now with the mystery still as profound and as bereft of logic as when the clatter of the sonic boom startled the consciousness of all within its hearing range, Thurber went to the phone once more.

"General Crowley," he said with a fluctuating feverishness, which at once exposed not only his honesty in dealing with the crisis, but his dismay over it as well, "I've come up with nothing . . . nothing at all, sir. The only possible move now, as I see it, is to continue efforts to track the ship. I have alerted Houston to initiate a global watch for the Galactic's trail."

"I'm not going to say don't do it," Crowley interrupted abruptly, "but the Strategic Air Command has already gone through that routine and struck out. There's absolutely no speck of activity anywhere to suggest where the ship might be."

"I'm dismayed by that situation, General," Thurber said but he showed clearly in his tone that he wasn't about to quit trying. With laudable initiative, he bared other strategy that he hoped would provide a clue to the spaceship's whereabouts.

"I've asked for an intense standby on all radio listening posts," Thurber explained, his tone now a bit more confident, more aggressive. "But even more importantly, I've called for an immediate astronomy watch by all observatories around the world. Kitt Peak and Palomar, understandably, won't be able to search and seek until tonight, but I'm told that the Haute-Provence Observatory in South Africa and the Soviet Union's Ratan facility are feverishly trying to pick up something in their night skies right now."

Crowley wanted to know what chance there was of spotting an object as minute as a spaceship in the universe with a telescope. Was Thurber just wishful thinking?

"No, General," came the assurance from Canaveral with increasing confidence. "They can pick up a dot in space."

Thurber paused as he thought the better of his answer.

"What I mean, General, is if that dot isn't too damned far away . . ."

All at once there was an interruption. Thurber asked Crowley for his indulgence. "General, excuse me a moment, please," he said

227

excitedly. "I'm getting a message . . . I think Simms is trying to make contact."

Thurber put the receiver down and turned his attention to Ensign Truman, who had just returned from the radio room with the startling news.

"Our receiver is picking up Dr. Simms, sir," Truman said eagerly. "He is asking to speak to you, Mr. Thurber."

The space boss spoke into the telephone again with an excited, eager tone.

General, please hang on . . . Simms wants to speak to me . . . I'll be back as soon as I talk to him."

Thurber again put the receiver down, this time in great haste, and rushed into the communications center. He was shown to the Varney-Edelson transceiver, which had been installed especially for two-way communication with the Galactic I spaceship program.

"You may sit here, sir," Truman said to Thurber in a respectful half-whisper. "The radio communicator, Mr. Hodges, will reestablish contact with Dr. Simms for you at once."

James Hodges, a civilian NASA radio operator, very quickly threw a switch at his console beside the one at which Thurber was seated, and spoke into a mike.

"Canaveral to Galactic I," he said imploringly. "Please come in, please come in Galactic I."

After a suspenseful dozen or more seconds, Hodges signaled with a jabbing finger that pointed to the mike in front of Thurber. "You may speak in there, sir, after you have received the message."

Thurber's heart beat faster as he waited for word from space. Then the pace quickened even more as a sound suddenly filtered out of the speaker.

"Maity, am I talking to you, old boy?" the voice in the speaker asked matter-of-factly.

Thurber appeared to be ecstatic that he was being addressed by the world's first spacejacker.

"It's I, Gordy, yes, please tell me what you're up to." Thurber rasped pleadingly.

"Maity, this is something I've been planning for more than two years," the voice from space began in a strident cadence. "I'm not going to do any explaining. The only thing I'll say to you is that I'm going to do for our world what no one has ever done for it before."

"Gordy, will you tell me where you are . . . what you're up to?" interrupted Thurber impetuously.

"No, Maity, I'm not going to tell you anything," the voice bounced back. "All I want to say is that, through your help and effort, you have contributed astronomically to the goal I hope to achieve . . ."

"I don't understand what you're saying," Thurber interrupted.

"You don't have to," Simms replied from the spaceship. "I'm cutting out all communication now. I will not be back on the air again because it won't be necessary."

Thurber continued to plead into the mike in

the hope of rousing further responses from Simms. But he was soon convinced that it was a hopeless pursuit.

Finally he returned to the phone, which still had General Crowley hanging on at the other end in Washington. He picked up the receiver and spoke into it in an idolatious, disappointed tone.

"General, the man who made off in Galactic I is a nut," Thurber said in a pained voice. "I pumped him but I didn't get a damned thing out of him. I have no idea where he is nor where he's going . . ."

CHAPTER XVI

Restless Reflections in Ravenna

At this very moment when the Cape Canaveral caper was about to explode into one of the twentieth century's most spectacular stories and command scintillating global attention, that hardy band of twenty-six men and women committed to the Kentucky coal mine in Operation WAMIS were destined to hear nothing about the awesome theft of a spaceship by the men who entombed them in the shaft for a full year's isolation.

They were in their second week of the survival experiment in the innards of the earth below Ravenna and already life underground was beginning to wear corrosively on some nerves.

"I'll never understand why we weren't allowed to have radio and television down here," complained Sandra Sheiler in a spasm of exasperation. "What difference would it have made? This place will drive me batty in a month."

As he listened to Sandra, Mervin Kotler took

a sympathetic stance alongside his companion from Super Bowl XXII.

"It's getting to me, too, Sandy," he murmured agreeingly. "But that's what it's all about, isn't it? We're supposed to be out of it, and we sure are."

Frank Waller was sitting beside Sandra and Mervin and overheard the conversation. He offered his own heady point of view about the isolation.

"It hasn't affected me yet but that isn't to say it won't," he snorted heavily. "For the life of me I can't understand Dr. Simms's motivation. I can see living it out here for a year, but without word of what's going on in the world? I just don't get it."

The flow of those remarks appeared to disturb Dr. Floyd Wayne Savage, who'd been making his rounds taking everyone's blood pressure as part of the daily morning medical routine.

"I think you guys are overreacting too quickly," he said in a softly scolding tone. "Dr. Simms very purposefully wanted everyone to live in total isolation so we could study its effects."

"Well, Doc, you can see what it's doing to us already," interrupted Elaine Pernick with a haughty air. "I'm going to hack it okay, so you've got nothing to be concerned with on that score. But that doesn't mean I've got to like it, and I'm not going to. This to me isn't exactly living it up."

Savage's face flashed with indignation at the young woman.

"You didn't agree to participate in this experiment to live it up," he said admonishingly. "We're simulating conditions that undoubtedly will be found on distant planets. You don't mean to say that if you were stationed on Mars you'd be listening to the news or your favorite TV and radio shows, do you?"

"If you want to know the truth, Doc," Joyce said, leaning toward Savage challengingly, "I wouldn't go to that God-forsaken place before those canals are paved and my favorite soap operas and murder mysteries are listed in the Martian edition of *TV Guide*.

Joyce provoked a groundswell of laughter with her fatuous remarks. Even Savage was impelled to chuckle some.

"All right, Joyce," he joshed, gripping her arm. "Just for that I'm taking your blood pressure now—just to see if you're alive."

Her anger all at once dissipated, the comical upstart settled back submissively and allowed Veronica Trees, the nurse, to wrap the pressure pack around her arm. When Veronica finished that chore, she took a step backward and Savage moved in. As he manipulated the instrument and studied the gauge and its fluctuating red fluid, he turned momentarily toward the nurse with a meaningful smile.

Her blue eyes stared straight ahead, but she finally shifted her glance at the doctor and her pixie face lit up brightly. While looking at each other now, they exchanged meaningful stares.

They were still being mature in their relationship with each other. They were playing by the interior rules of the experiment, which imposed restraints on emotions and applied brakes on desires.

Savage and Trees were abiding by the rules and it appeared the others were also sticking faithfully to at least that portion of the game plan.

Yet even the other impositions and ostensible inconveniences the students were experiencing in their seclusion—the circumscribed cuisine, the impersonal bathroom routines, and the general restrictiveness of their living conditions—were all being taken in comparative good stride.

It was only the lack of communication with the world that was starting to drive some of the indwellers of Operation WAMIS up a wall.

How odd that Dr. Simms had so insistently prohibited, of all the amusements that can be imagined and be most desired for a group so remotely removed from civilization, the accompaniment of such an innocent appliance as a TV or radio set to help relieve the mechanical drudgery of their voluntary durance.

For, indeed, if anyone had really bored down in thought about his logic in prohibiting radios, no stretch of the imagination could conceive of how even the earliest settlers on Mars could or would be deprived by NASA of such a simple and effecitve piece of equipment as Guglielmo Marconi's invention, which had been in use for nearly a century now, not only on Earth but throughout every reach of space that man and his machines had traveled.

Certainly the thousands of scientific readings from the robot landers on Mars and even far more distant Saturn and Jupiter were transmitted by nothing more complex than radio waves.

So if the voyagers on Operation Mars, as in fact were to have not only radio but even television, then why had Simms been so adamant in embargoing such receivers from the mine?

Could he have had an ulterior motive?

In light of the professor's galvanic getaway in Galactic I, the question now became of greater moment than ever.

But while his twenty-six guinea pigs remained in the ground oblivious to the earthshaking developments on the surface and in space, those being exposed to Professor Simms's incredible and incomprehensible escapade were so magnetized and stupefied by the event that they had no capacity to be concerned with something as seemingly irrelevent as Operation WAMIS now appeared to be . . .

CHAPTER XVII

Mixed Reactions

*SPACESHIP STOLEN
LOST IN UNIVERSE*

That was the two-line six-column 72-point type headline in *The New York Times* on the morning following Professor Simms's unprecedented spacejacking episode.

The last time *The Times* ran a head type that size was Monday, July 21, 1969, when Neil Armstrong and Ed Aldrin performed America's sensational space achievement. But the headline even then was only a one-liner:

MEN WALK ON MOON

The spectacular hijacking of Galactic I was a story of epic proportions and it commanded equally heroic scale in the handling it received in the world press.

Walter Madigan, *The Times* science writer, reported that the scientific community was baffled by Gordon Lyle Simms's motive in flying off aboard Galactic I.

"It is conceivable that Dr. Simms is perhaps bent on conducting an experiment in space that he knows could not otherwise be done unless he took matters into his own hands," wrote Sullivan. "Beyond that, there is no other explanation for the professor's weirdly odd exploit."

The *New York Daily News* assigned columnists Jimmy Breslin and Pete Hamill to look into the human and seamy sides of the story.

Breslin's first column was from Cocoa, the thriving metropolis nearest Cape Canaveral.

"All along the highway, flags bearing the names of Florida investors in real estate are waving in the breeze," wrote the perceptive Breslin. "This is the place that produced John Glenn and Neil Armstrong and all the other space heroes.

"But nobody did anything then about sending heavy construction equipment up to the Bronx to rebuild the tenements and apartments that the welfare families burned down in the 1970s.

"And they're not doing anything about the new apartments that President Carter had built for the people and that are now being burned down again by their children.

"Hey, this is a very terrible thing. Here is the Bronx being burned and down here they are worried about where Dr. Gordon Lyle Simms has flown to with the billion-dollar Galactic I, a spaceship this country needed as much as a hole in the head.

"Nobody seems to care in Cocoa what happens to the people on One-thirty-eighth Street and Morris Avenue when they got to move out of their apartment because they had a fire in it.

"Even Mayor Carol Bellamy seems more concerned about Dr. Simms's fate than what happened to Jesus Corvallo, who can't go back to his grocery store on Southern Boulevard and One-sixty-seventh Street because somebody firebombed it yesterday."

Pete Hamill had another view as he returned from Dublin, where he covered the peace pact signing by the Irish Republican Army and the government of Great Britain, the culmination of the long and bloody struggle at long last.

"On the way home to New York," wrote Hamill, "I wondered what relevance there was between the child with the small gray marbled body who was dug from the rubble of a Dublin bomb blasted store and what Dr. Simms has done.

"Common decency demands that we do away with such outrageous deaths. The English-Irish peace pact promises to usher in that happy day. But what do we do about scientists who make off with billions of dollars worth of spaceships and fly them off into the unknown?

"Clearly none of us can be safe if we allow the government to give these recalcitrants their opportunities to run our space shots any damned way they please.

"We can never be secure if we allow that practice. Now it's America's turn to take the lead and stop any damned scientist in the future from making off with a billion-dollar spaceship ..."

The New York *Post* was still covering the news differently, and by now had achieved some of the many goals Australian newspaper tycoon Rupert Murdoch had laid down in 1976, when he took over the publication. For one thing, he had eliminated all unions. For another, the newspaper was fully automated and its mechanical and printing processes were being handled in their entirety by just four people.

Moreover, the newspaper was experimenting with students as newsgatherers. Thus when Simms made away with Galactic I, a busty sophomore from Brooklyn with a tape recorder, a camera and a working press card, hopped up to Attica Prison for an interview with lifer David Berkowitz, the .44-Caliber Killer who called himself Son of Sam.

"I was a bad, bad man in my time," Berkowitz conceded. "I killed six young people and I shot seven others. I was real bad. But I want to atone for my sins. If NASA will let me, I'd like to take after Dr. Simms in a spaceship of my own ..."

What would he accomplish by doing that, the question was put to the man who had terrorized New York City and its suburbs for more than a year in the 1970s?

"Why, I'd shoot him down with my .44, what do you think I'd do?"

That interview produced the alliteratively eye-grabbing headline for New York's newsstands:

SON OF SAM
SPEAKS ON SIMMS!

Headlines of all shapes and sizes screamed for days about Simms's wildly improbable escapade. Television devoted hours upon hours to newscasts and analysis about the flight.

Walter Cronkite, Eric Severeid, and Howard K. Smith all came out of retirement and conducted symposiums on the professor's inexplicable dash off into space.

The American Broadcasting Company reunited Harry Reasoner and Barbara Walters after an eleven-year separation as anchorpersons on the ABC-TV Evening News. Harry also managed quick sidetrips around the country for interviews with Leonard Nimoy and William Shatner, the *Startrek* heroes, and Barbara went out to talk with See-Threepio, Artoo-Detoo, and Darth Vader from *Star Wars* fame...

Meanwhile, in Melville on Long Island, interest in Dr. Simms's space saga was no less gripping. Especially at the Chemical Bank on Broad Hollow Road, where Mary Spanacopito had just returned from lunch. She rushed up to the bank manager breathlessly.

"Tony!" she said almost in a shout. "You'll never believe who I saw on TV at Woelfel's Restaurant during lunch."

"Was it the bandit who pulled the holdup here last week?" the manager, Anthony Poosty, asked. His right hand shot up, palm facing out as though he were repeating the question in pantomime.

Mrs. Spanacopito hated it when Poosty pulled that routine because it only served to expose his abominably obnoxious character once again to her. Poosty had a total lack of empathy for his staff. He was always wisecracking and making inane remarks to persons working in the bank who came to him with serious and correct reflections on important business matters.

Of course, Mrs. Spanacopito's observation had nothing to do with the robbery her manager referred to. That had been staged the previous Friday, when a bandit with a paper bag and a note demanding money from one of the eight tellers on duty made off with $4,500 in cash.

"I'm talking about Dr. Simms, the space scientist," Mrs. Spanacopito said to Poosty in a level tone, trying to restrain her annoyance.

"Who's Dr. Simms, the space scientist?" the manager asked with a smirk.

"The man who made off in the spaceship," the answer came from the woman in his employ who was astonished that her boss hadn't yet heard about that fantastic story.

"Please bear with me, Mary," Poosty said coolly. "I don't watch TV or read newspapers until I get home in the evening. So if there's some monumental news story that's broken and you're aware of, I'd appreciate it if you'd let me in on it."

Mrs. Spanacopito took in a deep breath and rippled off what she wanted to say in a calm, even tone, which obscured her annoyance and anger at the manager's usual deliberately irritating reactions to serious approaches by bank staffers.

"The man I saw on TV was in here last week and he rented a safe deposit box," Mrs. Spanacopito stammered.

"What man, Mary?" asked Poosty in half annoyance.

"The scientist who flew off in the spaceship and disappeared," she said solemnly.

"Where did he disappear, Mary," he said ruggedly. Poosty had just returned from a three-martini lunch and his mind now was far from being all together. The three martini lunch, incidentally, had been restored as a tax writeoff again by President Mondale.

"No one seems to know," Mrs. Spanacopito replied. Her excitement and enthusiasm were almost unrestrained but Poosty couldn't be elevated to such heights. He was, in fact, bored stiff with the assistant's statements.

"Mary," he said gruffly, "I think you had one too many for lunch. If, indeed, someone did make off with a spaceship, I couldn't be less interested. I say, good for him if he did. And I'm willing to let it go at that. Now, if he happened to have a safe deposit box in our bank, again I say hooray for him. Beyond that, I don't think it should matter to me nor to you. This man doesn't interest me in the least bit. Nor should he concern you."

Mrs. Spanacopito turned and walked out of the manager's office with a miserable feeling. She had half-expected some atrocious reaction from Poosty because it was second nature with him to be that way. This visit lowered Poosty's physical decency still another rung on Mrs. Spanacopito's character ratings of him.

Poosty, she told herself, was a pure and un-adulterated unfathered misfit.

She went back to her desk. A customer was waiting to rent a safe deposit box. Mrs. Spanacopito smiled pleasantly as she greeted the man sitting beside her desk. She plunged into the transaction with the same eagerness to serve as she had when Gordon Lyle Simms had stopped by last week.

As she began preparing the application for the safe deposit box, all attitudes and recollections of what had brought her to speak with Tony Poosty soon evaporated from her mind.

Mary Spanacopito became so concerned with the business at hand that it took her mind completely off Gordon Lyle Simms's visit to the bank.

Even when she went home that night and watched the news and heard Dr. Simms's name on the telecast, she mentioned nothing about her experience with the professor to her husband.

At this precise moment, Mrs. Spanacopito

couldn't judge just what possible interest her encounter with Simms at the bank last week could hold for her husband when her own boss, Tony Poosty, didn't seem to give a damn.

CHAPTER XVIII

Eclipse!

The attention focused on Dr. Simms's spacejacking of Galactic I went the route of any spectacular news story after running its course. It received decreasing attention after entering its second week and by the middle of February only occasional news items appeared in newspapers or were reported on TV or radio.

Newsgatherers were now straining to harvest new angles but few succeeded. There was really nothing to report and soon the stories not only moved off page one but shrunk to a paragraph or two in the back of the paper. TV and radio barely breathed a word anymore about Simms and the missing space vehicle.

Besides, who cared about an apparently eccentric scientist and a missing spaceship that early afternoon of June 24, when all at once an eerie and terrifying darkness covered the earth!

It happened in swift seconds—much faster than the time it takes for a normal eclipse of the sun by the moon to obscure a portion of a country or a continent.

The eclipse was total. It was observed in the Eastern Hemisphere with greatest astonishment because it occurred when most of the country was bathed in a bright mid-day sun. It was 2:22 P.M. Eastern Standard Time, 1:22 p.m., Central, 12:22 P.M., Mountain, and 11:22 A.M. on the Pacific Coast.

No one realized what was happening in the beginning. The suddenness of the sun's disappearance caught everyone by surprise.

Tourists in Times Square cheered and applauded when total darkness engulfed New York City. Streetlights throughout the Big Apple's five boroughs went on automatically as though night had descended.

It was indeed night—six hours early!

Lights went on in skyscrapers, factory lofts, apartments, and wherever else people worked, dwelled, and played.

At the very moment when darkness came, Mayor Bellamy was holding a press conference in City Hall to announce that the New York Yankees weren't going to move from the city after all.

"The Mayor's study group," she was just beginning to say, "has decided to place a dome over Yankee Stadium and air condition the ballpark. The cost will be a very nominal six hundred million dollars. We feel the city cannot afford to lose the Yankees . . ."

The step to keep the perennial pennant-world series winners in the city was precipitated by inducements being dangled by Perry B. Duryea, Jr., New York's former two-term governor who retired from politics and headed up the Long Island Sports Authority.

Among the LISA's valuable sporting world acquisitions were Belmont Racetrack, Roosevelt Raceway, the Long Island Veterans Memorial Coliseum, and the Parr Meadows Quarterhorse Track. Along with that last-named property, LISA took over some eighty acres of undeveloped land in the Yaphank area, and it was there that Duryea and his sports authority were seeking to entice the Yankees to move.

As things stood, however, the loss of the Yankees did not mean that major-league baseball wouldn't come to Long Island. Duryea had a group of wealthy lobster fishermen in his hip pocket who were willing to buy the Boston Red Sox and move them from ancient Fenway Park to Yaphank . . .

As the sky went black and the lights were flicked on in the mayor's office, Miss Bellamy appeared as stunned as the reporters she'd been addressing. After a long bewildering silence, she remarked, "Well, this is one blackout we're not going to blame on Consolidated Edison."

That was good for comic relief but it did nothing to alleviate the consternation that all at once overtook the mayor and the press who, being sophisticated and knowledgeable about upcoming events, certainly were very much aware that no total solar eclipse had been forecast.

In Washington, the sudden blackness exploded at the exact moment on the clock—2:22 P.M.—as it had burst over New York, Philadelphia, Detroit, Boston, Buffalo, Pittsburgh, Dayton, Atlanta, Miami, Macon, and all other cities in the eastern time belt, Yaphank notwithstanding.

President Mondale had been speaking on the phone in the Oval Office with Frank Sinatra in Palm Springs about a $5,000-a-plate fundraiser for the National Democratic Party in mid-September. The conversation was proceeding along expected lines. It was all one-sided— Sinatra was laying down the terms for his appearance.

He wanted no reporters, photographers, or cameramen at the affair that was to be held in the New Orleans Superdome and patterned after the party showman Mike Todd had tossed in New York's Madison Square Garden in 1958, buffet-style.

Suddenly as he was speaking to Sinatra, Mondale gagged.

"Frank!" he exclaimed. "A most incredible thing has just happened . . ."

"Don't tell me, Fritz," Sinatra snapped back, "it got dark all of a sudden."

That ended the conversation abruptly as Mondale slammed the receiver down and turned to his special aide in charge of liaison, Bella Abzug, and demanded she get in touch with the National Oceanic and Atmospheric Agency and the Armed Forces for a possible explanation.

At the same time, the President rose from

his chair and walked around his desk to the hot line. He stood beside the phone in solemn contemplation.

It was an hour earlier—1:22 P.M.—when the sun disappeared from the landscapes of Chicago, Cleveland, Cincinnati, Birmingham, St. Louis, Dallas, New Orleans, Indianapolis, and every state, city, town, village, and hamlet in the central time zone.

The Stygian darkness affected urban, suburban, and farming areas with the indiscriminate sameness as in the eastern part of the country, as well as in the mountain and Pacific belts.

For Minneapolis, Denver, Butte, Boise, Tucson, Phoenix, Salt Lake City, Cheyenne, Great Falls, Pierre, and North Platte were just as mysteriously without sunlight as San Diego, Los Angeles, San Pedro, San Francisco, Seattle, and Portland.

Even Nome and Anchorage and Fairbanks, where it was 9:22 A.M. and the sun had barely risen in the eastern sky, were plunged in darkness.

Not only Alaska but in every square mile of Canada—from the Yukon and British Columbia, across Alberta, Saskatchewan, Manitoba, Ontario, Quebec, and to the Maritime Provinces, as well as over the great Northwest Territories and the District of Franklin—darkness was total, an absolute night.

The phenomenon wasn't limited to just those areas of North America. Mexico didn't escape the Sunstrike, as this weirdly unprecedented wonderment was soon to be labeled.

The same condition prevailed in Central America and Bermuda, the Bahamas and all of South America, from the tip of Cape Horn to the Caribbean shores of Venezuela and Colombia.

There was no immediate word from any source—not military, meteorological, astronomical, nor any other body scientific—on what had caused the Cimmerian nightfall.

Was it an eclipse?

Almost everyone among the approximately two billion inhabitants of the Eastern Hemisphere believed at the onset of the sun's fadeout that indeed an eclipse had occurred. Even as the condition continued into the second hour, and lacking official word from any knowledgeable sources about what had caused the blackness, people continued to believe the shadow of the moon had swooped down on earth.

But astronomers at Kitt Peak, Palomar, Harvard University at Cambridge, and other observatories in the Eastern Hemisphere were quick to realize that it wasn't an eclipse of the moon but a far more awesome force that had caused the sun to vanish so completely.

It took astronomers merely a matter of minutes to reach that determination, for there were several immediate and immutable scientific arguments to disprove a conventional eclipse had brought on the darkness.

First of all, eclipses are forecast years, even

centuries before they occur. Nowhere in any scientific calendar had anyone plotted an eclipse for this day of Friday, June 24, 1988.

But even if some incredible but really improbable sudden mutation in the lunar orbit had caused the eclipse, astronomers would still demand to know why the totality of darkness, the peak or umbra, was lasting so long.

Here it was now approaching the second hour of the blackout, a circumstance that never occurred in all recorded history and that scientists knew to an absolute conviction could never occur in the lunar orbit. The astronomers, moreover, were aware that totality never lasts longer than seven and a half minutes— nor is the umbra, or totality, any wider than one hundred and seven miles.

A second and still more curious aspect was that none of the standard advance warnings of an oncoming eclipse had been displayed in any way. There'd been no partial phase of the eclipse as when first "contact" of sun and moon takes place—a visible phenomenon to the naked eye, which observes the moon's invisible disk first "touching" the disk of the sun and appearing on earth as a small indentation in the western rim of the sun.

Nor did any astronomer or any other observer, professional or amateur, see the dark disk of the moon gradually moving into the sun's disk to make the sun appear as a crescent. In any total eclipse, it would take about ninety minutes for the crescent to thin out—a period

253

called the penumbra, or half shadow—and then disappear, at which point it suddenly grows dark.

Additionally, during this umbra or total shadow the brightest stars become visible.

True, the brightest stars and, strangely now, even some stars so small and distant that they previously could be seen only with telescopes, had suddenly become visible to the naked eye.

People everywhere in the Eastern Hemisphere cloaked in the coal blackness of night were remarking about the stunningly beautiful sight in the heavens—how many stars were glittering—and they were asking increasingly why that phenomenon was occurring.

Even of greater mystery to the astronomers in that first hour of studying the sky was the discovery that the dark disk of the moon was not projecting onto the pale arcane halo of the sun's corona.

This blackout, the astronomers had to conclude, was not being caused by the moon!

They advanced two very sound additional reasons for that deduction. One was their awareness that the general landscape illumination during totality is always a great deal brighter than on a night of the full moon, and it's only the quick transition from daylight that leaves an impression of greater darkness during an eclipse.

In this instance, the darkness—as measured with light meters and other devices—corroborated their suspicion that this was even deeper than that of a moonless night on any portion of earth.

To the astronomers across the United States who found themselves in the incredible stance of watching an inexplicable hemisphere-wide nighttime during a period when their portion of the globe was facing the direction of the sun, there was to be a still more disturbing development when contact was made with observatories in Europe, Asia, Africa, and Australia, where normal nightfall was occurring.

In clear, starlit skies over those four continents where the full moon should have been clearly visible in all of its shining orangey splendor over those lands, it couldn't be seen anywhere!

Inconceivable as it seemed now, not only had the sun disappeared, but the moon as well!

In those first hours of darkness, the scientific communities mobilized—almost as though they had been placed on a war footing—and strove to come up with answers to this unaccountable astronomical performance. They became even more puzzled as the sun now failed to rise over the Hawaiian Islands, the islands across the International Dateline, and to the Far East.

Now as the hours passed, it was no longer surprise and cheering, as those throngs in Times Square and elsewhere had done in the beginning. Now terror and fright were settling over the world and becoming more palpable as reports issued from Tokyo, Shanghai, Bangkok, Peking, Moscow, Dakar, Cairo, and from the rest of the world, which now was seeing no glimmer of a rising sun.

Then, as the Western Hemisphere went through its period of normal night, it was just as impossible to determine the difference from what it had been during the black period of "daylight" that had just passed.

Newpaper headlines screamed the alarming news in communities around the world. TV and radio pre-empted every show on their schedules and concentrated totally on continuous, uninterrupted coverage of the world-shaking worldwide blackout.

In the first twenty-four hours of the phenomenal eclipse, much of the civilized world was genuinely frightened, if indeed not terrified.

In the United States, some two-dozen Governors beat the gun on President Mondale in declaring emergencies in their states. Then, finally, when it became clear that the crisis was in no immediate prospect of ending, the Chief Executive went on the air and addressed an anxious nation.

"Not only America's but the world's scientists are working on this grave problem *day* and night," Mondale said in what surely had to be the biggest nonsequitur of his first term in office. He himself had been forced to cancel a swing through the Midwest in what was to have been the opening round of his campaign for reelection.

"There is no immediate danger that anyone

can foresee," Mondale went on in his attempt to allay fears. "It is merely a matter of having patience and placing faith in the world community of astronomers who are striving unrelentingly to find out what has happened to the sun."

The President pointed out that there was no reason America couldn't continue to function in the crisis, saying:

"We can continue to go to work, although it will not be altogether possible in all areas. Farmers and those others in outdoor activity will undoubtedly find it difficult if not impossible to perform their work. The government sympathizes with all those in such circumstances..."

But he was quick to assure the people that "everything humanly possible is being done" to come up with an answer to the mystery of "this puzzling phenomenon."

Meanwhile, Mondale pleaded, the public must try to maintain a low profile on the nation's streets and highways, which, he said, must be kept clear for essential transport.

He also pointed out that it would be no problem coping with a continuous night from the standpoint of energy supplies.

"Since the nation is now deriving almost all of its energy from nuclear power plants, I can foresee no problem relating to power outages or any of the other discomforts we might have faced in years passed when we were so dependent on Arab oil ..."

All in all, Mondale's speech was uplifting

257

and comforting to an extent, although he offered no immediate—or even long-range—solution to the baffling global disturbance.

Elsewhere around the world, presidents, prime ministers, monarchs, dictators, and other heads of state addressed their peoples in a similar way and begged them to bear up under the mystery of the blackout.

Perhaps in no part of the world were the varied reactions to the eclipse more dramatic than among the tribes of South America and Africa.

In a village in Surinam, the traditional conception of an eclipse had been that it involved a battle between the sun and the moon, who are brothers. The natives were convinced —after having observed other eclipses in years past—that if the sun didn't win out, the outcome could be perpetual night.

"Now it seems that this has happened," a radio announcer in Surinam said. But he had not given up hope that the problem would be solved.

"We must separate the combatants," the newscaster said. "We must make the most noise possible, beating on everything that is hollow and sonorous. . . . Furthermore, after the eclipse one must undertake a cleansing rite to rid the humans of blood that fell on them from the wounded moon."

One old man complained that he was having difficulty getting the younger generation natives to bang pots and pans with enough vitality to down the moon and up the sun.

Meanwhile, across the Atlantic on the continent of Africa, in a region of Niger, in the central Sahara, the native women there were decrying the eclipse as an evil omen devised by God to punish the wicked.

When the eclipse came, women drawing water from a well became transfixed. One moved away and knelt, her veil over her head, and she soon claimed to have become possessed by the spirits because her movements all at once became convulsive and uncontrollable.

Simultaneously three other women were seized by the spirits as the cries and weeping persisted throughout the entire period of occultation and for a while afterward.

Some observers offered the view that the demonstration by the nomads in betraying fear of the eclipse was a way of showing homage to Allah.

Even in Ethiopia, tribesmen of the Nyangatom tribe, daubing themselves with white clay, looked east as the eclipse descended, for they'd been told if they looked west they would die.

One medicine man explained that painting oneself white or yellow was an appropriate way to combat the darkness of the eclipse. Many Ethiopians followed the advice, but as the hours wore into the first all-black day, and then two and more days went by, the promise of emancipation from the continuing night faded and few of those who listened to the medicine man tended to believe him, even as he went through his ritual of spitting out masticated bits of leaf toward children, women, and others in the gathering.

While these reactions were being recorded among primitive peoples, the responses of those living in great population centers and areas of advanced civilization were much more varied and complex. For the most part, the overriding wonder was whether whatever up there was causing this gigantean eclipse was going to grace the earthly creatures with any kind of future.

For by now it had become more than a mere eclipse. The situation had grown ponderous and indeed evil. One of the most immediate and terrifying outcomes of the sun's disappearance and the totality of darkness was the alarming amount of looting that had broken out in thousands of communities, not only in the United States, as in past experiences when power failures plunged cities and communities in darkness.

This blackout was worldwide—and so was the epidemic of crime.

Plunderers roamed the streets of Toronto, Mexico City, Rio de Janiero, Bombay, London, Athens, Cairo, Capetown, Peking, Moscow, and literally thousands and thousands of other locales.

The rate of break-ins and thefts from stores, warehouses, and other commercial and industrial establishments was not as high in some areas because lights still could be left on at night. Yet the mere realization that this mysterious force of darkness had gripped the world, lowered peoples' morality and senses of values and generated a precipitous decline in regard for law and order.

Many people thought the end of the world was coming and didn't care about tomorrow. Millions began absenting themselves from their normal every-day pursuits.

Children cut classes and even stopped going to school.

Workers stayed away from their jobs.

Bills and accounts became due and weren't paid with such alarmingly uniform practice that many businesses, indeed many countries themselves envisioned bankruptcy and world-wide financial ruin looming ahead unavoidably.

Yet those crisis and the scores of others piling one upon another in ever-growing numbers, disturbing and frightening as they were, did not aggravate as much concern as was about to focus on a new fear after the world entered the second week of Sunstrike, as the phenomenon of darkness was officially designated by the United Nations in an emergency meeting of the full assembly of 172 member countries.

For several days now reports were coming in ever more frequently from all corners of the globe about severe and unprecedented weather conditions. Reports of severe snowstorms and blizzard conditions in Australia, for example, were disturbing enough, although some climatologists argued that a lack of sunlight was undoubtedly the cause for the harsher weather in a continent that normally, at this time of year, expected to experience only moderate winter-style climactic conditions.

If these conditions weren't moderate but extreme for Australia, then what could the experts say about the sudden and even more drastic weather changes elsewhere in the world?

In such historically hot and tropical lands as Brazil, Bolivia, the Republic of the Congo, Gabon, Nigeria, Cambodia, the Philippines, the Hawaiian Islands, Cuba, Bermuda, and the Bahamas, among many others, were experiencing temperatures now plunging far below freezing and their warm landscapes were being buffeted by the rarest of all climactic occurrences—snowstorms!

Terrible, terrifying, treacherous killer snowstorms. . .

CHAPTER XIX

Killer Snowstorms!

It began snowing lightly at first. The time was 5:15 P.M. on that June 27, 1988, the fourth day of the still-unexplained and increasingly terrifying global eclipse that affected more than seven billion inhabitants on earth.

And while the fright had been no less palpable in this part of the world than in any other, the sight of snowflakes glistening in the direct and reflected light of the gas vapor street lamps along Bay Street in the business district of Nassau generated a rare excitement among the residents and those few remaining visitors, the last remnants of the tourist trade who had not fled home to New York, Boston, Chicago, Los Angeles, São Paulo, London, or wherever it was that they had come from to spend a holiday in the capital of the Bahamas.

Never had it snowed on this island paradise in the more than one hundred and fourteen years of meteorological record-keeping begun by Great Britain in 1874.

The snowfall was a novelty to the populace—

but only during the first hour. Then all at once the welcoming smiles, the spasms of gaiety and jocularity, and the bubbling excitement that had been greeting that rarest of all sights in this enchanted ocean island ended stunningly.

For all at once the snow had begun to be driven by a high wind.

What an incredible turn!

In any study of the Bahamas's historic past, the climate was one of the most delightful in the world. Eighteenth-century travelers had recognized its extremely desirable features and had made the most of it by returning there repeatedly for vacation stays and visits.

Its weather had been regarded as the British colony's greatest asset. Frost was unknown; during winter months temperature averaged 72 degrees Fahrenheit while summer temperatures varied from 80 to 90 degrees; the highest recorded temperature had been 94 degrees and the lowest 51 degrees.

Rain had varied from forty to sixty inches yearly in the different islands and was always heaviest in June, September, and October.

This was now, of course, June of 1988 and it should have been the Bahamas's heaviest month of rain. But now, all at once, instead of rain the precipitation was in the form of snow.

Unprecedented snow. Heavy snow. Snow that now suddenly began building toward a disaster in Freeport.

Never before had snow fallen on the Bahamas and now it was swirling down so furiously that it paralyzed the entire chain of islands.

Within just a few hours, drifts of up to ten feet had isolated thousands in their unheated homes and stranded other thousands of natives on roads where they foundered helplessly.

For a pitifully large number there was to be no rescue, for the Bahamas was ill-prepared to cope with the crisis created so abruptly by the unexpected near-blizzard. There were no snow plows, snowmobiles, or other emergency rescue vehicles to perform errands of mercy.

Many enterprising householders organized neighborhood mutual assistance groups and began digging out with shovels, only to find that the trail to the street led nowhere. There was no municipal equipment to clear the narrow roadways.

The storm continued to rage mercilessly for eight uninterrupted hours and then mercifully abated. But by then hundreds of buildings that had not been built to withstand the weight of so much snow were crushed.

There was no immediate count on the numbers of persons killed and injured, but the toll even by the most conservative estimates was extremely high.

What made it all the more pitiful was that the hurt couldn't be removed to hospitals or even be given emergency medical treatment. All transportation had ground to a standstill.

Worse still, a bitter cold was blowing in from the surrounding Atlantic Ocean and the thermometer was plunging. An hour after the snow subsided a howling gale-force wind buffeted the Bahamas. The temperature went below the 32-degree freezing mark—and continued to plummet.

Governor Hugh Grace Bowen frantically appealed to the nearest prospect from where help might be sent—Washington, D.C. He begged for snow-removal equipment and for emergency supplies of warm clothing, which the Bahamas never stocked. But Washington sent a shatteringly disappointing response.

For, incredibly, an outbreak of widely prevalent ice and snowstorm was occurring in virtually every part of the United States. Even the fiftieth state—the Hawaiian Islands—was engulfed by a cataclysmic snowstorm that rivaled the intensely savage and deadly visitation upon the Bahamas.

The snowplows, snowmobiles, and all other snow removal equipment were needed desperately on the domestic fronts.

Snow had begun falling over Kansas, Oklahoma, Nebraska, Iowa, Missouri, and other Midwestern states a little after the eclipse had gone into its third day. For several hours before the snows came, it had been raining. It'd been a normal, gentle, early summer's precipitation, which farmers traditionally welcomed at this time of year. The rain was part of a weather system that had moved across California and the mountain states from the Pacific.

The rain that changed to snow over the Midwest was a different weather front than

the one that raked the Bahamas. That one was
a tropical air mass, which had streamed over
the Atlantic northward and was cooled precipi-
tately by the underlying surface of the sunless
Bahamas. The air mass there became extremely
stable and stationary as its water vapor content
condensed and produced the low stratus clouds,
which released their precipitation in the form
of snow.

Normally that thirty-six inches of snow, as
it was officially recorded after the storm subsided, would have been a relatively severe tropical storm delivering an unwelcome three
inches of drenching rainfall over those eight
hours when instead those frozen white crystals
fell so devastatingly.

The cloud formations, of course, could only
be surmised in this period of perpetual night.
For there was no way to judge from the
ground when it was cloudy—except, of course,
when the stars and other planets in the solar
system couldn't be seen.

Weather forecasting systems had suffered a
crushing setback by Sunstrike. Weather satel-
lites were useless in this constant, unceasing
darkness and the only method the meteorological
services could employ in predicting when precipitation might be expected was plotting the
course of weather conditions from reports of
activity in other regions.

Now as snow instead of rain cascaded from
the skies over the central United States and
Hawaiian Islands, it was quite obvious that so
long as the sun remained hidden there would

be no rain but only snow. Brutal, driving, destructive, murderous snow.

But the Bahamas, the Midwest, and the fiftieth state weren't the only lands on which snow was falling in that first week of summer. Parts of Canada and Mexico, where temperatures dipped to the low twenties, were being hammered by heavy frozen precipitation. The spectacle of snowfalls in Acapulco, Monterrey, Tampico, Chihuahua, and other temperate locales of Mexico as far south as Guatemala was a phenomenon as outlandishly unprecedented as it was in the Bahamas.

As the solar eclipse went into its fifth day on that June 28, the incidence of cataclysmic weather conditions had spread over virtually the entire surface of the globe. No earthly region with a past history of even the very slighest measurable trace of rainfall in normal times was immune from the icy scourges infecting lands that never before had experienced the icy visitation of hail, sleet, and snow.

The most stunning of these improbable precipitation wonderments were those that began occurring in Africa and South America.

The crisis on both continents was pitiful, for natives who had never known a need for more than a loincloth or sari as garments suddenly were left without protection against the bitingly cold elements. The more ingenious of those primitive inhabitants of the Amazon regions quickly fashioned thick-layered capes that were sewn with mangrove leaves as well as the leaves from palms, myrtles, laurels, acacias, cedrelas, and dozens of others in the rain forests and regions along the length of the great river of South America.

Across the Atlantic, in Africa, the natives of the Congo, Angola, Tanganyika, Gabon, Uganda, Kenya, and other localities of the dark continent were likewise caught in the grip of the extreme weather changes, which plummeted temperatures from the high nineties to the middle twenties on that fifth day of the inexplicable eclipse.

The inhabitants of those regions also frantically garbed themselves in makeshift robes of leaves, reeds, straw, and whatever other vegetation they could thatch into body coverings.

In such normally arid areas as Algeria, Egypt, Libya, Niger, Chad, Morocco, and the rest of the so-called low latitude desert areas where precipitation was always negligible, an unparalleled meteorological occurrence began taking place indiscriminately almost over the entire expanse of North Africa.

Though very little water vapor was traditionally carried in the air over those regions and thus there'd always been a dearth of rainfall, the temperatures now had reached such a dramatic low that the crystals of the filmy cirrus clouds that form in the high levels of the atmosphere were being shaped and a remarkable spectacle was occurring over those northmost regions of the dark continent. Ice crystals were forming spontaneously in the cloudless skies and dropping onto the landscape, as though they were formed in the heavens through a concentration of water molecules and released when they exceeded the number that could be supported aloft in vapor form.

In short, the phenomenon was marked by snow falling during a cloudless, starlit sky—and at a time when that portion of Africa was gripped in the throes of Fahrenheit temperatures now dropping into the teens.

Indeed, the temperature's descent by now, still only the fifth day of Sunstrike, was almost universally the same all over the earth. It approximated 50 to 70 degrees below the average of every community, country, and continent at that time of year.

"Without sunshine for any substantial length of time, we will all freeze, regardless of how great our fuel supplies may be," declared Dr. Peter Cushing Morchelson, the director of the National Oceanic and Atmospheric Agency in Washington.

"This is a potentially catastrophic occurrence. I don't wish to sound like an alarmist, but if we continue without solar heat for an indefinite period, all life on earth will cease . . ."

His terrifying statement was given during an interview by Jim Hartz for the "Today Show" on the NBC-TV network. In the background as Hartz questioned Dr. Morchelson on the steps of the floodlit marble-columned NOAA Building in Washington, a driving snowstorm—the second in this, the tenth day of Sunstrike—was raking the nation's capital.

Could Dr. Morchelson give the viewers of this live telecast an idea of how the weather patterns might behave in the immediate and foreseeable future?" Hartz wanted to know.

"It will be dreadful for a period of time," Dr. Morchelson explained in a grim tone. "There is no way to predict precisely how quickly we will reach absolute zero temperatures on earth, but if we do it will be the end of everyone—that includes all animal life as well as vegetation."

Hartz asked the director to explain what absolute zero meant.

"It's the temperature in space," Dr. Morchelson responded. "It's two hundred seventy-three degrees below freezing on the celcius scale. No life as we know it can survive in that cold."

But if people were to remain warm by staying indoors, couldn't they survive?"

"For a period of a few months, yes. But . . ."

Dr. Morchelson shook his head and frowned in contemplation.

"Please go on," Hartz urged.

"Let me state the situation hypothetically . . . that is, let us assume the sun never shines again. Here's what will then happen . . ."

The director looked across at the swirling snow and gestured toward it menacingly with a clenched fist.

"That stuff you see out there will continue to come down with increasing fury for a few weeks more, perhaps two, three at the most. It will snow as heavily and as fiercely in the tropics as it is snowing in Washington right now. No part of the earth will be immune from these awesome storms. And it will continue to storm until the weather gives out . . ."

Just what did that mean? Hartz wanted to know.

"Temperatures will plunge to the lowest depths. But not all at once, because the reserve heat from the earth's interior will still provide a modicum of warmth. But heat escapes quickly from hot bodies, when the exterior reaches the sort of cold I anticipate will come. Then the weather systems die out and we gravitate toward absolute zero conditions."

Hartz regarded Dr. Morchelson with a dour expression.

Dr. Morchelson put his hand on the newsman's shoulder and smiled wanly. "But Jim," the director rasped, "you and I won't be concerned with absolute zero temperatures for very much. Because long before the earth has gone into that condition every bush and tree will be in a dormant state. And when that happens, the process of photosynthesis ends. Oxygen is no longer manufactured by our plant life. Our atmosphere will be gone . . . and so will we."

The broadcast was the most chillingly incisive explanation that Americans, or for that matter any peoples in the world, had heard so far. Until now most governments had been trying to downplay the cataclysmic consequences that so obviously were threatening the earth.

Dr. Morchelson's interview was picked up by

the Associated Press, United Press International, Reuters, and other news agencies and flashed around the world. Almost immediately scientists in the United States, the Soviet Union, and England uniformly confirmed the NOAA director's assessment.

"No question that the earth faces extinction," the renowned Soviet meteorologist, Dr. Evgeny Zorzivkov finally agreed. "The American's prognosis is proper in all respects, although I do not believe that the heat from the earth's interior will have an appreciable effect in slowing down the advent of absolute zero conditions."

From London, Dr. Rutherford Ernshaw, the leading British meteorologist and Nobel laureate, also concurred with Dr. Morchelson. In the interview over the British Broadcasting TV-radio hookup, Ernshaw said it made no difference whether earth's interior "body heat" dissipated quickly or slowly.

"The bloody thing that we should be concerned with is finding out what has caused this Sunstrike and properly putting an end to it. I really can't understand the thinking in Washington. Why don't they launch a squadron of space shuttles to conduct an intensive search of the solar system to ascertain what is causing this weirdly strange phenomenon?"

Ernshaw slammed to top of his desk with his open palms.

"I really think someone should tell us why the damn sun is smiling on every blasted planet in the universe except on our earth and moon. I know the sun is still up there. It must be."

It was indeed weirdly strange. Mercury, Venus, Mars, Jupiter, Saturn, Uranus, and Pluto were visible in their normal positions in the solar system. Obviously, they were receiving light from the sun as they had had been for several billion years. Why then were the Earth and Moon the only heavenly bodies being totally deprived of sunlight?

What was causing the eclipse?

Sunstrike was in its second week now and the devastation was growing hourly. Tens of thousands all over the world were dead and the toll was mounting frighteningly.

And still not one spaceship had been launched to investigate.

In fact, even the space stations in lunar and earth orbit had by now been evacuated of all personnel. That move was directed by NASA after it became obvious they couldn't conduct experimental observations of the inky black surfaces of the two globes they had been girdling. And none of the orbiting labs had succeeded with all of their sophisticated telescopes in detecting what force, power, or contrivance had blotted out the sun—just on the earth and the moon.

The United States was the only nation that had the wherewithal to conduct an extended search in space for the source of that disturbance. But it could not perform such a mission with the conventional space shuttles, which had served to ferry people and equipment to

274

the various orbiting stations. Those shuttles didn't have any adequate fuel capacities to carry them on extended flights into space.

What was needed was a vessel of the type in the Galactic series, the nuclear-powered ship in which Dr. Gordon Lyle Simms inexplicably made off into space almost five months before.

But a sister ship, the second in the series of twelve Galactics that Rockwell International was building for the space program, was on the assembly line nearing completion.

President Mondale had ordered a drastic speedup in fabricating the ship immediately after Sunstrike. As a result, the initial target date for the Galactic II's readiness for flight was moved up five months.

Delivery to NASA was scheduled for July 15—less than a month away.

The flight was to be launched at Cape Canaveral and the same astronautic team that was to have flown in Galactic I to Mars was reassigned to take Galactic II up in a search of space for the cause of the deeply enigmatic eclipse.

The ship's readiness was deemed critical now, for the earth was being buffetted more cruelly than ever with worsening snowstorms and howling blizzards.

CHAPTER XX

Disaster, Disaster . . .

July 4 was a day of record snowfalls in two-thirds of the continental United States. It was the day that Galactic I and its ten-member crew was to have taken off on the year-long expedition to Mars.

But on that 212th anniversary year of the nation's independence, the 15,000-foot runway at Cape Canaveral was buried under four feet of new-fallen snow and crews with bulldozers and earth-moving machines were trying to clear the strip. They were under emergency orders from Washington to keep the runway open and in readiness for the forthcoming flight of Galactic II, now less than two weeks away.

The task of bulldozing the snow was becoming increasingly difficult because of the extremely low temperatures—they were hovering around 30 degrees below zero in Florida now. For that matter, the temperatures almost everywhere from Miami to Montreal, from Melbourne to Mecca, from Moscow to Madrid were uniformly the same readings—35 degrees below zero, give or take one or two degrees.

Now Dr. Peter Cushing Morchelson, the director of the National Oceanic and Atmospheric Agency, had worked out with other meteorologists a timetable for the onset of the colder temperatures that inevitably would come as long as Sunstrike continued.

They had charted the plunging mercury over the critical ten days just past, recorded its increasingly sharper day-by-day declines, and worked out the following forecast of thermometer readings on the centigrade, or celcius scale for the next twenty days when finally absolute zero would be reached.

July 4 —	-33 degrees
July 5 —	-36 degrees
July 6 —	-40 degrees
July 7 —	-46 degrees
July 8 —	-52 degrees
July 9 —	-59 degrees
July 10 —	-67 degrees
July 11 —	-76 degrees
July 12 —	-87 degrees
July 13 —	-100 degrees
July 14 —	-116 degrees
July 15 —	-135 degrees
July 16 —	-157 degrees
July 17 —	-169 degrees
July 18 —	-193 degrees
July 19 —	-215 degrees
July 20 —	-238 degrees
July 21 —	-257 degrees
July 22 —	-270 degrees
July 23 —	-273 degrees

There it was, as precisely as any scientist or meteorologist could predict doomsday, as it soon would be called—the day when the thermometer hit the very bottom, that absolute zero or 273-degree-below-zero, which Dr. Morchelson had discussed a few days earlier with Jim Hartz.

The temperature calendar was released to the news media and instantly received the broadest distribution and attention. At least it did in those areas of the world that had not been isolated by the ravages of the storm and bitter freezing.

By now commerce and industry, which had come to a standstill in the first few days of the world-wide blackout, resumed functioning in limited and restricted fashion despite the terrible blizzards and roof-high drifts that by now—July 4, 1988, the eleventh day of the cataclysm—had brought virtually all activity to a standstill.

Only those areas of the Northern Hemisphere accustomed in years past to cruel winters and heavy accumulations of snow were able to cope with the crisis to any extent. Only there was survival a matter of some hope. Elsewhere, in the normally warmer climes, it was merely a question of how soon the end would come.

The temperature calendar meant nothing to those millions, indeed billions, who were unable to cope with the present minus 37-degree temperature gripping the earth on that July 4—actually July 5 west of the International Date Line in the Pacific.

No one actually believed that any living being would be around to witness that day of absolute zero, even though Dr. Morchelson suggested survival was possible in a properly sheltered environment.

But properly sheltered environments were rapidly running out even in the northernmost regions most accustomed to the harshest winter conditions.

In Malmo, Sweden, for example, the waters froze to such great depths that the ice literally crushed several freighters moored to the piers in the seaport harbor when the eclipse came.

One freighter, which was being loaded with such export products as chocolate, sweetmeats, and cheese, was split with such force by the crunch of the ice it seemed as though a bomb had exploded inside the cargo bay. The chocolate, sweetmeats, and cheese were blown out of the hold and scattered over the snowy landscape for several hundred yards.

Elsewhere in Malmo, the frozen harbor waters visited utter destruction on the Kockum Mechanical Works, which housed some of Europe's finest shipbuilding facilities. The inordinate pressure and force of the frozen water acted almost like a glacier, pushing relentlessly inland and crushing piers, gantries, cranes, lifts, and other facilities in the shipyards, as well as destroying the dry dock and patent slip in the inner basins of the harbor.

In Venice, the tenth day of Sunstrike was an alluvian nightmare, as the headwaters of the Adriatic froze into such solid cakes of ice that they split the two and a half-mile road and rail causeway linking the island to the Italian mainland.

On Venice itself, the Grand Canal began to heave its frozen banks on the fifth day of the eclipse, and now as Sunstrike was ten days old the devastation was total.

Some seven thousand gondolas had lain in their canal moorings waiting to be disgorged by the ice, as the freighters in Malmo had been.

Here the high winds and driving snow served as the agents of destruction.

The colorful and celebrated flat-bottomed boats, the characteristic conveyances on Venice's canals for centuries, were tossed like matchsticks over the frozen snow-covered landscape.

Some were driven with such force by the cyclonic 140-mile-an-hour winds that they were smashed to smithereens against the nearby buildings lining the shores of the canal.

Some of the extravagantly decorated boats with their elegant iron peak *ferros* and halberd-like designs were lofted through the air like airplanes or missiles and sent crashing into such revered centuries-old structures as the Church of St. Giovanni e Paolo, where the doges are buried and the site of numerous noble mausoleums.

Other gondolas were catapulted against the revered Church of St. Marks, smashing some of its exterior facade, its marbled columns that had been brought from Alexandria and other cities, and also damaging some of its ogee gables.

But worse in terms of irreparable damage was the way building foundations were cracked by the expanding floating masses of ice that were heaved out of the Grand Canal and its many tributaries.

The pressure in hundreds of instances not only split foundations but caused many buildings to topple. One of the most frequent occurrences during this catastrophic upheaval was the destruction of the square brick shaft campaniles, or bell towers, that had been among Venice's most stirring and striking features for centuries.

Earthquakes in times past had caused the collapse of the great tower of San Marco and that of Sansovino's beautiful Logetta, on its east side, to mention only two. These had been rebuilt, but now, in the onrush of glacial ice from the canal, combined with winds Venice had never experienced in its history, the towers once again tumbled.

No one wondered now or even gave thought to the day when they might be rebuilt, when any part of Venice might be rebuilt and restored to its former splendor and beauty, truly one of the world's most remarkable sights—before Sunstrike began changing the face of the earth.

Before departing Venice for a look at other devastation, perhaps the description from Byron's *Beppo* should be recalled about those once-proud gondolas that were destroyed almost to the last one:

'Tis a long cover'd boat that's common here
    Carved at the prow, built lightly, but
      compactly
Rowed by two rowers, each call'd
    "Gondolier,"
    It glides along the water looking blackly,
Just like a coffin clapt in a canoe.

Looking blackly. That's how the world looked on that tenth day of Sunstrike as the winds raked the Church of the Latter Day Saints, the gigantic Mormon Tabernacle.

The temple was filled with several thousand refugees who had been evacuated from their heatless Salt Lake City homes by snowsleds and four-wheel-drive jeeps over a five-day period. An early ice storm hit before a crippling two-day blizzard completely paralyzed the state of Utah, felling power lines and cutting off electricity to nearly 30 percent of Salt Lake's 250,000 residents.

This was truly a time of challenge for the Latter Day Saints' theology and philosophy, which takes note of time, space, matter, and the extent and nature of the universe with fixed notions in its doctrines and covenants. For, it is the church's belief that duration is without beginning or end, space is limitless, matter in its elemental status is eternal and, while subject to infinite changes, may neither be created or annihilated.

There was no response immediately either from anyone in the church, not from its president or those in the responsible hierarchy, to challenge Dr. Morchelson's timetable for the freezeover and annihilation of earth—now a mere thirteen days left in the countdown to absolute zero, the terminal minus 273-degree day that will end all weather on earth and mark the doom of all life on the planet.

Perhaps the most terrifying occurrence in Utah was the systematic formation of ice on the shores of the Great Salt Lake, lying northwest of the capital. Never before since James Bridger and Etienne Provost discovered it in 1824 had ice ever been known to form on that shallow, briny water.

Yet now when temperatures had reached an incredible and killing minus 76 degrees, even the extremely salinated waters of the Great Salt Lake were beginning to freeze. Dr. Perry G. Mangrove, a marine biologist at the University of Utah, gave his assurance that the lake would not overspill its banks and send glacierlike floes off on destructive courses.

"The ten-foot maximum depth of the Great Salt Lake obviates that possibility," he said in a statement to the *Salt Lake Tribune*. "But I do fear greatly about the fate of those islands..."

He was referring to Stansbury, Antelope,

Fremont, and numerous smaller islands and islets used for grazing by the migratory flocks of white pelicans, great blue herons, cormorants, terns, and gulls. The waters of the Great Salt Lake had risen as a result of the freeze, inundated those islands, and destroyed the grazing grounds.

But it didn't matter much to the migratory birds—the cold had killed almost all of them off anyway . . .

In another part of the United States, the Great Lakes-St. Lawrence region, concern was mounting hourly about the fate of some eight million inhabitants living on the perimeter of those great bodies of water and their connecting waterways.

For there now, the largest group of lakes in the world—Superior, Michigan, Huron, Erie, and Ontario—were beginning to spill their banks along some four-thousand miles of shoreline in Minnesota, Wisconsin, Illinois, Indiana, Ohio, Pennsylvania, and New York, as well as Ontario and Quebec in Canada.

Already on that eleventh day of Sunstrike, the banks of Lake Michigan had overflown and glacial sheets, flat as pancakes but deadly behemoths in their four and five foot thicknesses and fifty-foot diameters, were sent by the expanding pressure of the freeze upon the snow-covered shore, which had the effect of being a greased sliding pond.

One such saucer-shaped iceberg crashed into the Edgewater Beach Hotel and destroyed the entire lobby and main ballroom. Inspectors from the Department of Buildings quickly determined that the structural integrity of the hotel had been damaged. They promptly ordered its evacuation and shuttered it.

Other ice floes rose out of the lake like slow moving ships, traveled over the beaches along the North Side's "Gold Coast," and plowed into other hotels and apartment buildings on Lake Shore Drive with devastating impact, forcing thousands more to flee to safety.

Further inland, the Chicago River also overflowed its banks and not only sent crushing ice floes into buildings lining its shores but also uprooted several bridges spanning the waterway for a mile inland from its mouth on Lake Michigan.

Chicago's highway and sanitation crews toiled relentlessly to keep main roads and expressways open for emergency vehicles. No other travel was allowed, although the executive order from Mayor Michael Bilandic banning all traffic was more an act of protocol than of practicality. No one with an ounce of sense would—or even could—drive in those unprecedented weather conditions.

Especially now as a blizzard piling up twenty-foot-high drifts had delivered the most crippling blow Chicago had ever known . . .

Detroit and Windsor suffered similar devastating consequences from the freeze that lifted Lake Erie's waters into destructive moving glaciers. Yet some of the nation's worst encounters with the howling storms occurred in San Francisco, where the populace had never experienced extreme deviations in weather, a city whose climate was generally mild, cool, and where mean temperatures historically ranged between 56.5 degrees on the low side to a maximum of 62.6.

With the thermometer skidding to minus 35 degrees on that tenth day of Sunstrike, the Bay Area was overwhelmed by a savage snowstorm that swept in from the Pacific on July 2 and raged for two full days. By the time it subsided, forty-four inches of snow had inundated the City by the Golden Gate and turned it into a disaster area of the first magnitude.

Ruin and suffering were widespread. The waterfront area was hit severely as ice floes from the never-before turbulent San Francisco Bay and the Golden Gate gushed in fury during the storm. The frozen water packs were sent by the 80-mile-an hour winds sliding over famed Fisherman's Wharf and smashed the storefronts of some ten of the area's famed seafood restaurants.

The *Balclutha*, the restored three-masted sailing ship that had rounded Cape Horn seventeen times before the turn of the century and had been moored next to Fisherman's Wharf, weathered the storm as truly it was expected of the last surviving ship of the hundreds that once sailed out of San Francisco and made the dangerous voyages around South America's Cape Horn.

But the *Balclutha* didn't escape unscathed.

The heavy seas, high tides, and raging winds broke her from her mooring and sent the three-master, prow first, into Joe DiMaggio's Restaurant on Fisherman's Wharf.

The worst of the storm's destructive effects was felt after the snows had stopped falling. Drifts more than thirty feet high had formed at the crests of the city's many steep elevations, particularly Nob Hill, Russian Hill, and Telegraph Hill.

Then some five-and-a-half hours after the battering blizzard had ended, a terrifying sequence of events occurred. The snow in the drifts on the hilltops were inexplicably dislodged by the raging winds and sent downhill in a screaming series of avalanches.

Several thundering snowslides reaching two-story heights cascaded down Nob Hill and struck like bombs in Union Square. Building fronts were demolished by the impact of these avalanches but there were no deaths or injuries because by now the danger had been anticipated and all occupants were evacuated.

The New York City scene was no better than it was in Chicago, Salt Lake City, San Francisco, or those other cities that had been visited by the killer storms. It was no better at this point of time—2:50 P.M. of July 4, 1988. The situation, in fact, was due to get worse. Much worse . . .

A screaming snowstorm driven by gale-force winds narrowly missed the National Weather Service's designation as a blizzard in the first hours of its arrival. But it certainly carried the punch of an outlandishly high-powered storm.

Snow removal operations in the city ran into a snag from almost the moment the snow began falling. Although Mayor Bellamy had put the Big Apple on an emergency footing just after the eclipse began, Department of Sanitation forces were unable to get a beat on the swift one-two punch the surprise storm threw at the metropolis.

It started very quickly with swirling winds that resembled a hurricane or an extratropical cyclone, moving very slowly on its path and depositing snow as the wind circled and swirled counterclockwise.

In the second hour the storm's intensity increased and the Weather Service at Rockefeller Center officially recorded the measurement of snowfall at four and a half inches—a one-hour record fall for New York City.

The storm's ferocity was all the more terrifying because it was accompanied by deafening thunder and brilliant lightning, dramatized and highlighted by the uninterrupted, around-the-clock darkness.

Thunder and lightning were not unusual during snowstorms in New York during daylight hours. But they hardly ever commanded attention because they were seldom noticed. But in the perpetual darkness of Sunstrike now the slighest flash of light in the sky was starkly eye-catching.

Despite repeated implorings to motorists to stay put and not risk being stranded in the intensifying storm, the warnings were heeded with the usual disregard. Thus several thousand Metropolitan Area residents were trapped in their cars on such heavily traveled arteries as the Long Island Expressway, Belt and Grand Central Parkways, and numerous other highways.

Unlike times past, however, when rescue vehicles took stranded motorists to shelters, few carriers were available for such errands of mercy now. A crisis earlier in this dismal day before the snows had come had required every available rescue conveyance for duty along the shores of Manhattan, Brooklyn, Queens, Staten Island, and the Bronx.

Five hours before the snow began falling, sudden, stark terror swept over the New York City area, hitting hardest along its shorelines. It happened shortly before 10 o'clock that Monday morning as New Yorkers again absented themselves from their jobs by the tens of thousands and huddled in their apartments and homes, trying to keep warm against the unparalleled sub-zero freeze.

For hours a whining wind had been buffeting the city and at times its velocity was exceeding fifty mph. But then all at once the gusts boiled up with snarling fury, slashing over the landscape with awesome abandon. As its speed increased, the spiraling, cyclonic swirl of the wind began taking its toll.

The suffering people on the streets, most of them emergency workers on errands of mercy, had already been numbed beyond belief by the unbearable cold. But now the violent wind, striking as it did, swiftly and stunningly as a tornado might hit, caught them by surprise in its icy, vicious grip.

Before they could flee to the safety of shelters, people everywhere on the streets were snapped up and hurled like ragdolls through the air. Some were carried in their palpable terror for mercifully short distances before being slammed or crushed against buildings, lampposts, trees, and vehicles on the street.

Others were catapulted for hundreds of feet and smashed into objects with such force that death again was swift and sparing of lingering pain. But some were suddenly dropped from the heights to which they were lofted by the wind, whenever the vortex of the storm paused an instant, as cyclones often do. In those instances, victims plummeted like leadweights straight down, screaming terrifyingly, to be flattened against the rock-hard blacktop streets and the even harder-surfaced concrete sidewalks.

Death of many was marked by lingering suffering. For some who survived the agony, pain, and torment, shattered and mangled bodies were all that were left of them.

Human life wasn't the only target of this awesome killer wind. It also cut a path of unbelievable destruction on property, ripping signs and advertising displays from storefronts and rooftops and hurling them with a fearsome force against other buildings, other roofs, and upon the street.

Times Square became a litter-strewn depository for uprooted and smashed billboards and signs. The shredded and mangled metal and shards of glass were scattered knee deep over Broadway and Seventh Avenue.

Perhaps the eeriest sight on the Gay White Way was the rooftop scene where the Great Atlantic & Pacific supermarket chain's billboard at 43rd St. and Broadway had stood before the wind wrenched it off its supports. The metal facing of the display was catapulted across the street against the skyscraper at 1515 Broadway, between 43rd and 44th streets, where the old Astor Hotel once stood.

The debris narrowly missed several editors from Fawcett Publications who were arriving for work despite the cataclysmic conditions to put out a quickie paperback on the eclipse that was to be called, for lack of a more imaginative title, *Eclipse!*

It wasn't until days later that the pipes behind the billboard, which gushed steam from a giant brimming cup of fresh brewed 8 O'clock brand coffee, were noticed. The remorseless wind had twisted them, remarkably, into the shape of a cross or crucifix.

Even more extraordinary was the uncanny course taken by a twisted and gnarled sheet of metal that had been torn from a men's clothing billboard on the roof of Bond's store two blocks to the north.

That segment of metal had been ripped from the portion of the billboard displaying a bearded man in jockey shorts. And, incredibly, it was flung through the air by one of the more forceful cyclonic gusts and thrust against the A&P pipes that had been twisted into the shape of a cross.

The impact of metal against pipes was so strong that it stuck in place. It was after the winds and massive snowstorm subsided and people ventured into the rubble-strewn slag-heap that was Times Square that they noticed the amazing freakish sight of pipe and metal upon the roof where once reposed the A&P coffee billboard.

The twisted pipe, the mannequinlike metal billboard of a man in shorts had stuck together in such a fashion that it looked like a pop-art version of Jesus Christ on the cross!

This wonderment precipitated an outpouring of TV cameras and newspaper photographers and the resultant publicity brought religious fanatics descending upon Times Square. They set up streetcorner revival meetings and clarioned calls amidst the debris and rubble for a return to Christ to spare the world from a heading that everyone now began believing was inevitable doom.

Human bodies and signs and billboards weren't the only casualties of the violent giant whirlwind. Cars, trucks, and buses were over-turned or catapulted through the air and pounded into scrap heaps. Lampposts, traffic signal stanchions, and other standing objects were ripped from their moorings with remorseless fury by the thrashing storm and hurtled all over the city.

Virtually half of New York's shops and buildings were windowless by now, the fourth hour of the cyclone's hammering onslaught. Thousands of stone and metal cornices and ornamental filigree adornments were ripped from the buildings and shattered on the ground.

After the wind causing the devastation and destruction had attained its peak in the city proper and just as quickly had dissipated, police and rescue workers lifted corpses and bleeding bodies from the rubble that littered the streets. Victims were rushed to hospitals for consignment to the many makeshift morgues, or the emergency rooms for medical treatment.

Meanwhile, the shorefront communities required at least an equal amount of special attention from rescue teams. High hurricane-force winds blowing in from the Atlantic and Lower New York Bay caused a special brand of devastation and destruction along the city's many miles of coastline.

Whipped up by the rampaging windstorms and rapidly forming ice floes, the waters rose in ugly, fifty-foot high waves and crashed angrily against the shore with splashing bursts that visited destruction wherever they fell.

In just minutes the violent tidal waves washed away two-thirds of the Coney Island boardwalk and surged over Bowery Street and into Surf Avenue, smashing through the rows of refreshment stands, games, and rides of the famed amusement park.

The Cyclone, Tornado, and Thunderbolt rollercoaster structures were smashed and their steel and wooden girders and tracks splintered and washed helter skelter over the streets and lawns of the sprawling Coney Island Houses apartment project.

Going eastward, the waves pounded destructively against Brighton, Manhattan, and Oriental beaches, then rose to such heights of savagery in Sheepshead Bay that hundreds of fishing boats were torn from their anchorages in the frozen waters near the shore, lifted by the violent waves over bulkheads and sea walls, and driven against the rows of stores and shops on Emmons Avenue.

One forty-foot trawler was split in two by the impact of a titanic wave, then another mountainous wall of water and ice roared along and sent the separated sections of the boat careening across the street. The wave hit with such fury and power that it carried both forward and aft sections of the boat crashing halfway into famed Lundy's Restaurant.

The wind-driven tides wrought more havoc on long stretches of Staten Island and Long Island shorefronts, gouging out miles upon miles of irreplaceable beaches and destroying hundreds of valuable properties.

And after the hammering cyclonic-hurricane bursts had rent New York almost helpless, the blinding blizzard came.

Although the government weathermen at Radio City didn't officially designate the storm a blizzard in the first hour or so, they had no choice but to do so after then—for anytime a record four and a half inches of snow falls in one hour, combined with winds of seventy mph, that is nothing less than a blizzard.

For forty-one hours the snow fell, dumping an unprecedented sixty-four inches over the Metropolitan Area. It was estimated long before the storm came to a merciful halt that several thousands had died or would die before rescue teams could reach them. Actually, there was no way any count could be kept of lives lost at a time such as this. Statistics just couldn't be compiled under such traumatic conditions. It would be weeks, perhaps months, before the full count of casualties was known—if then.

For the deep freeze that followed the snow was unrelenting. Indeed, it was a progressively worsening factor. This was now July 12, 1988, the nineteenth day of Sunstrike. And conditions on earth were never worse.

Even during the Pleistocene epoch, the Ice Age, the glacial climate and continental ice sheets formed much more slowly and temperatures dropped over a far longer period. In fact it took centuries for the temperatures to plummet, and even at that they never reached the interminable cold and the promised colder readings soon to be experienced as the earth headed toward absolute zero, or minus 273 degrees.

During the Ice Age, the sun shone just as it always had on this planet. It kept a reasonable control over cold, as it did over Antarctic and Arctic lands in normal periods of the earth's history. For the Pleistocene epoch was caused by what some scientists and astronomers believe was a periodic change of the earth's motion, such as eccentricity of the orbit every 91,800 years, inclination of the axis to the eliptic plane every 40,000 years, and the shifting of the perihelion every 21,000 years.

Those changes were found to have altered the distribution of solar heat upon the earth's surface—yet those changes never reduced the total amount of such heat received at any one time.

But Sunstrike had altered that concept totally. It wiped out every ray of sunlight on earth, as well as upon the moon.

So far as scientists could determine, none of those three factors that brought on the last Ice Age—the eccentricity of the orbit, the inclination of the axis, and the shifting of the perihelion—had occurred in this dread crisis of 1988.

In a desperate effort to cope with the terrible predicted condition of absolute zero, which the earth was due to reach in a matter of eleven more days, scientists struggled and groped for possible ways to stave off the intense cold.

But how?

One group of oceanographers suggested that the Bering Strait separating Alaska from Siberia might be reconnected to allow the warm Japanese current to provide a milder climate over Asia and North America.

This was viewed as a stop-gap measure and not a long-range solution, for as the director of the National Oceanic and Atmospheric Agency, Dr. Morchelson had pointed out, the day of absolute zero was inevitable and only the earth's interior heat would provide a ray of hope in that it wouldn't let the crust or surface cool as fast as it might otherwise.

Yet, when the earth cooled finally—life would ultimately come to an end once the atmosphere were gone. Unless, of course, the particle accelerator could be used to provide a vacuum that would again make possible the formation of life-giving oxygen.

But without sunlight, how could even the particle accelerator establish the condition necessary to manufacture atmosphere?

Impossible!

Knowing that the particle accelerator was no solution, scientists turned to other ideas. Even science reporters and writers, as well as columnists busied themselves posing ideas of how to save the earth.

Rupert Murdoch's New York *Post* jumped immediately on the scientists' suggestion to dam the Bering Strait by saying it wasn't a new idea. The newspaper reprinted Harriet Van Horne's column, which she'd written more than a decade before—on February 6, 1978, during a particularly severe winter that most of the nation had suffered through.

"When people talk of the weather—and they talk of little else this year—somebody is sure to ask, 'Why can't we find a way to control the climate?' " wrote Miss Van Horne.

"I always stay for the answers, because they're fascinating. If you're 'into weather,' as they say, you probably know about the plan to dam Bering Strait. This would be done with rock mined in Alaska, so diverting the currents that rainfall and temperature patterns would change throughout the planet. And *beneficially*. But the project has about 750 drawbacks, so don't count on it.

"Another plan calls for blackening the polar caps—with soot, if you please—to lower the 'albedo,' or ratio of light. This would allow more solar warmth to penetrate the ice and melt it, producing in reality Homer's 'wine-dark sea.' "

No one had suggested the soot plan in 1988 inasmuch as there was no longer a source of solar warmth. There couldn't be with the sun blotted out. But even when there was sun back in 1978, Miss Van Horne saw not much of a future to the idea.

"The big drawback to this plan," she wrote quoting Fitzhugh Green, "is the problem of finding enough soot—millions of tons."

Then the columnist asked:

"Has he ever thought of New York as a possible source?"

As matters stood at this very moment in New York and everywhere else on earth, there were no thoughts about damming the Bering Strait or sooting over the polar icecap. There wasn't enough soot anywhere to cover the endless blanket of unbearable snow and ice that had wrapped itself around the world.

CHAPTER XXI

Someone Remembers Dr. Simms . . .

While the nation and the world were gripped in the relentless frozen holocaust of Sunstrike and as its increasing savagery was claiming hundreds of thousands of lives daily, the arduous task of running the government was being attended to in Washington with a passion that once and for all should have put to rout all those critics indulging in the fancy that Congress was a do-nothing body.

Certainly the debate raging in the hallowed halls of the Senate at the very moment when another forty inches of snow had buried the capital anew, should have stood as a monument to the lofty goals and ideals of the legislative process as it was decreed for practice by that ancient and revered testament called the Constitution.

As in generations past, the Congress again was demonstrating that those who are the hardest at work in time of peril are not necessarily the ones who are reaching solutions to our country's crises.

301

Yet at this very moment a debate the senators judged to be of inordinate significance was being waged, as it had been for nearly six weeks. New York's two senators, Mario Biaggi and Andrew Stein, were in the forefront of the raging controversy, which had spilled over into the first dozen days of Sunstrike.

The Senate was trying to decide whether additional funds should be allocated by Congress for the completion of the Westway on Manhattan's West Side.

This was a project that had been started during the administrations of Mayor Edward Koch and Governor Hugh L. Carey back in 1977. But spiraling inflation had not treated construction costs kindly.

The initial estimate of $1.16 billion for the 4.2 mile six-lane superhighway that was to replace the old elevated West Side Highway from the Battery, at the tip of Manhattan, to 42nd Street, had run into many roadblocks, most of them financial.

The federal government had come to the rescue time and again—five times since 1980, to be exact. At total of $23.5 billion had been appropriated by the beginning of 1968, but a need still existed for more funds now to complete a 1.1-mile portion of uncovered road sunk below street level between Canal Street and the exit ramp of the World Trade Center 110-story Twin Towers, now the forty-fifth tallest buildings in the world, since the Michigan General 160 story earthquake proof skyscraper became the world's tallest in Los Angeles in the latter part of 1987, replacing the 144-story Anheuser Busch beer-bottle-shaped edifice in St. Louis, which had held the distinction of towering over all other buildings.

The debate in Congress had bristled for many weeks over whether another $9.7 billion should be appropriated for the completion of that downtown section of the Westway. Until Sunstrike blotted out the sun, Senators Biaggi and Stein had been battling each other at cross-purposes.

Biaggi, a former policeman and still the most decorated cop in the history of the NYPD, had been blustering loudly to redirect the highway dollars to beef up the subway's transit police force, which he said was necessary so members of the NYPD could ride to work and home in safety from muggers, rapists, and pillagers who'd been granted immunity from arrest by the City Council so long as they didn't mug, rob, or rape passengers during the 7-to-9 A.M. and 5-to-7 P.M. rush hours.

There were no restrictions on weekends except that women over seventy-two years of age and men past eighty were out of bounds because so many had been victimized in the past that they were designated as endangered species by the City Council.

On the other hand, Senator Stein wanted the $9.7 billion federal highways funds used instead to build a new convention center somewhere in his old East Side congressional neighborhood, known as the Silk Stocking District. The center, he argued, was gravely needed to restore confidence to New York City after the previous convention center, which had been built in 1981 on 32nd Street, had been burned down by roving gangs of arsonists.

The pyromaniacs had turned to the pursuit of firing public buildings because they had burned the last of the city's old-law, free-standing tenements and apartments—and even almost all of the new apartment buildings that were built with the federal funds appropriated during President Carter's administration, to replace the houses wilfully destroyed during the Bronx-and-Brooklyn-Are-Burning years of the 1970s.

But when Sunstrike came, many concerned senators offered the suggestion that debate over Westway funds be set aside temporarily so Congress could devote attention to the crisis brought on by the sun's disappearance.

The motion was put to a vote on the second day of the eclipse and lost 40-38, with twenty-two abstentions. So the debate continued.

But then, on July 12, the nineteenth day of Sunstrike, when the entire world was not only buried under mountains of snow but freezing in near-minus 90-degree temperatures, the Senate finally voted to postpone further action on Westway.

At the same time, the legislators in the Upper House approved two emergency appropriations.

One measure introduced by Senator Jane Fonda (D.-L.-C.-R.-Ind., California) provided for $106 million to form a committee of leading civic and business leaders to study the causes and effects of the eclipse on industry and commerce. This was totally independent of the commission of lawyers, doctors, and other professional people that had been formed a week earlier with a $180-million budget to look into the feasibility of appointing an exploratory ad hoc committee to determine whether or not Congress should appropriate funds for disaster relief to disadvantaged nations, particularly in Africa, where snow removal equipment and warm clothing were desperately needed.

The second measure, passed after the Westway issue had been shelved, was introduced by Senator Stein. The Senate passed it by a narrow 44-43 vote (seventeen abstentions). This bill provided an allocation of funds to pay for the evacuation of Jews from the Soviet Union who were not allowed to receive emergency shipments of warm clothing from the United Jewish Appeal or other relief organizations.

But Moscow had agreed that if the expense of emigration was paid for, any Jew who wanted to leave the Soviet Union would be allowed to.

The six o'clock news on New York's CBS-TV Channel 2 came on the air after the opening commercial for McDonald's, which carried the sad tidings that the hamburger chain was closing its 51,342 outlets in the United States and 4,320 stores elsewhere in the world for the duration of Sunstrike.

"But we shall be back when the sun goes on again all over the world," said the announcer, borrowing a somewhat familiar refrain from a World War II song. Then, after reminding viewers that McDonald's had sold nine billion egg McMuffins and eighty-eight billion Big Macs since the beginning, the announcer faded into a misty snowbank outside one of the franchises and Chris Borgen began intoning the solemnities of the Sunstrike crisis.

"The news tonight is grimmer than ever," Borgen said cryptically and arrestingly. "The terrible toll of frozen deaths, fatalities by the tens of thousands mounted again today and are expected to climb even higher. Perhaps the most sobering word is the one just reaching us from Peking, where an official government announcement has listed more than one million dead in the newest blizzard that swept across the southern half of China. Monsoon winds . . ."

As the terrible and worsening events of the eclipse were spieled by Borgen in his crisp, staccato style, Mary Spanacopito let out a sudden anguished cry and threw her head back against the pillow-backed arm chair in her living room.

"John . . . John, what is this all about," she sighed dispiritedly. "What is happening to the world . . . what is going to happen to us?"

Her blue, worry-strained eyes stared at her husband who was sitting in the Betsy Ross high-backed rocker. He took his eyes off the TV screen and glanced at his wife.

306

"This is our punishment, Mary, the world's punishment," he said somberly. "Let me read this . . ."

The dour-faced Spanacopito reached toward the coffee table for a book. An executive with the Metropolitan Life Insurance Company, he had not been to work in five days, since Long Island was placed under an emergency no-travel ban issued by Nassau County Executive Alphonse D'Amato and his counterpart in neighboring Suffolk, Regis Neal.

The book Spanacopito picked up was the black leather-bound new Catholic edition of the Holy Bible. He turned to chapter seven in Genesis and ran his finger down page twenty-three. Then he began reading . . .

"Then the Lord said to Noah, 'Go into the ark . . . for after seven days I will send rain on the earth for forty days and forty nights, and I will wipe from the ground every living thing that I have made . . ."

His wife interrupted Spanacopito with an excited offering.

"Yes, the Lord was going to destroy the earth and all that was on it in forty days," she said heavily. "But did you see the countdown to absolute zero . . . just half the time, a mere twenty-three days before all life will die . . ."

Her husband hadn't lifted his eyes from the Bible when Mrs. Spanacopito had cut him off. Now that she had spoken and went silent, with his gaze still fixed on the book, Spanacopito went on reading grim-voiced.

". . . The flood continued forty days upon

the earth. The waters increased and bore up the ark and it rose above the earth. The waters rose higher and increased greatly on the earth; but the ark floated on the surface of the water. The waters rose higher and higher on the earth so that all the highest mountains everywhere under the heavens were covered . . . All flesh that moved on the earth died: birds, cattle, wild animals, all creatures that creep on the earth, and all men. All that were on the dry land in whose nostrils was the breath of life, died. And every living thing on the earth was wiped out, from man to beast, from reptile to bird of the air; they were wiped from the earth . . ."

His voice trailed off now and he turned his eyes toward his wife.

"Mary," Spanacopito said in a throaty whisper, "this is the end of the world. . . . Billy Graham has been screaming his bloody head off for the past week that we must repent, that the end of the world is coming. . . . Mary, we've nothing left but to sit back and wait for our time to come. It won't be . . . it can't be much longer . . ."

Spanacopito rose and walked to the kitchen archway. He pointed inside. "That's the trouble right now," he said grimly. "The food . . . the food is gone. There's not a damned thing to eat and there's no food to be had . . ."

Earlier in the day, Spanacopito had trudged across shoulder-high frozen drifts to one of the several Town of Huntington emergency food centers that had been set up by Supervisor Mary Rose McKee. This one was nearest his home in the Melville Sunoco station, opposite the Melville Firehouse, on Broadhollow Road. The depot was open when Spanacopito reached it—but all the food supplies were gone.

"We ran out of everything early this morning," Spanacopito was told by Lawrence Doran, the service station owner who'd volunteered his premises for a food emergency station when it became obvious after the first of many brutal snowstorms and blizzards that pumping gas and repairing autos had to be suspended for the duration of Sunstrike.

Doran told Spanacopito the outlook for delivery of more food stores in the immediate future looked grim. "The trouble is the trucks can't run in this cold," he explained. "They tell me they're going to try and attach portable nuclear generators to the engines, which will blow heat and keep them from freezing. But I don't know when they'll get around to doing that."

Now in their home, Spanacopito turned away from the kitchen after he made his point about the empty cupboards to his wife, and returned to his rocker. Borgen was still reciting the news and Mrs. Spanacopito was listening intently.

As her husband sat down, he began saying, "It's a lucky thing we have gas heat. I understand that the homes with oil are running out and there's no way they'll get any deliveries . . ."

All at once his wife screamed, "Shush, John! Keep quiet! I want to hear this . . ."

She reached for the volume control and turned up the sound. A photo of Dr. Gordon Lyle Simms was being flashed on the screen behind Borgen, who was now talking about the professor who'd flown off in Galactic I and hadn't been heard from again in the more than five months since his spectacular disappearing act in space.

"National Air and Space Administrator Maitland Thurber said today that one possible solution to the earth's blackout and the storms that are threatening to wipe us all out could be Dr. Simms, who is out there somewhere in space," Chris Borgen was saying. "But it has been all too long since Simms has been heard from and it isn't likely we'll ever hear from him.

"However, Galactic II is coming off the assembly line at Rockwell International and will be ready for its scheduled takeoff to search for the cause of Sunstrike on July fifteenth . . ."

As a commercial replaced the newscaster on the screen, Mary Spanacopito turned to her husband excitedly.

"John," she shrieked, "that man . . . that man was in my bank!"

Spancopito looked at his wife with a puzzled frown.

"Honey," he said benignly, "what are you talking about? What man?"

"Him! Him!" she almost jumped out of her chair. But by then the commercial had erased the screen portraying Professor Simms.

"What man, who?" her husband persisted.

"Dr. Simms," Mrs. Spanacopito stammered. "The man . . . who's picture was behind Chris Borgen. He's the man who came into my bank and rented a safe deposit box . . ."

Now Spanacopito was truly bewildered.

"Mary," he rasped with an effort. "What the hell are you talking about?"

"Did you see the man behind Chris Borgen on the screen?" asked his wife.

"Yes," Spanacopito replied. "I heard Borgen say something about Simms, that loony who hijacked the spaceship."

"Yes, but don't you understand what it means?" Mrs. Spanacopito shrieked in excitement.

"What, honey?" her husband asked with a look of trepidation mixed with wonderment.

"Dr. Simms was in the bank back in January . . . he rented a safe deposit box."

"Mary, what are you trying to tell me?" Mrs. Spanacopito's husband demanded sharply. "Supposing he was, what significance has that with the situation that faces us and the world?"

"I don't know, John," Mary Spanacopito said quickly. "But all I'm trying to say to you is that he put something in that safe deposit box, which I feel could have significance with his disappearance in space."

"Did you see it?" Spanacopito asked, now intensely interested in his wife's observations.

"No," she admitted readily, "but the whole thing seems to be crying for some kind of an investigation. I don't know why I feel this way but I feel he took that box to put something in that he didn't want anyone in the world to know about. He lives in California . . . why did he come to a Long Island bank to rent a safe deposit box?"

"Did you mention this to anyone else?" her husband asked Mrs. Spanacopito.

"Yes, to Tony Poosty." she responded haltingly.

"And what did that stupid person have to say to that?" her husband asked with prior awareness of the bank manager's I.Q.

"He ignored the whole thing," she replied. "He almost scolded me . . . I just couldn't understand that jerk."

"All right, sweetheart," Mrs. Spanacopito's husband said loudly. "The time has come to do something about all this. I'm calling the FBI."

CHAPTER XXII

Breaking Into the Mystery

John Spanacopito had to wait three hours for a dial tone. Finally a breakthrough hummed in the earpiece and he pushbuttoned the call numbers—661-6711—and reached the Federal Bureau of Investigation office at 215 Deer Park Avenue in Babylon.

Agent Bryan Dudley listened intently. The information held more than inordinate interest for him. Spanacopito's call was one of those incredible turns in an investigation, which, for lack of a better phrase, is called a million-to-one shot.

Just a few hours earlier, the agents in that Suffolk County office had received urgent instructions from Washington to investigate Dr. Gordon Lyle Simms's itinerary during the period he'd been on Long Island last January.

The inquiry was mandated by the stunning discovery that Maitland Thurber made quite by accident. It happened when Thurber spoke with Dr. Furth Koenig, the astronomer from Kitt Peak whose letter warning about that strange, radioactive gaseous cloud in the vicinity of Mars had precipitated the drastic change in Galactic I's flight schedule—the change that led to Dr. Simms's spectacular solo into space.

Koenig had gone off to the International Convention of Astronomers in Moscow at the time Thurber received the letter. As it turned out, Koenig suffered a heart attack at that conclave and was confined to a cardiovascular center in the Soviet capital for the next five months. He was finally discharged on June 23 and arrived home in Arizona the day before Sunstrike began.

He returned to his duties at Kitt Peak and was immersed in the massive investigation of the universe by trying to unearth a solid scientific answer to the mystery of the incredible eclipse. Among Koenig's most immediate findings was that a grouping of constellations and certain stars normally visible during that quarter of the year from the Northern Hemisphere had also mysteriously vanished. Among the heavenly bodies that no longer shone were Leo Minor, Ursa Major, Hydra, and Canis Major. Even the Magellan Clouds were no longer visible.

Then on July 12, the nineteenth day of Sunstrike, Dr. Koenig phoned NASA's boss at Canaveral to provide astronomical coordinates and navigation data, which Thurber had requested from various observatories in preparation for the impending flight of Galactic II, the mercy ship that was to search space for the cause of Sunstrike.

During their conversation, Thurber asked Koenig in all seriousness, "I don't suppose that you've made any other observations of dangerous radioactive clouds, have you Furth?"

Koenig was stumped.

"What clouds, Maity?" he asked. "Are you pulling my leg?"

Although he'd given the original letter to Simms, Thurber had a photostat in his files. His secretary retrieved it and Thurber read the letter to Koenig, who listened with utter disbelief to the language.

"Maity, old boy," Dr. Koenig finally almost roared, "you've been had. I never sent you that letter. There's no such thing as a gaseous radioactive cloud between Earth and Mars. That's a crock . . ."

Immediately following the shock of learning that the letter he believed was written by Koenig was a phony, Thurber said goodbye and slammed the receiver down in palpable fury. He sucked in a deep breath and exhaled it noisily in a high state of exasperation. Then he grabbed the phone and asked his secretary to get the Justice Department.

"I want to speak to the Attorney General himself, Sam Dash."

Thurber's tone was solemn, as if the memory of that utterly astounding revelation that he'd been had was too much to bear. About three minutes went by and his secretary buzzed. The Attorney General was on the line.

"Sam this is an urgent request . . ."

Thurber's voice was so tremulous that he

had to stop and take a deep breath again. After exhaling he was somewhat more in command of himself. He was now able to spell out his suspicions about the letter.

"The postmark on the envelope shows it was mailed January 16 from Tucson," Thurber said, twitting the envelope nervously between his right thumb and forefinger. "That was a Saturday. But I remember distinctly when I received it. It was the following Tuesday in the morning mail."

"Why do you remember that so well?" Dash interrupted, his curiosity aroused by the space boss's exceptional recollection of when he got the letter.

"Because," Thurber said quickly in a reassuring voice, "I went to dinner with Dr. Simms the next evening, Wednesday, the twentieth, and I read the letter to him . . ."

Dash knew at once what sort of investigation had to be launched, but he was also anxious to learn whether Thurber had any particular area that he surmised should be probed more intensely or given greater priority than others.

"Yes, very much so," Thurber offered helpfully. "There's no question in my mind now that Dr. Simms was behind this plot. To what extent and for what reason I can't say. But it was his idea to equip Galactic I with a full response from the particle accelerator, that is, to have it operate on colloidal suspension. That was even before the counterfeit letter arrived and reported the danger of that nonexistent radioactive cloud."

"But where do you think I should have the FBI begin its probe, Maity?" asked Dash insistently. "There's got to be a beginning—last January, last October, when in your view did he act in ways that now seem suspicious to you?"

"Begin with January, the day he left Ravenna after putting those people in the experiment down in the mine . . ."

Thurber gasped all at once.

"Oh, my God," he rasped. "They're down in that mine in this remorseless weather. I must do something about that . . . I don't even know if their equipment is affected, if it is functioning."

The Attorney General cut Thurber short. He suggested that the twenty-four UCLA students and their doctor-nurse team overseers may very well be in far better shape than the rest of civilization on the surface of the earth. At least they had protection from the snow, ice, and intense cold. Moreover, Dash right now wanted more than anything a lead or two from Thurber in picking up Dr. Simms's trail after he deposited his human guinea pigs in the mine for Operation WAMIS.

"He flew to New York," Thurber said, looking his NASA key personnel diary for Simms's travel schedule after leaving Ravenna. "He should have arrived there sometime Monday night. He stayed at a motel called the Kings Grant in Plainview on Long Island."

Thurber then informed the Attorney General that Simms met Boyce McMorrow, the Grumman aerospace engineer the next day, Tuesday, January 19.

"They had lunch at a place called the Marcpierre," the NASA director said. "I know that to be a fact because just now as I'm talking to you, the voucher he submitted for that lunch—ninety-seven dollars and thirty cents—is staring me in the face. I just pulled it out of Simms's expense folder. Come to think of it, that's a hell of a lot of money for a lunch, isn't it?"

"Just a second, Maity," the Attorney General cut in, "I'm not going to have the FBI investigate what the Marcpierre charges for lunch . . . I'm only concerned in Simms's itinerary. Believe me I don't care what he ate or what he paid for lunch."

Thurber deviated because he was stuck and stalling to come up with an answer. The mystery very clearly thickened now, for Thurber had no rundown on Simms's movements until the next day when he flew to Florida and met the space chief for dinner in the Ramada Inn.

"I'm totally in the dark about where he went or what he did after lunching with McMorrow," Thurber confessed straightforwardly. "All I can really add is that he ate dinner at the motel that Tuesday night and had breakfast on Wednesday morning, both at the motel . . . Oh, yes he spent ten dollars for cab fare from the airport to the motel, then he also rented a Hertz car. It was delivered to him at the Kings Grant and he turned it in at the airport, Republic Airport in Farmingdale, before flying down to Florida."

That was all that Sam Dash wanted to hear.

"Stay cool, Maity," the Attorney General offered comfortingly. "I'm going to put the FBI on this right away. Chances are you'll be contacted by agents. But I wanted this information first-hand from you so I could put the Bureau on it without delay."

Bryan Dudley, who was in charge of the FBI office in Babylon, put three agents on the case. Although the snow had stopped falling, the roads were virtually impassable. So Dudley had the G-men conduct their preliminary investigation by phone of Dr. Simms's unaccounted nearly twenty-four hours on Long Island.

The inquiry brought some fast facts into the fold but added nothing to the tapestry of the professor's movements during his day-and-a-half sojourn on Long Island.

Hertz's office in Jericho Turnpike in Huntington Station revealed that the car Simms rented was driven a total of twenty-seven miles from the time it was brought to the motel until it was turned in at the airport.

Based on information relayed from the Justice Department—that Simms had lunch at the Marcpierre with Boyce McMorrow—the G-men hit Rand-McNally's Nassau-Suffolk County map and calculated the precise distance between the motel and restaurant was 6.5 miles.

"He drove there and drove back," Dudley said to the other agents, so make that thirteen miles even."

One of the G-men had already spoken with McMorrow on the phone. In that conversation the engineer explained that while he didn't see Simms arrive in the car at the restaurant, he had to assume the professor had driven to Marcpierre.

"I say that only because when we left the place, he went to a car and drove away," McMorrow told the FBI agent who phoned him at his Huntington Hills home where he was snowbound for the past six days. "I must believe he had also driven the car to the Marcpierre."

McMorrow, however, was unable to provide any further information about Simms's activities. He only saw him during lunch and had no idea what the professor's itinerary was for the rest of his stay at the motor inn in Plainview.

"That leaves fourteen miles unaccounted," Dudley continued as he measured the distance now from the motel to Route 110 along the Long Island Expressway, then south to Republic Airport.

"That's four miles on the expressway and five more on one-ten, for a total of nine miles. We know he drove from the hotel to the airport in that 1988 hatchback Ford Airflow because he paid the ninety-six-dollar rental with his American Express Card at Republic. So nine miles and the thirteen we know he drove between the restaurant and the motel makes it twenty-two miles. Now where are those five missing miles?"

Questioning the clerks on duty Tuesday, January 19, and Wednesday, January 20, when Simms checked in and checked out of the motel elicited no recollection of the professor. Obviously the motel staff was too absorbed in the Alice Crimmins movie being filmed there to pay close attention to guests on those days.

No one at the Kings Grant even recalled the man who took the rental car, since it was only a paper transaction that required only moments for Simms's show of identification and to sign the forms.

The same response came from the airport, where payment for the use of the car was a fast credit card transaction, as was the ticket purchase for Eastern Airlines Flight 456 to Titusville.

Within an hour, however, the FBI in Babylon had two seemingly direct leads on Dr. Simms's apparent detours on Long Island, ostensibly from the time he left the Marcpierre and Boyce McMorrow's company and his arrival at the airport early the next afternoon—a period of approximately twenty-three hours.

Actually, however, Dudley and his fellow agents very quickly and logically had eliminated seventeen and-a-half hours and narrowed the time span for wherever those five unexplained extra miles had been driven to a mere four and-a-half hours.

"It doesn't seem likely he went to either of

these banks after he left McMorrow at the restaurant," Dudley concluded as he studied the scribbling of figures and information on a scratch pad. "McMorrow told me they broke up around two-thirty P.M. Both the Chase-Manhattan and Chemical Bank close weekdays at three P.M., except that back then before Sunstrike the Chemical also had drive-in banking hours until four-thirty P.M. But we're not concerned with that because whatever transactions Simms negotiated at either bank was inside the office. These checks paid for something—but what? It's strange as hell that he would issue checks at both banks for identical amounts."

Dudley reached those conclusions and the final one, which he'd soon spell out, after a phone call from the Los Angeles office of the FBI. One of the first steps taken by the Bureau in Washington after assigning the case to the Babylon branch was transmitting teletype requests to all FBI offices in the locales where Simms was known to have been in the past year or so, requesting every bit of information dug up about him.

One of the first areas the G-men on the Coast checked was Simms's banking habits. They found, among other activity, that he had a personal checking account at the Bank of America branch in the Century City section of Los Angeles. The checking account interested the G-men the most, for when they looked into it, the microfilm record of Simms's most recent transactions before he flew off into space on January 26 showed very telling activity.

That quickly narrowed the search considerably since the FBI was really interested only in what Simms had done on Long Island during January 19 and 20, when his movements couldn't be accounted for in totality by Maitland Thurber or anyone else up to now.

Of course, what came out of the bank microfilm records were the two canceled checks for twenty-four dollars each, which Simms had issued the morning of Wednesday, January 20, first at the Melville branch of the Chase-Manhattan bank to rent the safe deposit box which he didn't use, then for the safe deposit box in which he deposited the eighteen-page memo at the Chemical Bank on Broad Hollow Road, which, most significantly in the rapidly moving events of this period, it should be pointed out, was situated directly across the street from the Melville Sunoco station that was serving as an emergency food depot in the Sunstrike crisis.

The information about the issuance of those two checks by Simms was immediately transmitted by the Los Angeles Bureau to the agents in Babylon. And it was the dates written on both checks—January 20—that told Dudley and the other agents that it was most unlikely Simms had conducted his mysterious transactions at those two nearby banks in that half hour of Tuesday, January 29—from the time he left McMorrow and the time those banks closed at 3 P.M.

That left Wednesday morning to be checked out for whatever business Simms had conducted at the Chase-Manhattan and Chemical branches. If the information from Los Angeles had done anything, it certainly narrowed the time factor to a reasonable certainty about when Simms traveled those heretofore-unexplained five miles in the Hertz car. He had to have put on that mileage on the odometer before he flew off to Florida on Wednesday, January 20.

Dudley and the other agents reached that conclusion confident that they weren't an inch off course in their calculations. For when they measured the distance over the roads from the Kings Grant Motor Inn to the Chase-Manhattan branch, then to the Chemical Bank, and finally to the airport—their computations justified the unaccounted five miles almost to the last foot.

Now that the G-men had solved the mystery of *where* Dr. Simms had been, they resolved to learn *why* he'd been to the two banks.

The call to the Chase-Manhattan branch was answered with a recorded announcement:

"Under President Mondale's national emergency orders, the Chase-Manhattan bank has closed all its branches and suspended all business for the duration of the crisis caused by Sunstrike. We hope this situation does not inconvenience you . . ."

"Damn it!" exclaimed Dudley as he hung up without waiting to hear the rest of the message. "Now what do we do?"

When he dialed the Chemical, a recorded message again informed him that this bank also was adhering to Mondale's emergency order closing down all unecessary business. The President had decreed that among such businesses were all those involved in finance, ranging from the stock market to trading in commodities, gold, futures, and banking as well. Thus they suspended all activity until further notice.

"That really queers it," Dudley said disgustedly and slammed the phone into the cradle. He turned to the other agents.

"It looks as though we've got to find some of the people who work in those banks so we can get somebody to open up for us," Dudley said sharply. "You guys hit the reverse directories and get people in the area who can get us some leads."

And it was just minutes after Dudley had issued those instructions to the other G-men that the call from John Spanacopito came through . . .

Spanacopito didn't bandy words about. He was extremely brief. He related what his wife had told him, and was about to put Mrs. Spanacopito on the phone when Dudley cut him off.

"Don't explain any further, Mr. Spanacopito," Dudley almost gasped in excitement. "Just give me your phone number and, most importantly, your address. We're going to come over to see your wife."

Spanacopito provided the G-man the phone

number and address, which was on East Lyon Street in Melville, less than a mile from the bank. Then . . .

"By the way, may I speak to your wife for a second, please?"

Mrs. Spanacopito came on the line.

"Do you have a key to the bank, ma'am?" Dudley wanted to know.

"No, I don't," Mrs. Spanacopito answered. "The person who can help on that account is the manager, Tony Poosty."

She then gave the FBI agent Poosty's home phone number.

"Thank you, ma'am," said Dudley. "We'll be over to your home as soon as we can. Within the hour hopefully. You must know what it's like trying to get about out there."

"I certainly do," Mrs. Spanacopito chuckled. "You'll find me right here. I won't be going anywhere."

The call to Poosty, who lived in the Deer Park section, some eight miles from the bank, introduced Dudley to a man whose mood and temperament were just as nasty and obnoxious as everyone who worked with him already knew them to be.

"I can't go out in this weather," Poosty snapped on the phone. "Besides, if you want to open the bank you'll have to talk to the main office downtown. I have no authorization to open the bank. You know what the President's emergency order is—you of all people should know. I hope you're not suggesting that I do something illegal, are you?"

Dudley slammed the receiver down without responding.

"That guy's a real S.O.B.," Dudley almost screamed. "He then turned to the other agents. "Let's go and see Mrs. What's Her Name."

"Better dress very warmly, Mrs. Spanacopito," Dudley said through chattering teeth as he and Agent Terrence O'Donnell warmed their hands over the gas burner of the kitchen stove. "We nearly froze getting here on the snowmobile."

Mrs. Spanacopito slipped into her fur parka, pulled a warm knitted wool ski cap-mask over her head and face, and shoved her hands into her ample lambswool-lined leather mittens.

"I'm ready," she said in an eager but apologetic tone. "I only hope I haven't started you people on a wild goose chase. I want you to know that I didn't see what, if anything, he put into the safe deposit box."

"But we know it was something," O'Donnell said to Mrs. Spanacopito, who had provided the phone number of Anita Tersey, the guardian of the vault who supplied Dr. Simms with the keys and safe deposit box he rented. Mrs. Tersey had almost total recall of that transaction when she spoke on the phone to Agent O'Donnell.

"I remember it distinctly only because that person . . . I don't remember his name nor his face, but I know the day . . . it was the only rental transaction that I had handled the first two months of the year. But I especially recall that when I tipped the box something inside shifted. I remember that only because I had told myself that the thing the man put in for safekeeping for the first time with us seemed compact and solid, like a packet of money or some tightly folded papers . . . nothing loose like so many people put in those boxes. When you've handled as many safe deposit boxes as I have, you almost have a feel of what people are putting in and taking out of them."

Meanwhile, Agents George Farnsworth and Elmer Weiss had gone on their snowmobile directly to the Chemical Bank branch on Broad Hollow Road to scout the place. They found the snow drifts had reached over the terraced entrance, which was well above street level. Although access to the main lobby entrance of the building was partially blocked, they quickly determined there'd be no problem getting into the bank itself.

One of the several huge plate glass floor-to-ceiling windows on the street side of the building had been blown out by the cyclonic winds, which had raked New York City and its environes the other day, and the opening had been boarded up temporarily with plywood. That'd be no problem ripping away so the G-men could get into the bank.

Although they'd brought the required tools to break open the Mosler safe lock on Dr. Simms's box, they didn't have anything to pry the plywood board loose. But they quickly hit upon a solution. The Melville Sunoco station across the street had hammers and a crowbar. And they were borrowed.

As soon as Dudley and O'Donnell came cruising over the hard-packed snow on their snowmobile with Mrs. Spanacopito, the board was ripped away.

The agents and Mrs. Spanacopito scampered into the bank and descended the stairs to the lower level. The barred safe deposit vault door was locked but Mrs. Spanacopito obtained the key and opened it. She then looked hastily through the card file and came up with Dr. Simms's registration for H000423. But, of course, Simms had both keys and it was impossible to open the customer's lock.

But that proved no problem after Mrs. Spanacopito opened the bank lock with the master key. The G-men were prepared to handle the second lock.

Farnsworth went to a nearby outlet and plugged the electric cord attached to his drill fitted with a half-inch diamond bit. Then he placed the point of the bit against the customer's lock—and began drilling.

Some six minutes later he pulled the drill out of the hole. He had bored through. Weiss moved in with a viselike device. He inserted a shaft into the hole drilled in the lock, then applied pressure on a lever until the small door protecting Dr. Simms safe deposit box snapped open.

Farnsworth reached in, pulled out the box, and handed it to Dudley who quickly lifted the lid. He pulled out the eighteen-page memorandum that Simms had penned to himself on yellow legal size paper. It was folded over three times, making the compact packet that Anita Tersey had described so accurately.

Dudley began reading the memo. Before his eyes had traveled even a third of the way down the first sheet, he gasped.

"This is incredible!" he exclaimed aghast.

By the time he had reached the bottom portion of the first page, he was compelled to scream, "The man's crazy! He's doing all this . . . Simms is causing the eclipse and the cold."

Very quickly now he thumbed through the memorandum, which was actually described by Simms at the very beginning as a guide for himself, a reference work of sorts that would come in handy when he wrote his memoirs.

As Dudley read through the pages with ever-increasing disbelief and astonishment, the other agents and Mrs. Spanacopito stole occasional glimpses over his shoulder at the writing, especially those several times when Dudley gasped at some particularly startling passages that he came across.

One thing was eminently clear by now. And Dudley expressed it accurately when he reached the last page and then hurriedly went for the phone to dial the FBI headquarters in Washington.

"This document," he said, "is a confession of how the eclipse is being caused and what is causing it. Dr. Simms is behind the whole thing. He wants to conquer the world."

His words drifted off as he tried to catch his breath from the excitement that gripped him while waiting for the call to go through.

"He wants," continued Dudley, "to kill us all off . . ."

CHAPTER XXIII

Confession: Plan for World Conquest

Although Agent Dudley had been instructed to report directly to FBI Director Ellen Fleysher if he made a breakthrough probing Dr. Simms's activities on Long Island, that order was easier issued than carried out. Dudley found that even the terrible crisis of Sunstrike had not breached the insufferable red tape of bureaucratic government agencies. He was compelled to go from one level of Bureau officaldom to the next higher one. Only after some fifteen precious minutes was he able to reach the top.

Miss Fleysher was the first woman to head the FBI in its long and distinguished history. By now the scandals of the 1970s brought on by Watergate and charges of illegal break-ins on the Weathermen and other terrorist groups had finally blown away. Largely the credit for restoring confidence in the Bureau belonged to Director Fleysher, who had introduced a multitude of innovative changes, which generated a new high level of efficiency and credibility in the methods the G-men employed now in their investigations.

No sooner had Miss Fleysher heard what agent Dudley had discovered than she signaled her secretary to switch the call to Sam Dash's office.

"You must tell the Attorney General about the confession," the FBI chief said quickly.

Dash listened for a brief few moments. Alerted ahead of time about the nature of the call, the Attorney General had already phoned the White House, and President Mondale was standing by to speak with Dudley.

"I'm switching you to the Oval Office," Dash said. "The President is waiting to hear about the confession."

In a moment the call was transferred and Mondale was on the line.

"Mr. Dudley," the President said in a voice edged with excitement. "Please read the confession to me. I will be recording this conversation."

Although classified immediately as top-secret and invoking absolute prohibition against disclosing any portion of the confession to the public, the presidential ban didn't remain in force for even a day.

The very next morning, *Newsday*, the Long Island newspaper, went into Federal Court in Brooklyn's Eastern District and made an application to lift the presidential directive for secrecy.

Newsday's executive editor-in-chief, Manny

Topol, himself presented the arguments for his newspaper.

"Your honor," he addressed himself to Federal Judge Stephen P. Scaring, "under the Public Disclosure Law the President does not have a right to withhold the contents of Dr. Simms's confession. We demand that this court issue an order releasing the entire text to the media."

U. S. Attorney Marvin I. Bernstein opposed the motion strenuously. "Judge," the prosecutor argued, "under Friedgood vs. Sutter, there is precedent to deny plaintiff's application. I cite the United States Supreme Court ruling by Joe—I beg your pardon, I mean by His Honor—Mr. Justice Joseph Suozzi . . ."

All at once the silence in the packed courtroom was cracked. A door in the back opened and Assistant U. S. Attorney Barry Grennan hurried into the courtroom and stormed down the aisle with quick, urgent steps. In his hand he was clutching a newspaper. He went directly to the counsel table and laid the newspaper down in front of Bernstein, who then leaped to his feet shaking his head in obvious dismay.

"Judge," he said disconsolately. "This whole preceeding has been a waste of the court's time. While Mr. Topol was here lulling us with arguments about why Dr. Simms's confession should be released, his newspaper has already hit the street not only with the verbatim confession, but with a photostatic reproduction of the whole original document!

Indeed, *Newsday* had the confession. The whole confession, all eighteen pages of it!

How the newspaper obtained it was never revealed. But here is exactly how the confession appeared in the Thursday, July 14, 1988, edition of *Newsday*:

I am preparing this while seated at the desk in my room at the Kings Grant Motor Inn.

7:30 P.M., Tuesday, January 19, 1988

This memo is written to myself and I have placed it in this safe deposit box for my own guidance and reference for the time when I write my memoirs.

I have undertaken to rewrite world history completely by blotting out the sun and destroying the maddening civilizations that have ruined this no-longer beautiful earth.

I intend to start a new human race on earth with my hardy band of survivors who are in the Ravenna mine.

Here now is my plan to conquer and rule the world by freezing it until all life, except those twenty-six people in Kentucky, is extinct:

As my calculations tell me, vegetation will wither, too. But it will not die, for the period I require to effect my mission will be relatively short—no longer than six months, or merely the length of a fall and winter's sleep, which plant life and flora routinely go through with the change of seasons. But human life will not survive, for the total freeze will paralyze civilization completely. Man will not be able to maintain heat during this artifically created ice age, for the snows and bitter freeze will immobilize and render useless all transportation and power generating facilities.

No one will survive beyond the fourth month of darkness, because by then the last stores of energy and foodstuffs, like all life itself, will have frozen in the 200-below zero temperatures.

I plan to achieve these ends by *blotting out the sun*!

Not until two and a half years ago was the idea born in my mind. At that time, I had occasion to have access to the Galactic I plans and design specifications.

At the same time I became aware of the particle accelerator that was being installed on this new spaceship. I thought it was a remarkable machine, for to create a vacuum that will sustain an atmosphere on an airless planet in space is indeed a tremendous advance.

But the particle accelerator's ability to produce colloidal suspension and spin an infinite amount of plastic in space was, to me, a far more intriguing aspect.

It was that awareness that started the wheels in my mind spinning. At first the thought of blotting out the sun was merely a momentary, passing illusion. Then as the idea of turning off all sunlight on earth reoccurred, it fascinated me increasingly.

The decision to carry out my plan was reached when I realized how utterly simple it would be for me to take off in the Galactic I

337

and achieve this fantastic scheme to take over the world.

Only one setback occurred during the preparations—Boyce McMorrow had not provided the instruction booklet for the operation of the collodial suspension phase of the particle accelerator. That was why I made such a fuss with Thurber. My argument about the need to protect the crew in Operation Mars from the dangers of radiation won out—fortunately.

And with McMorrow providing those instructions, coupled with the first-hand information he provided today at lunch, the stage for my plan to take over the earth was set.

Only one possible flaw can surface in my plan. No one, not even McMorrow, knows for certain that the particle accelerator will manufacture plastic in the vacuum of space. The only way to determine whether it will is to test the machine in space.

That means taking the Galactic I on such a test run. But no preliminary flight is contemplated for the ship, because it has been put through its shakedown flights and passed them with flying colors.

Thurber will never consent to a test flight just to check out the particle accelerator. I had enough difficulty convincing him of the need to obtain the colloidal suspension instruction booklet.

Right now I'm still not certain that we'll take the Galactic I on such a preliminary flight. It will all depend on my daring ruse—

the letter I sent Thurber, under Dr. Furth Koenig's name, from the Kitt Peak National Observatory.

If Thurber bites the lure—that a dangerous radioactive cloud has been discovered near Mars—then the chances of taking Galactic up for the test flight will be greatly enhanced. It will be up to me then to convince him of that necessity.

On the other hand, there's that possibility that Thurber's curiosity may drive him to question the laboratory further about that peril. Of course, he won't be able to speak to Koenig directly because his schedule has taken him to the International Convention of Astronomers for the balance of this month.

If Thurber discovers the fraud, he will probably conclude it was some practical joker. He'll never know who wrote the letter. Certainly, he'll never suspect it is I—since I didn't write it.

But even if Galactic I doesn't go for a test flight for colloidal suspension, I'll still make off into space to carry out my wonderful plan to blot out the sun. . . .

Now for the details of how I plan to execute the takeover:

There are certain incontrovertible scientific measurements that I must deal with.

First, the earth's diameter is 7,918 miles. Merely to cast a shadow over that area—to completely blot out the sun—is not so monumental a task.

But there are other factors. The moon,

whose diameter is only 2,159.9 miles, must also be blotted out—otherwise my scheme will be immediately detected. The sun, everyone will know, is not blotted out if the moon is shining.

Now the big problem is not only blotting the sun from the earth and moon—but the space between them. That's a distance of 252,710 miles at the moon's maximum distance from earth.

Thus the total miles to be covered are:

$$
\begin{array}{r}
7,918.0 \\
2,159.9 \\
255,710.0 \\
\hline
262,787.9
\end{array}
$$

The very widest total shadow or penumbra cast by the moon during an eclipse is only 167 miles. That is when the moon is at its minimum distance from earth—221,463 miles.

Therefore, to cast a total eclipse, or a penumbra, over the entire diameter of earth, moon, and distance between them, I must employ this formula:

$$
\frac{2,1599.9}{167} \div \frac{X}{262,787.9}
$$

2,1599.9 ÷ 167, X = 13, × 262,787.9 = 3,416,231 miles at minimum orbit of the moon.

To double the distance—which I feel is absolutely necessary so as to prevent any possibility of the sun's corona showing during the blackout—I must double the size of the plastic screen. Also I must place the screen far enough away from the moon so no observation of the

340

screen can be made from the space laboratories in lunar orbit.

$$3,416,231 \times 2 = 6,832,462$$

That will be the size of my plastic screen, 6,832,462 miles square at 442,926 miles from earth.

To work with round numbers, I am going to place the size of my screen at 3,500,000 miles square.

To spin the screen in the framework I have set up to create the freezeover of earth, I must exceed the limits set for top speed on Galactic I by a considerable rate.

It will be necessary to achieve a speed of 1,862 miles per second, or 1/100th the speed of light (186,282 miles per second or the theoretical top flying speed of the Aere Perrenius).

My speed for the flight translates to 6,706,-150 m.p.h., a seemingly incomprehensible rate. Yet, as I've already noted, it is only 1/100th the maximum capability of the engine, which is 670,615,200 m.p.h., or the speed of light.

I calculate such speed is perfectly safe and will not invite even the remotest likelihood of an encounter with the possibility of experiencing any of Einstein's theories about time going backwards, etc.

By flying at 1/100th of the speed of light— 6,706,152—I will criss-cross a section of the solar system in the approximate region of Venus's orbital path. I will build up the screen on a plane not observable to Earth:

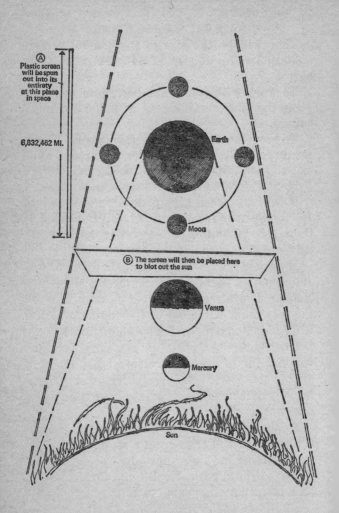

A Plastic screen will be spun out into its entirety at this plane in space

6,832,462 Mi.

Earth

Moon

B The screen will then be placed here to blot out the sun

Venus

Mercury

Sun

My timetable will be set to function within these parameters:

A. First pass to form screen will be executed twenty-four hours after I have blasted off from Cape Canaveral.

B. First length of screen will be 3,500,000 miles $\times$ 1,000 miles. It will take thirty-one minutes, twenty seconds to spin.

C. I must then allow approximately fifteen minutes to slow the ship, make a turn-around, and accelerate for the next pass. That totals to forty-six minutes plus for one complete run in producing the screen, 3,500,000 $\times$ 1,000 miles.

D. Since it will require 3,500 passes to complete the curtain of 3,500,000 miles, the duration of this project dictates other elements to be considered.

E. I must have time to eat and to sleep. Therefore, I shall add fourteen minutes to every forty-six minutes for a complete pass for those purposes.

F. Now, then, the screen will be spun in 3,500 hours or about 146 days.

G. I must also allow four more days to tow the screen into place 500,000 miles from earth—and set it into the precise corresponding orbit as earth's around the sun.

When all these steps have been completed, the penumbra, or total shadow, will be cast on the earth, moon, and all space between these bodies. I will maintain this posture for the next six months, which is the time I have estimated is required to completely freeze the earth and its life. When I finally remove the curtain and return to earth, I intend to drag the plastic screen with me. I will ship the screen in an orbital path around the earth—this will set the screen afire as it reenters the atmosphere.

I calculate that the heat from the fire of more than twelve quadrillion square feet (12,250,000,000,000 to be exact) will cause an immediate heat wave, which will greatly facilitate in warming up the earth, now bathed in the welcome warm rays of the sun.

The great thaw will be stepped up and the devastating ice and snow will begin to melt.

I will then proceed to release my guinea pigs from their lair. They will no longer be guinea pigs but the nucleus of the new civilization I have planned.

I will start life anew on earth in my own image or mold, as God had done. When I release my people from their underground cave, I will not bare the truth to them. I will hoke them with a story that I alone survived the great cataclysm on earth because of my inordinate knowledge and ability in coping with the forces that took all the other lives.

I will be their hero—and leader.

I shall proceed to set up my own government in Washington and begin the world anew with a fresh civilization.

It is my intention to take measures to protect my small band of survivors against the ravages of pestilence and disease certain to threaten the world as six billion human bodies and several trillion animal bodies begin decomposing.

I will keep my people in the mine for several months, sustaining on their food supplies. From time to time they'll emerge to plant crops on nearby farmlands with seeds in plentiful supply in farmers storebins, which were not damaged by the devastating freeze.

What bodies in this desolate area may be lying about will be buried and the threat of disease will be eliminated from our immediate environment.

In a short time decomposition of human and animal remains will be completed and the bodies and carcasses that once roamed the earth will have been reduced to skeletons.

With the threat of disease ended, I will bring my survivors out of the mine and start my new world.

Of course, it will be a totally vegetarian society in the beginning—except for meats, poultry, and fish in cans in warehouses around the world.

But animal life will come back. For through the temporary ice age, I am certain that many hardy creatures inhabiting the frozen northern regions—bears and other such denizens—will have survived.

These will be the font of the new civilization's early supply of the fresh meat. And since the earth's population will be minuscule for generations to come, the propagation ratio of these animals will certainly exceed the food demands of earth's few early inhabitants.

Children born to the survivors will be entitled to all the riches abounding on the world's undamaged face. All lore will be found in libraries and in the teachings of their parents and those others who instruct them; the villages and towns and cities, and all their structures and institutions, yes, even the skyscrapers of New York, Chicago, and everywhere else will belong to my people—and me.

As the new society grows, I will send groups of offspring to begin new enclaves of civilization, in the once-teeming communities of the United States and later, as the order grows still larger, the entire world.

They will start modestly at first, but as the population increases, activity will heighten. In a hundred years, perhaps, New York, for example, will be coming back to life with its business and commerce, theaters and restaurants, libraries and museums. But it will be far from the frenetic and fantastically overpopulated city it is today.

It will be a new world, a much better world, and it will all belong to me.

Now to get some sleep, get up in the morning, and put this document in a safe deposit box for what will one day be my complete diary of how the world was reshaped by me.

—GORDON LYLE SIMMS
finished this writing at 11:35 P.M.,
Tuesday, Jan. 19, 1988

11:10 A.M., Wednesday, January 20, 1988

Although I first rented a safe deposit box at the Chase Bank, I did not use it. It was on street level and I was afraid that when the thaws come, the flood waters would destroy the vault and this document. Here at the Chemical, the high rise of the first floor makes it quite safe.

CHAPTER XXIV

Seek and Destroy at All Cost!

The afternoon of that Wednesday, July 13, 1988, was unequivocally the most brutal for the world since the advent of total darkness. Storms raged over the seven continents and most of the other parts of the world, the islands, peninsulas, and smaller land masses such as Greenland and Iceland.

No part of the globe seemed immune from the savage snowstorms, hammering winds, and numbing freeze. For the first time known to man, who had not begun recording temperatures until the thermometer was brought into being in 1654 by the Grand Duke Ferdinand II of Tuscany, the mercury dipped to minus 100 degrees on that twentieth day of Sunstrike.

But that wasn't the bottom line of the scale, for the earth faced a drop of another 173 degrees to that absolute zero of space—minus 273 degrees—in just another ten dreadful days.

And then the helpless planet would enter a phase of its existence from which there could

349

be no hope of survival for any human, beast, fish, or plant life.

But the discovery of Dr. Simms's confession in the safe deposit box changed that ill-boding outlook suddenly and dramatically. Incredibly, the answer to the mystery of what was causing Sunstrike came on the very eve when Galactic II was scheduled to fly into space and seek that very same answer.

Now the answer had been provided by Dr. Gordon Lyle Simms's written confession. He had spun a plastic screen 6,832,462 miles square and drawn it across the sun's path at a distance of 442,962 miles from earth, merely twice the distance to the moon.

At the very time that G-man Dudley and his team of FBI operatives had followed Mrs. Spanacopito into the bank, broken open the safe deposit box, and found Dr. Simms's confession, the team of space fliers scheduled to guide the ill-fated Galactic I on its journey to Mars were checking out the controls and navigational equipment of Galactic II in El Segundo on the outskirts of Los Angeles.

They were already in the countdown phase and were readying the spaceship for blastoff at 9:15 A.M. of Friday, July 15. Their course in space was uncharted. How could the journey have been mapped? No one knew what was causing the eclipse and certainly no one had any idea of where to look for it.

If you're wondering why Galactic II was in El Segundo and not at Cape Canaveral for the takeoff into space, the answer is quite simple.

There was no way to transport Galactic II across the deep frozen snowdrifts and treacherous ice floes marring the land and sea routes to Florida. Thus, the decision was reached that, despite the dedicated efforts of the groundskeepers who kept Canaveral's runway open for the flight of Galactic II, the ship would have to take off from California.

But how could this gigantic spacecraft lift itself into space where there wasn't a 25,000-foot concrete runway? Indeed no runway at all under those more than ninety inches of frozen snow.

That detail was ultimately attended to by the State Highway Department and Los Angeles County's road gangs. They joined forces, manned bulldozers, plows, and graders and cut a level surface on those ninety-plus inches of hard-packed snow that had fallen on the Los Angeles area the past three weeks.

In the end they had prepared a 25,000-foot stretch of snow-covered ground into a substitute runway for Galactic II's takeoff.

The grading work was completed by 5 A.M. of that Friday, July 15, just a shade more than four hours before the blastoff. The makeshift strip was examined by Maitland Thurber and other NASA officials and engineers who'd flown to El Segundo to supervise the last-minute details for the takeoff.

Thurber then faced a massive assemblage of newsmen who had managed to reach the site under the most trying travel conditions. But this was an event of unheard of dimension. It was, as Thurber put it for want of a more original phrase, "the moment of truth."

As he stood before the reporters to explain what was about to happen, a speaker in the background attached to a makeshift control tower outside Rockwell's administration offices, blared, "The time now is seven forty-five A.M. . . . ninety minutes to blastoff and counting . . ."

Thurber instinctively checked his watch.

"I don't believe I have to stress too emphatically how important this takeoff is . . ."

He let the words fade away momentarily to prepare everyone for the point he was about to make.

The reporters were bundled in their heavy storm gear and although the temperature now was a shivering minus 100 degrees, few of the journalists seemed bothered to any great extent by the intense cold. They didn't have to be told what Thurber was about to say to them, because they were well aware of the absolute and finite extremities of this flight.

In all respects, it was the most important mission any four members of the human race had ever embarked on.

For all the world now looked to Captain Randolph Stuart, and Lieutenants Rigby Deems and Frank Perlman, and Commander Phoebe Swedlow as the earth's saviors.

There could be no room for error and yet, dammit, none of the multitudinous steps required for a launch had been taken.

Virtually every rule in the countdown

procedure that NASA had formulated through experience and trial and error over its long and illustrious history had been broken in the haste to put Galactic II on the runway on this momentous day in the history of the earth.

"We know this is a monumental gamble, putting this spaceship on the runway for a launch this morning," Thurber said to the reporters. "Galactic II has just been rolled off the assembly line. It has not undergone the extensive shakedown that all space vehicles are submitted to nor, most importantly, has it been flight-tested. Yet, as all of you certainly know, there's no time for any of those preliminaries, vital as they may be. Time is extremely short. We must launch immediately."

Thurber looked at this watch.

"It's a mere . . ."

Just as he was about to utter the time that was left for the takeoff, the loudspeaker interrupted with, "It is nine-oh-five A.M. . . . there are five minutes to launch."

Thurber shrugged and threw up his hands as though he were resigned to the time announcements on the loudspeaker instead of having to rely on his own timepiece. He churned up a few chuckles among the reporters with his gesture, but not many newsmen appeared receptive to frivolity. The situation was deadly serious.

And Thurber was quick now to make that point as time for launch rapidly approached.

"If I were to tell you that the fate of our earth is going to be decided in less than ten minutes, I am quite confident that I'll not get any argument from anyone. You ladies and gentlemen of the press know this ship *must*, I repeat, *must* take off if we are to survive."

Once more he was interrupted by the loudspeaker.

"Attention, please," the voice droned. "This is the final countdown. One minute to launch . . ."

Then, "Ten seconds and counting, nine, eight, seven, six . . ."

And with the sound of "one" there was a fearsome roar of the Galactic II's Aere Perennius atomic engine and a fiery sheet of flame shot from its jets. The spaceship surged forward and all at once the reporters and NASA officials watching the launch gasped in horror.

The wheels suddenly began to slide over the ice. While there was no power driving the wheels, the inordinate high rate of acceleration had caused a centrifugal force reaction—a tendency as in the immutable laws of force and motion enunciated by Sir Isaac Newton, to spin away from a circular path and seek to pursue the attraction of gravity.

But just as the ship began to slide, just as quickly Captain Stuart sensed the problem, let up on the power momentarily, and the wheels ran their true straightline course once more. The ship continued moving forward with ever-increasing speed.

It passed the 10,000-foot mark doing every bit of 300 mph and by the time it had coursed midway along the packed-snow runway the craft was doing 550 mph. Then in another ten seconds it had traversed the full length of the 25,000-foot runway—and by then the wheels were off the ground.

Galactic II was airborne!

Its takeoff was a success!

In the darkness of the eclipse, in the utter blackness of Sunstrike, Galactic II disappeared from view the instant it had lifted off the runway. Although exterior lights were ablaze on the ship, these remained visible to the ground observers for a mere few seconds. For the craft was out of sight almost immediately, so swift was its ascent into the heavens.

And thank heaven for that . . .

"Galactic II to mission control . . . Galactic II calling Rockwell tower . . ."

"Come in, Galactic II."

"We have fantastic news . . . we are in contact with the sun . . . repeat, we are in contact with the sun. It looks terrific! It is still shining brightly as ever . . . and we shall soon have it smiling down on you all again!"

"Have you spotted the interference? . . . Please acknowledge . . ."

"Interference is dead ahead. We have also sighted Galactic I . . . but, hold on!"

Astronette Swedlow's voice suddenly choked.

"What is wrong? . . . what is wrong? Acknowledge please . . . what is wrong?"

Phoebe was too overcome—as were the others aboard Galactic II—to be able to describe immediately the incredible turn in the cosmic heaven. Simms apparently had spotted the spaceship from earth approaching and panicked. His vessel had been parked at the edge of the multimillion-square-mile black plastic screen, which had blotted out the sun from the earth and moon and was traversing in an orbit coinciding precisely with that of earth's around the sun.

But then all at once his ship broke from its seemingly stationary stance and rocketed away from approaching Galactic II.

Lieutenant Perlman, the navigator aboard the rescue craft, was the first to spot it, and he screamed an alert to the others in the control cabin.

"He's seen us . . . he's fleeing!"

Suddenly the crew of Galactic II was stunned by the voice that came over their receiver. But their astonishment was no less than that of the people in mission control at Rockwell International's makeshift tower.

"Everyone listen to me . . . pay close attention . . . this is Dr. Simms."

"Come in, Dr. Simms, we are receiving you, sir," the radio operator at mission control said at once. "We are awaiting your message."

Even as his first words were spoken, Simms's spaceship had veered away from its fixed orbital position and was flying at what seemed to the observers aboard Galactic II as an incredible rate of speed.

"Slow down, Dr. Simms, slow down!" cried

356

Lieutenant Perlman. "You're heading into the gravitational pull of the sun. You cannot proceed on that course. It will destroy you, sir."

"Stop jabbering, damn you," Simms snarled back. "I know what I'm doing. This is the way I want it to go for me now. I had thought I could rule the earth but I know now that I have failed. Are you listening to me?"

"We are listening, Gordy . . ."

The voice was Maitland Thurber's.

"Is that you, Maity?"

"Yes it is, Gordy . . . what made you do all this?"

"Too many things wrong, too many . . . the world, it's gone crazy . . . I . . . I . . . Maity, listen, I wish I had the strength to tell you all the things that have been wrong with this earth of ours . . . too many things . . . no justice . . . no equality . . . too many rotten people, selfish . . . looking out for themselves . . . greedy, hungry, self-serving . . . prejudiced, no good people . . . those are the ones I wanted to get at . . . to do away with them, to make the world over into a decent, less-crowded, happy, and habitable planet for humanity."

"Gordy, you must come back . . . Gordy . . ."

But Dr. Gordon Lyle Simms's voice had faded away and was never to be heard from again. It could never be heard from again because the professor had turned the Aere Perennius engine up to nearly the speed of light and was heading at what was judged to be approximately 170,000 miles per second toward his inevitable destruction.

At the rate of speed Simms was traveling, it was estimated that his fate was sealed within the next eight and a half minutes, but most probably much sooner than that. For that speed would have taken him in that time to the boiling circular disk, where only the most elemental forms of matter could exist at the temperatures encountered even at the very surface—6,000 degrees Fahrenheit.

Since it happened to be a fact that all of the bits of matter, electrons, and protons that exist at the sun's center, where the temperature is believed to be 35,000,000 degrees, participate in a process of continual interchange of energy between radiation and motion of particles, one could assume that Dr. Simms and Galactic I had perhaps contributed the first additional rate of power gain to the sun's mechanical equilibrium and output of energy since the beginning of time.

The last word about Dr. Simms that was flashed from aboard the rescue spaceship was:

"Galactic II to mission control . . . Galactic II reporting that Dr. Simms and his ship have disappeared from sight in our optical equipment. He is obviously sailing into the sun for self-destruction. There is no way to save him."

"We receive you and acknowledge," mission, control crackled back. Then . . .

"Galactic II proceeding to primary mission. . . . We will remove plastic screen causing Sunstrike . . . please acknowledge . . ."

"No further instructions, Galactic II . . . please carry on . . ."

Aboard the Galactic II now the crew was mapping strategy for the most important mission ever undertaken by the human race.

"What do you think, Phoebe?" Captain Stuart asked. "Shall we just let the plastic sheet fly off into space after we remove it or should we bring it down into the atmosphere to burn and perform the warming function on earth, which Professor Simms expected it to do?"

Commander Swedlow was prepared with her response almost before Stuart had finished asking the question.

"Get rid of that terrible thing," she shouted. "Rip it away and let it float into space. Don't dare bring it back to earth. Let's get the sun to warm the globe. Get rid of that crazy plastic sheet . . . get rid of it."

Lieutenants Deems and Perlman concurred totally. And so Stuart maneuvered Galactic II into position and slowed the ship to a parking orbit at an edge of the plastic sheet. The crew then extended one of the ship's automatic mechanical service arms and took a solid grip upon a portion of the plastic.

"We have it . . . we have it!" exclaimed Rigby Deems. "Let's get going!"

With Galactic II's mechanical arm firmly clutching the forward edge of the black screen floating in the northeast sector of the universe as viewed from the earth, the plastic that had blotted out the sun was now being tugged from its fixed orbit.

"Accelerate . . . accelerate!" Deems shouted.

Stuart immediately called for more power, which increased the ship's speed to 50,000 mph. The direction of Galactic II's path now was the same one taken by Simms—toward the sun. The crew had decided to send the plastic sheet into the sun, too, so it would never be encountered in space as a navigational hazard or, inconceivable as it seemed, to return and perhaps circle the earth again, which might cause another eclipse, brief as that one might be.

"Success! . . . Success!" shouted Deems excitedly. "Look . . . at the earth!"

That old planet suddenly appeared in the distance as the moon might during a first-quarter phase—except that the shadow-causing the rapidly diminishing eclipse was not a curve but a straight line.

It was a very rapidly moving shadow. No moon went through its phases as swiftly as the shadow of the plastic was torn away from its place in space. The Eastern Hemisphere, the portion of the earth facing the sun, was lit up all at once in a most remarkable glow.

From Galactic II it was truly a blue marble in space now, for the solar system's only life-supporting planet had never before been seen so clearly. The three horrendous weeks of Sunstrike, a period without any evaporation and of epidemic snowstorms, had virtually exhausted the earth's cloud layers. Thus the earth looked to Galactic II's crew just as it might on a model of the globe sitting on a desk. That was how clear it was.

Light returned to earth now as quickly as it had left. New York, Chicago, Dallas, Los Angeles, San Francisco, Rio de Janeiro, Acapulco, Mexico City, São Paulo, and all other cities—as well as villages, towns, and hamlets—saw the sun again. Even in London, Paris, Madrid, and other Western European cities they viewed their first sunset in twenty-two days.

And as the world turned, Honolulu, Tokyo, Brisbane, New Delhi, Moscow, Warsaw, Cairo, Johannesburg, and all parts of the world that had not experienced this phenomenon when the Eastern Hemisphere had, were now bathed in it . . .

LIGHT! SUNLIGHT! Beautiful, fantastically welcome, glorious sunlight had all at once interrupted the twenty-two terrible days of darkness.

Sunstrike had ended!

Beautiful, fantastically welcome, glorious sunlight was back!

In the days and weeks ahead, the sun melted the snows and ice. The earth experienced a period of inordinate suffering brought on by cataclysmic floods.

Yet, throughout the world, the return of the sun's warm rays and the promise of the new life they augured was more than anyone had hoped for during that period of darkness and world-wide suffering.

Joy was universal—even for the twenty-six persons in Operation WAMIS who were left in the mine in Ravenna. When they were emancipated finally from their long bondage, they had no idea what had happened to the earth. They'd had no means to communicate with the outside world and thus remained unaffected in their isolated environment.

"I'm glad it ended this way," shrugged Sandra Sheiler. "I can't imagine Dr. Simms thinking that I was going to be part of his new world order. I am really such a very imperfect person. Here it is, more than six months after the Super Bowl and I still don't know who won between the Seattle Seahawks and the Tampa Bay Buccaneers. See, I don't know the score about anything . . ."

A lot of other people didn't seem to know the score either. The cataclysm of Sunstrike taught the world very few sets of new values. As things returned to normal, more and more of the same mistakes were being repeated.

CHAPTER XXV

Cheers—Jeers

The United States Army Band completed its rendition of "America the Beautiful" and the last melodious echoes faded into the clear blue skies and bright sunshine smiling down upon the White House Rose Garden.

A beaming President Mondale turned with glowing pride toward the assemblage of distinguished guests before him. Their posture was almost militarily stiff as they waited eagerly to receive the thanks of a grateful nation, indeed a grateful world.

Without question this was the most exhilarating single moment in Mary Spanacopito's life and her husband felt no less joy and elation than she did, standing beside his wife at this momentous ceremony.

This, too, was a memorable, once-in-a-lifetime happening for the heroic astronauts, Randolph Stuart, Rigby Deems, and Frank Perlman, as well as astronette Phoebe Swedlow, who ripped down the plastic screen that the satanic Dr. Simms had deployed in space.

They had saved the earth as it lay helpless on the brink of the precipice, waiting to be toppled to the cataclysmic end Sunstrike threatened on all life.

Now the heroes stood before the President, presenting themselves in the traditional manner of intrepid warriors and spiritual achievers. They had, all of them, attained greatness under fire, they had overcome trying moments of duress that test men's souls.

And so then Mondale spoke to them with great ardor and sincerity. "Civilization will be eternally grateful to you for as long as life exists on this planet. Words cannot express what we owe you . . ."

Meanwhile, less than a mile from the White House, a horde of reporters and photographers, perhaps four times greater than the group at the Rose Garden ceremony, stood outside the U.S. District Court, a short distance from 1600 Pennsylvania Avenue. They were covering an unusual event.

Hundreds of demonstrators had positioned themselves on the steps of the courthouse and now all at once broke out in cheers for the four defendants just coming out after being arraigned.

It was a nonviolent protest by men who carried nothing more formidable than attaché cases and not even one picket sign. They were FBI agents, outraged by a turn of events that at this moment threatened possible jail sentences of up to ten years and $10,000 fines for Bryan Dudley, Terrence O'Donnell, George Farnsworth, and Elmer Weiss.

The world had gone full circle after its convalescence from its nightmarish encounter with Sunstrike. Or, as the big black headline of the *Washington Post* put it on that afternoon of September 15, 1988:

4 FBI Agents Indicted
In Bank Break-In
Which Saved World

The agents had committed the unpardonable sin of not obtaining a search warrant from a judge to enter Dr. Simms's safe deposit box!

Preview

KILLSHOT

by Tom Alibrandi

> The following pages are excerpts edited from this new novel scheduled for publication in January, 1979.*

Killshot:

more than a game.

Killshot:

When one player, by virtue of perfect execution and precise coordination, drives the handball in such a fashion so it strikes the front wall low to the floor, allowing his opponent no possibility for a return shot.

The Arte of Handball
by S. O'Dwyer
Dublin, Ireland, 1815

But there is a second kind of Killshot:

When a certain breed of renegade player attempts to hit his opponent with such force so as to maim or otherwise injure him . . . for life.

By the time Coldiron and Barry worked their way into the South, they had been on the road for a little over five months. They were also more than $60,000 to the good, and it looked like they had only dipped into the till. The road promised them much more. Everywhere they went, the best handballers wanted a crack at Barry West. His growing reputation was attracting them in flocks.

The kid had been winning more handily than ever. Though his competition had grown keener as they went, and in spite of the grueling schedule Coldiron had been arranging for him, West seemed to be improving weekly. His victories were coming easier.

It had also become evident to Barry that the old man was in some kind of a hurry, like they had to do it all in a certain period of time. The kid was pulling on his gloves at least three times a week. Sometimes as many as five times. His coach seemed obsessed with tearing the country apart behind the abundant talent of Barry West.

If Coldiron hadn't been so driven with arranging Barry's schedule of matches; if he hadn't spent so much time and thought glorying in their growing pile of money; and if he hadn't been so intent on moving up that triangle his mind showed him every night before he passed out from Green, he might've noticed earlier.

Sure, the kid was unbeatable. He was winning big. He was demolishing everyone who Coldiron put him up against. But it was how he had been winning that was to finally become evident to his coach. Barry West had begun hitting people.

At first, Tate hadn't noticed. Once he did, he was sure it was coincidence. It was a game in which the ball travels in excess of one hundred miles an hour; it was a sport in which each player sweated so profusely the ball could easily get away from someone. Accidents could and did happen in handball. Players often got hit with the bullet-like shots. It was considered part of the risk of playing the game. It was regrettable when it did happen, and the man who accidentally hit his opponent felt bad. It just happened sometimes. Sometimes.

It took until Fredericksburg, Virginia, for Coldiron's attention to be drawn to what was happening. It was in a match against Mike Montague that the change in the kid began to come into focus to Coldiron's bleary eyes.

368

Montague was a year older than West, and was equally as aggressive on the court. He had just driven an alley pass along the left side wall, in an attempt to move Barry out of the center court zone. The shot had gotten away from the Southerner; it was too high, above the shoulders and two feet off the side wall. To be effective, an alley pass needed to be as close to both the floor and side wall as possible. As it was, West was left with an excellent opportunity for a rollout kill. He was in good position and the ball hung in the air like a ripe apple. The dozen or so people in the gallery, Coldiron, and even Montague himself figured West would easily put it away.

Only the kid didn't go for the rollout. He exploded out of the rear corner, catching his opponent's hard drive in its full momentum, and proceeded to drop Montague with a vicious shot to the back of the neck.

Montague was unconscious on the floor. Coldiron stood in shocked concern with the others in the gallery. He wondered if the others had seen what he had. Montague hadn't even been in the kid's shot-line to the front wall. It appeared ʻat West had deliberately hit his opponent, like he had ꓱed the guy up in a rifle scope. Tate hoped his eyes had ꓱd.

The place was quiet as Montague's second held a vial of ꟷꟷꓱelling salts to the fallen man's face. The player's head jerked. His neck spasmed around the area where he had been struck by the ball. He came out of it, but not before his stomach had its say. Montague vomited on the man bent over him; it was the involuntary reflex that sometimes accompanies a deadening blow to the base of the skull. The stricken man was helped to his feet, and walked unsteadily, holding on to his attendant.

Coldiron shifted his attention to West. What he saw sent a chill through him. He was looking at a face without remorse. It was the face of a man without shock. It was the look of someone who had just completed a mission.

Montague was done. He had been hit in such a way that the energy had left him like the air being let out of a balloon. West had nailed him in one of the spots. Mike Montague was unable to continue within the fifteen-minute forfeiture time allowance. West had won the match in the first game. He had barely broken a sweat.

369

Coldiron waited until they were packing their car to leave to talk with West.

"You got off easy today. Too bad about that kid getting hit."

"Yeh. I felt real bad. He's okay, though. Lucky he was only shaken up."

"Yeh. Real lucky. What happened down there? Didn't you see him when you teed off?"

"No. The guy jumped in front of me after I had already pulled the trigger. There was nothing I could do. I really hated to see it happen."

"Right, kid. Those things are a bitch. Sometimes a guy just seems to jump in front of your shot. I know how it goes."

"That's what happened. Montague seemed to just jump in front of me at the last second.

"Where to next, Tate?"

"South. Way South," Coldiron said and climbed into the passenger side of the car. He'd try to forget what happened in Fredericksburg. He really wanted to believe the kid.

That night Coldiron tried to shut off his mind with Green. His thoughts made it through the alcoholic haze. He lay in bed and tried to answer the questions that sliced at him. The same ones came at him. Over and over.

Why was Barry doing it? The kid had more talent than seven guys. Maybe Fredericksburg was an accident? Maybe the way Montague got hit, looking like he was set up, was just imagination?

As the questions were the same, so were his answers to them. Barry had started hitting people on purpose. There was no mistaking that. Fredericksburg had only turned his mind to it, allowed Coldiron to add it all up.

An occasional hit could easily be an accident. Even a couple of them. But Barry had picked off seven people in the last month. That was more than coincidence. Especially with a player of West's caliber. The kid could put an egg in a china cup at fifty feet, without breaking either. Barry West could put that hard rubber ball anywhere he wanted.

Which is what Coldiron knew he had been doing. West was sticking people in the spots; he was hitting them in the right places to slow them down, force them into losing their concentration or, as in Montague's case, into forfeiting the match to him. What was especially frightening to Tate was that the kid had the skill and power to cripple a man. Even kill him. Coldiron had showed him how.

Tate was wracked with indecision. It was making him crazy. Should he confront the kid? Lay his cards on the table? Let West know he was heading for big danger? Then what? What if he did? What if West told him to shove it and walked? What if he ended the partnership and went on without Coldiron? The kid could make it without Tate. But Coldiron knew he sure as hell couldn't make it without the kid. And he was so damn close.

Barry's next match destroyed any doubts Coldiron might've had that the kid was hitting people on purpose. It happened in the third and match-deciding game. West had his hands full with Corley Stinson. His dark-haired and handsome opponent was playing an extremely skillful game of handball. Midway through the third game he hit Stinson. West was trailing 10-11 at the time. He was running out of gas when he paralyzed Stinson with a bullet to the groin. The Southern man's scream had hardly stopped rebounding from the stark walls when it was discovered that his left genital had been shattered. He was still writhing on the floor when the ambulance attendants wheeled the gurney into the court. The match was over.

Tate walked back to the hotel. His legs were killing him. The pain in his heart was even greater. He had to have time to think. Coldiron had a killer on his hands. The kid would stop at nothing to win.

Even winning was no longer enough. The kid was addicted to the thought of becoming the best in the game. He had tasted the sweetness of fame. He was a top gun. They were lining up to take a crack at him. Lining up to play a hitter who liked the taste of blood.

One part of Coldiron knew clearly what he must do. The kid had to be dealt with before he killed somebody. Another part of the old fox refused to accept the obvious. Tate had been a loser for twenty-five years, clawing for crumbs. That made it easy to deny, not that the kid was a hitter, that West had to be dealt with. A very convincing voice in him said the kid would turn it around before it got too far.

Fear helped Tate consider that Barry would stop hitting people. Maybe if he lightened up on the kid's schedule, so West could get more rest, more time to let off steam. Maybe if Barry were less pressured and frantic he would go back

371

to playing honest fourwall. Maybe it wasn't too late. Maybe the obsession to be the best wasn't too great. Maybe the taste of blood wasn't too strong in the kid's mouth. Maybe those who voted to take out the hitters hadn't yet noticed. Maybe he could forget the whole thing. Maybe.

There was the triangle. And the appointment Tate had promised himself he'd keep that night in the alley in New Orleans. Coldiron was gripped with his own obsession. It was every bit as strong as Barry's compulsion to win.

In the final analysis he knew it was only a matter of time. He could only push it down so far with Jack Daniel's Green. The inevitable could be postponed for only so long. Coldiron's prayer was that his own compulsion and the Green could dull his conscience long enough until he could hobble up what was left of that triangle. He had to keep that appointment.

THE MANITOU

"Like some mind-gripping drug, it has the uncanny ability to seize you and hold you firmly in its clutches from the moment you begin until you drop the book from your trembling fingers after you have finally finished the last page."

—Bernhardt J. Hurwood

squamacus—An American Indian sorcerer. In the seventeenth century he had sworn to wreak a violent vengeance upon the callous, conquering White Man. This was just before he died, over four hundred years ago. Now he has found an abominable way to return, a perfect birth for his revenge.

en Tandy—A slim, delicate, auburn-haired girl with an impish face. She has a troublesome tumor on the back of her neck, a tumor that no doctor in New York City can explain. It seems to be moving, growing, developing—almost as if it were alive! She is the victim of

THE MANITOU
GRAHAM MASTERTON

A Pinnacle Book
P982 $1.75

If you can't find this book at your local bookstore, simply send cover price, plus 25¢ for postage and handling to:

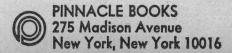

PINNACLE BOOKS
275 Madison Avenue
New York, New York 10016

HERE ARE 11 WACKY, ZANY, ALL-IN-GOOD-FUN TWO-IN-ONE JOKE BOOKS FROM LARRY WILDE, AMERICA'S MOST POPULAR JOKESMITH

Order the ones you want today!

___OFFICIAL POLISH/ITALIAN
    JOKE BOOK   P548   1.25

___OFFICIAL JEWISH/IRISH JOKE BOOK   P320   1.25

___OFFICIAL VIRGINS/SEX MANIACS
    JOKE BOOK   P634   1.25

___OFFICIAL BLACK FOLKS/
    WHITE FOLKS JOKE BOOK   P722   1.25

___MORE OFFICIAL POLISH/ITALIAN
    JOKE BOOK   P772   1.25

___OFFICIAL DEMOCRAT/REPUBLICAN
    JOKE BOOK   P818   1.25

___OFFICIAL RELIGIOUS/NOT SO
    RELIGIOUS JOKE BOOK   P904   1.25

___OFFICIAL SMART KIDS/DUMB
    PARENTS JOKE BOOK   P40-011   1.25

___OFFICIAL GOLFERS JOKE BOOK   P40-048   1.50

___LAST OFFICIAL POLISH JOKE BOOK P40-147   1.50

___OFFICIAL DIRTY JOKE BOOK   P40-19-0   1.50
              and

___THE OFFICIAL ETHNIC
    CALENDAR 1978   P40-145   3.50

If there is a Pinnacle Book you want—and you cannot find it locally—it is available from us simply by sending the title and price plus 25¢ to cover mailing and handling costs to:

    PINNACLE—Book Mailing Service
    P.O. Box 1050
    Rockville Centre, N.Y. 11571

___Check here if you want to receive our catalog regularly.

ALL NEW DYNAMITE SERIES

THE DESTROYER

by Richard Sapir & Warren Murphy

CURE, the world's most secret crime-fighting organization created the perfect weapon —Remo Williams—man programmed to become a cold, calculating death machine. The super man of the 70s!

rder		Title	Book No.	Price
_____	# 1	Created, The Destroyer	P361	$1.25
_____	# 2	Death Check	P362	$1.25
_____	# 3	Chinese Puzzle	P363	$1.25
_____	# 4	Mafia Fix	P364	$1.25
_____	# 5	Dr. Quake	P365	$1.25
_____	# 6	Death Therapy	P366	$1.25
_____	# 7	Union Bust	P367	$1.25
_____	# 8	Summit Chase	P368	$1.25
_____	# 9	Murder's Shield	P369	$1.25
_____	#10	Terror Squad	P370	$1.25
_____	#11	Kill or Cure	P371	$1.25
_____	#12	Slave Safari	P372	$1.25
_____	#13	Acid Rock	P373	$1.25
_____	#14	Judgment Day	P303	$1.25
_____	#15	Murder Ward	P331	$1.25
_____	#16	Oil Slick	P418	$1.25
_____	#17	Last War Dance	P435	$1.25
_____	#18	Funny Money	P538	$1.25
_____	#19	Holy Terror	P640	$1.25
_____	#20	Assassins Play-Off	P708	$1.25
_____	#21	Deadly Seeds	P760	$1.25
_____	#22	Brain Drain	P805	$1.25
_____	#23	Child's Play	P842	$1.25
_____	#24	King's Curse	P879	$1.25